THE BOND

Be it known to everyone, that the people of the Dale of Uri, the

Community of Schwyz, as also the men of the mountains of

Unterwald, in consideration of evil times, have full confidently

bound themselves, and sworn to help each other with all their

power and might, against all who shall do violence to one or any

of them.

That is our Ancient Bond.

*Excerpt from the *Pact of the Eidgenossen* (Oathbound). Signed in August of 1291, somewhere deep in the forests of modern day Switzerland.

By J. K. Swift

The Forest Knights Series:

ALTDORF

MORGARTEN

The Hospitaller Saga:

ACRE

MAMLUK

HOSPITALLER

ALTDORF

The Forest Knights
Book 1

J. K. Swift

Printed in the United States of America

UE Publishing Co.
First Edition

10 9 8 7 6 5 4 3

ISBN-13: 978-1468012903
ISBN-10: 1468012908

Acknowledgements

Many people made my trips to Switzerland and Austria a true pleasure, but I would especially like to thank Peter and Akiko Huber for their kind hospitality. Also to Maya Huber and Thomas Hildebrand, thank you for dragging me through the hills of the Bernese Alps and sharing so many wonderful dinners together. And to Alex Jarosch and Lina Hedinsdottir, thank you for opening up your home to us. Some day I promise to write something where the Austrians are not the bad guys.

Dedication

For Phyllis and Roy: a mother who read to me every night, and a father never too busy to cut a piece of wood or plastic pipe into whatever I could imagine. Some children never have a chance, but a few have it all.

And for Sonja, my muse, who saves me from myself everyday.

ALTDORF

The Forest Knights Book 1

Prologue

"WHAT WILL YOU DO with all this coin?" Foulques de Villaret, Knight Hospitaller of the Order of Saint John asked as he dropped two large bags on the slab-carved table worn smooth from years of use.

The village hall in Schwyz was small, but had a peaked roofline and thick post and beam framework that slotted into itself seamlessly. Although simple, it gave off an aura of permanence. The builders had left the interior walls plain and unadorned, yet so much care had gone into selecting the best natural materials from the surrounding forest that only the finest of tapestries could have improved the simple décor.

The room could accommodate fifty villagers standing shoulder to shoulder, but today it held only five. One woman and three men sat behind the long trestle table at the front of the hall. The villagers were all younger than forty, but those years had not been kind. Their clothing of worn, homespun wool and brown callused hands marked them as farmers, while their knobby limbs and sunken eyes hinted at a hard existence in a densely forested land too mountainous to be tamed by ploughs.

The woman did not look at the heavy bags in front of her. She stared at the young knight, her hard eyes searching his face, daring him to judge her or the men who sat at her side.

"We mean to buy animals for our people. Sheep, goats, pigs. Maybe a few oxen. We hope it will give us enough to breed more stock," she said.

Foulques de Villaret shook his head. He was a powerfully built man wearing a black surcoat with a large white cross on his chest; a thigh-length chainmail hauberk glistened beneath. As the white cross contrasted against his black clothing, so too did his ice-blue eyes jump out against a mass of wild hair and a full beard of darkness.

"You could buy much more than a few beasts with that gold. Perhaps you should count it and make sure the sum."

The woman's husband, a gangly man, shifted on his hard stool and exhaled. He stroked the ridge of his brow with his thumbs as he fixed an unfocused gaze on the bags of coin.

"There is no need," he said. "You are a Hospitaller Knight and our people are poor. Your Order's oath to care for the poor and sick is the very reason we chose your brethren over the other orders fighting in the Holy Lands. We believe you mean to honor that oath and treat with us fairly. Did you know, Sir Foulques, the Templar Knights offered half again the number of coins before us?"

De Villaret nodded and corrected him. *"Brother*

2

Foulques. I relinquished my title and possessions when I joined the Order."

Just as the Templars kept an ever-watchful eye on their rivals the Hospitallers, there was not much the Knights of Saint John did not know about the Templars' activities. In the war against the Saracen infidels in Outremer, a world away across the Mid-Earth Sea, de Villaret had been witness to more suffering and cruelty than most sane men could bear. But flesh and blood enemies were not to blame for the pain etched in these villagers' faces.

Yes, the Austrian ruling family, the Habsburgs, taxed these lands to help support their armies scattered throughout Europe, but the land was so poor it contributed no more than a pittance to the treasury. The real hardships came from the land itself. Carving farmland out of the forested mountain slopes only resulted in stunted crops that struggled through the long winters and short growing season to a single harvest, if any.

De Villaret felt the woman's eyes on him, searching, assessing. Attempting by force of will alone to draw out and reveal his innermost flaws, picking at them like a loose thread to see if he would unravel. Was he a man to be trusted? He shifted his weight, his black hair bunching about his shoulders, and addressed the villagers seated before him, making a conscious effort to look at the woman as he spoke.

"It is not a simple thing you do, but rest assured you have chosen wisely in putting your faith in my order, and in God."

The woman stood so quickly her chair shot out behind her and toppled to the floor, causing everyone to

—

jump, including the young knight.

"Desperation is not faith," she said, leveling a thin finger at de Villaret. "We put no faith in you or your kind—only in our own people." She jerked her head towards the door, her eyes never leaving his face. "Go now, before we come to our senses."

Upon becoming a Knight of the Order of Saint John, besides taking vows of chastity and poverty, de Villaret had sworn to accept the poor as his lords. But being born into a noble French family, he was unaccustomed to being dismissed by a peasant, nevertheless a woman. He hesitated and looked to the other men. Their downward cast eyes told him who held sway in these lands.

He willed his clenched hands to unfold.

It mattered not. He had what he wanted. He bowed his head, ever so slightly, and without a word strode to the exit, his chainmail making a metallic rustle. He threw open the door and stepped out into the summer's early morning light.

The quiet was disconcerting, unnatural, for it should have been deafening.

Spread before him, overflowing the town square, were five hundred children lined up in flawless marching formation. They varied in age from five to thirteen-years-old. All orphans or second sons sold by their families or villages. Fifteen of de Villaret's fellow Hospitallers, knights clad in the same black surcoats and cloaks, and grizzled sergeant men-at-arms dressed in brown, all with white crosses displayed on the chest, were interspersed amongst the orderly group. The few men stood out like giants as they were head and shoulders above even their tallest charges.

Without a backwards glance into the village hall, de Villaret strode to take his place at the front of the column, next to a knight leading a string of pack mules, aware with every step that the woman's eyes were still locked upon him. Burning, boring deep into his being.

The column began its long winding journey toward Saint Gotthard's Pass. It was the fastest route de Villaret could take to cross the treacherous Alps, jagged abominations the Devil himself had placed in the middle of Europe in his continuous efforts to divide faithful Christians. Eventually, God willing, they would descend into northern Italia, and make their way to Genoa and the shores of the Mid-Earth Sea. There, he would load his new charges onto ships and set sail for the Holy Land.

He glanced over his shoulder and took in his army of children stretched along the narrow road as far as the eye could see. These were no common slaves he had purchased. Every child was dressed in a new cloak and laden with the best traveling gear their families or villages could afford. Although, in most cases, that accounted for little more than an eating knife and a walking stick, perhaps new shoes for some. The children were still fresh and bore the difficulties of the road well. But that would change soon enough.

May the Good Lord protect us all.

Chapter 1

LIKE SHEPHERDS FROM HELL, the demons drove their flock of evil spirits and twisted minions over the Alps far into the valleys below, spreading disease, insanity, and chaos. The only warning of their approach was the *föhn*, a warm, dry wind that preceded the horde's arrival. It was not superstition or myth to the locals, but simply an event that occurred a scattering of times every year, and the föhn in the late winter of 1314 was longer and warmer than any could remember.

At first, as the warm breeze reduced great banks of snow to puddles, it was a welcome respite to a hard winter. But as the air continued to warm and the moisture was wicked out of the countryside, throats dried out, and animals became uneasy. Once the people recognized it for a föhn, the wise ones hastened to the safety of their homes to latch their shutters and bar the doors. They knew what chased the wind.

Erich felt ill at ease, but he could not be sure whether

the cause was the föhn or the six horsemen that had appeared with it. He had shadowed them from the woods for the past hour.

Their mounts were great long-legged beasts, with heads held high and chins tucked in; not the sturdy mountain ponies that fared better in this land of hills and steep mountain passes. At first he thought they might be soldiers on patrol to Einsiedeln, or one of the other wealthy monasteries in the area under protection of the Holy Roman Empire, but they were not dressed like any Austrians Erich had ever seen.

Unlike the heavy wool and sackcloth garments Erich had on, the riders wore layers of simple dark clothing of lightweight fabrics, the likes of which Erich had never seen. In addition, each man wore a black chainmail shirt, the mesh so fine and light, it seemed more a vest than armor.

A single one of the mail shirts would fetch a price large enough to keep a family in these parts fed for years. But first it would need to be removed from the man wearing it, and that, Erich knew through experience and by looking at the weapons each man wore at his side, could only be accomplished one way.

He waved to a man concealed in the woods a hundred yards up the road, who in turn, relayed the signal to more men hiding beyond a bend in the road ahead.

Brigands. Highwaymen. Desperate men turned predators, who singled out the weak to provide for their own existence. Now in his late twenties, Erich had made his life amongst men such as these for nearly fifteen years. His band of almost thirty men was one of the most lucrative gangs working the road leading north out of

—

Saint Gotthard's Pass. Traffic had been good of late, and by targeting nobles with insufficient escorts, the occasional small trade caravan, and local peasants as poor as the raiders themselves, Erich's group managed a comfortable existence, unlike most in the settlements surrounding the Great Lake.

But they never ascended far up into the pass. The craggy peaks were the domain of demons, and were to be avoided lest one risk the corruption of his soul. And, besides, there was no profit to be had on the other side.

A number of years past the Duke of Milan had purchased the area and built a great fortification, the Castelgrande, which sat atop a rock bluff overlooking the southern approach to the Saint Gotthard Pass. Regular patrols from the castle had almost eliminated all banditry in the valleys on the south side of the pass. However, once the merchants managed the winding climb from the narrow valley floor out of the tree line and over the barren summit, which was covered in snow eight months of the year, they were in Austrian lands, and there were no longer any Milanese patrols to protect them. Austrian patrols were rarely seen this far south.

It was this pass that the six men had recently climbed, and they now rode slowly, relaxed. The weary slump to their shoulders told of a great distance traveled. Although tired of the road, they exchanged easy banter and laughed often, with one man standing out by his immense size.

Clean-shaven and blonde, he sat astride one of the largest horses Erich had ever seen; yet the animal seemed no more than a pony the way the man's legs dangled around its torso. He talked non-stop, emphasizing his words and laughter with grand gestures from his brazier-sized hands.

—

The fair-haired man was such a spectacle that Erich was surprised to find his attention always drifting to the darker man riding beside him. Though he appeared small compared to the giant, Erich could tell he was taller than most men. He wore his chestnut brown, neck-length hair untied, and although beardless, his face was darkly stubbled, except for the area that a long, jagged scar passed through. The thick, pale tissue started under the man's left eye and ran down his face in a graceful curve to fold over the line of his jaw.

He led a riderless spare horse, two hands taller than his own, saddled and ready to be mounted. On his belt he wore a long knife, and hanging off his saddle was a mace with a heavy flanged head. His movements were relaxed and his eyes never once left the road ahead to search the woods on either side, but there was an uneasiness about the way the man sat straight in his saddle that bothered Erich.

Erich scanned the woods for his three hidden archers. He could not see them but he knew they would be ready. Around the bend ahead the road narrowed with thick stands of pine on either side. At his signal, he and his archers would open fire on the horsemen from the rear and then the bulk of his men would emerge from the woods to chase them, leaving the riders with no option but to flee straight up the road. More men would be waiting with ropes stretched across the road that would unhorse the men from their galloping mounts. It was a tried and true system that had passed many a test.

Erich nocked a noisemaker arrow to his bowstring, aimed into the sky, and let fly. A piercing whistle shrilled through the air. Seconds passed—nothing happened.

Where are my archers?

A sinking feeling sifted through him and settled in his guts. Something was wrong.

He scanned the woods to see twenty of his men scrambling out of the trees, shouting and screaming as they charged up the road towards the six horsemen. For bandits, they were well armed with heavy clubs or decent swords taken from previous conquests. Some wore unmatched pieces of armor, usually leather, but the occasional gleam of chainmail could be spotted when one of the intermittent patches of sunlight found it through the trees.

Erich tried to wave them off but to no avail. They were too caught up with adrenalin and bloodlust to spot him in the foliage as they rushed by, each man mindlessly intent on being the first to reach the victims.

At the sound of the screams from behind, the six horsemen turned their mounts and formed up in a single line, the road just wide enough to accommodate all of the large horses. Their movements were precise and unhurried. As one, they drew their weapons. The tall man said something and held his mace high into the air. He turned his head and looked directly to Erich's hiding spot; his features obscured by the forest's shadows save for the long pale line, which even at this distance, seemed to pulsate with a cool white light.

He reined in the riderless destrier close to his side with one hand, and lowered his mace in the other to point at the attackers running up the road. The horsemen seemed to merge together into a single, multi-headed beast as they began to trot ahead, each man's knees close enough to touch the man's next to him. Then, as one, the great warhorses leapt into a full gallop.

Destriers bred and trained for this very situation, they

snorted with excitement as they gathered speed and charged through the band of brigands as though they were nothing more than tall blades of grass. Men screamed as they tried to dive out of the path of the frenzied animals. Bodies were blown aside like leaves in a maelstrom; bones snapped, shoulders dislocated, and chests caved in under the heavy iron-shod hooves. Once through the tangled maze of bodies, the riders turned their mounts with their legs and formed up for another charge.

The road was littered with men on hands and knees, some still and lifeless, others groaning, crawling, trying to pull themselves to the safety of the woods. Those that were fortunate enough to have avoided the charge stood on trembling legs, their eyes darting from their trampled comrades to the demons on horseback readying their mounts for another charge.

The horsemen were only twenty yards from Erich now. He stood and nocked an arrow. The tall man held his hand high again as the warhorses snorted and pawed at the earth. Erich took aim at the leader's throat and pulled his bowstring back.

"Hold," came a whisper so close to Erich's ear he felt the word's heat. A sharp point contacted the back of his neck and he felt the coolness of blood trickle from the scratch.

"Lower the bow and let that shaft fall to the ground," the voice said softly.

The riderless horse.

Erich grimaced. There were seven—he had led his men into a trap. Erich's back muscles trembled with exertion as he eased back the string and dropped the weapon. The arrow slithered beneath a tangle of scrub still brown from the winter snows, and disappeared.

He turned slowly to see a mahogany-bearded man pointing a small crossbow at his face and holding another larger one at his side. His hair was cut short but the reddish brown beard was braided into a fork that reached down to his upper chest. The man lightly pressed the point against Erich's forehead.

"It may be small, but it will tear a hole clear through your head, boy. In fact this bolt is under so much pressure, and the tickler so touchy, it goes off by itself sometimes. Stay very still."

He raised the other heavier crossbow, took his eyes off Erich for a moment to sight down its length, and shot one of Erich's men standing forty yards away through the chest. With a pop, the bolt spread apart the man's chainmail like thin spring ice and embedded itself far into his chest, the leather vanes on the back end of the shaft all but disappearing.

He turned to Erich and said, "Walk."

On the road the horsemen began their second charge. A few unwise bandits raised their swords and tried to sidestep the horses but were cut down by the riders' weapons. Most fled into the trees, as did the others further up the road that came from around the bend to see what the screaming was all about. In minutes it was over.

The bearded man marched Erich through the trees. They passed Erich's three archers crumpled in the underbrush, lying in pools of their own blood with their throats cut. One of them still in his teens. Erich knew the circuitous route back to the road was taken solely for his benefit. He fought to push down the guilt building inside.

Thomas took a slow drink from a water skin and then rotated his mace arm to work out the throbbing in his shoulder. The ligaments had been stretched one too many times, but he refused to admit he needed a lighter weapon. He watched Ruedi march his captive out of the trees and force him down hard on his knees in front of the small group of men.

"This one is the leader," Ruedi murmured through his forked beard.

Thomas nodded, his dark eyes narrowing. He appeared tall because of his lean, wiry build, but he was still a full head shorter than Pirmin Schnidrig, the fair-haired titan of a man standing next to him.

"Just a kid," Pirmin said, his words strongly accented.

"Old enough to put a knife in your back if you show it to him," came another voice. Hermann Gissler, an angular man bordering on gaunt, with small eyes and black hair greying at the temples, strode forward and put the tip of his long sword in the middle of Erich's chest. "Do we hang him? Or spare the tree, and run him through now?"

"Not worth the rope," said Urs, a short, stocky man with forearms thickened by years at the forge. "Let us take him to Schwyz and turn him over to the Vogt. Judging from the size of his band they must have been quite active in this area. Might be a reward."

"Waste of time," Gissler said shaking his head. "He will only slow us down, and no village in these lands has money for a reward. Besides, they would just hang him anyway."

Thomas gave his sore shoulder a hard squeeze to get

the blood moving, and looked at the dead men littering the road. He turned to the man on his knees, who looked straight ahead, head held high and eyes unseeing. A small crucifix hung from the man's neck.

He was healthy and better fed than the few people they had seen since crossing the Gotthard, nevertheless, his eyes showed no hope. He had the look of a man who knew he was going to die. And perhaps that is what he deserved. Thomas had no way of knowing how many innocent deaths this man was responsible for, and he did not care.

He had, of course, killed Christians before. But they had always been a threat in some way to the Christian Kingdom in Outremer; Saracen spies, or lowly mercenaries loyal to God only until the gold ran out. But here, in this cold valley, hidden in the shadows of rocky peaks so high and numerous you could ride for hours without seeing the sun, it felt different. Senseless. As though God had no interest in how the lives of these people played out.

"We let him go," he said.

Gissler looked at Thomas, eyes wide in disbelief. "We might not spot him next time. To show his appreciation for the mercy you have shown, he will put a quarrel in your back first chance he gets."

"You confuse mercy with indifference. We are God's soldiers, chosen by Our Lord to protect those who follow the one true faith. This man wears the cross at his neck. It is not our place to discipline half-starved ruffians."

He looked at the brigand, whose eyes had come alive and were darting side to side with a newfound hope that he may not be killed.

"You forget Thomas, we no longer fight in His army," Gissler said. His mouth moved to say more but he stopped himself.

"Bind him to a tree. By the time someone sets him free, we will be hours away," Thomas said. His tone left no room for debate.

Gissler narrowed his eyes but lowered his sword. He knew there was no point arguing with Thomas once he decided on a course of action. But then he brightened, as a new solution presented itself in his mind.

In one fluid motion he reversed the grip on his sword, stepped in and slammed the pommel into Erich's forehead. Stunned, Erich fell forward and reached out his hands to catch himself on the ground. Gissler whipped the blade onto Erich's right hand, cleanly severing away half of his first three fingers. The sword clanged as the steel made contact with the rocky ground, and just as swiftly, Gissler wiped and resheathed his blade.

Erich screamed and pulled his hand into himself, curling up into a ball.

"No need to waste rope on his likes. He will not be any good with a bow for the rest of his miserable life," Gissler said, his mouth turning up slightly.

Ruedi leaned on his larger crossbow and laughed. "Gissler the problem solver," he said, shaking his head. "Of course he could still use one of these," he said holding up his small crossbow with one hand.

Thomas let out a breath and stared at Gissler, but said nothing. It was not his fault. The others stood around drinking water, checking their weapons, or comforting their mounts. No one was surprised by Gissler's sudden action for they were all men shaped by a lifetime of war, Thomas included. It was, after all, common practice to cut off the fingers of enemy archer captives.

Finally, Anton, a small man with several earrings in his right ear who had taken to wearing perfume and bathing as frequently as the Saracens, wandered over to the writhing form on the ground and skillfully tied off the man's fingers, stemming the flow of blood. Then he began gathering kindling for a fire.

"It will not take me long to cauterize this mess. Go on ahead—I will catch you soon enough," he said to Thomas.

"Once you are done, take a moment for those on the road," Thomas said. "No man should die unshriven, but since they did not unburden their souls in confession, I am afraid a blessing is the best we can do. We leave them to God's mercy."

"Yes, Captain," Anton said. His face paled briefly as he contemplated the horrors of facing his maker with an unshriven soul, and then he remembered the groaning man at his feet who was still alive. "Max, leave me some of your kirsch."

Max, a barrel-chested man with a sour face and hair more grey than black, balked at Anton's request. "Get your own—this is one of my best batches. Who knows when I will have the means to make more?"

"Oh calm yourself. Soon you will have all the cherries you want. You are back in the land of kirsch, remember?"

Grumbling, Max rooted through his saddlebag filled with packets of saffron, turmeric, pepper, and other exotic spices he had hoarded and brought from the east. It was worth a small fortune in the right hands, and if he remembered correctly, his family in Zug had connections

---

with buyers. He found a small flask of one of the poorer quality cherry alcohol batches he had distilled himself and tossed it to Anton.

"That should be for drinking, not burning," he said.

"Was hoping to hear that," Anton said. He popped out the stopper and took a long swig, grimacing as the hard alcohol burned its way down. Then he roughly pulled Erich up to a sitting position and forced the young man to drink a few mouthfuls. He coughed and sputtered, but managed to keep most of it down.

Max turned his back in disgust.

The men mounted up leaving Anton building his fire in the middle of the road amidst a handful of motionless corpses. Erich moaned beside him, cradling his stumped fingers.

They resumed their traveling pace. By nightfall the party would be in the village of Schwyz, where they would split up and go their separate ways. After so many years together this weighed heavily in the thoughts of each man, but with no desire to speak of it, they rode mostly in silence.

"I hate to say it, but Gissler was right Thomi," Pirmin finally said in his melodic Wallis accent. "We should have made an example of the leader and left him twisting at the end of a rope."

The way he sung his words made even a hanging sound like a cheery event. He came from the Matterhorn area and everything about the man was big, from his almost seven foot frame to the custom-made, eight-foot long battle-ax he carried. He was larger than life; an oversized blonde Adonis, both terrifying and beautiful to behold, and he was Thomas's closest friend.

"A year ago you would not have taken any chances

with that outlaw. I fear you are getting soft. As usual God only knows what is rattlin' around in that head of yours."

Thomas first looked slowly at the thick woods, patches of snow still visible at the bases of most trees, and then higher up at the white-peaked Alps surrounding them on every side. He could not recall any particular memories of this road, but breathing the clear air and taking in the majestic scenery of the Alps stirred up a warm, comforting feeling that was at the same time both new and familiar.

Strange, he thought. There was no reason for him to have any feelings for this land. Unlike the others he rode with, he had almost no memories of family here. None that still lived, that is. He did not even know his true last name. For that matter, when he thought about it, he only knew two of the men's original last names. For the purpose of making record keeping matters simple, the Hospitallers gave all the boys from the alpine areas the same last name: *Schwyzer*, meaning 'one from Schwyz'. The boys were forbidden to use any other last name. Hermann Gissler refused to surrender his family name. He got around the rules by telling the monks his first name was Gissler. As for Pirmin Schnidrig, well the monks tried to beat his last name out of him, but that only made him all the more determined to make sure everyone knew he was a Schnidrig.

"Not soft. Just tired. I think I am getting too old to be one of God's soldiers," Thomas said.

Pirmin laughed and rolled his eyes. "Thomi, you were an old man when you were five."

This made Thomas grin just enough that he could feel the scar tissue tighten and resist along the length of his face.

His saddle leather creaked as he twisted and looked behind them. A thin tendril of smoke rose above the trees from Anton's fire in the distance.

He turned back to the road ahead and wondered what God had in store for him. He had been a leader of men and a war galley's captain for twelve years, a soldier of the One Faith for over twenty. Almost a year ago to the day, Grand Master de Villaret had said, "Gather the Schwyzers, Thomas, those who remain, and take them home. This is the last order I shall give you."

In a few short hours, that order would be fulfilled.

They rode on in silence, and no one looked back when the brigand leader screamed long and hard, like he was being dragged away by the furies of hell.

***

Seraina was leaning against a young oak, listening to the wind, when she heard the far-off scream reverberate gently through the woods and drift up to where she stood. She opened her pine-needle green eyes and stood up straight; her long, auburn hair sticking to the bark of the oak as though the tree were reluctant to give her up. Although it came from miles away, she could hear the scream because she stood at the edge of a clearing shadowed by the towering presence of the Mythen.

The Mythen were two mountains, standing side-by-side, one taller with the upper reaches treeless and jagged, while the shorter one had a mane of green running up the side closest to its companion. They jutted out of the earth with a statement; distinct from the low-lying hills surrounding them, their pyramidal shapes too grand and

19

symmetrical to be ordinary. They were sentries of the ancient world, forgotten now by most, and although their rock surfaces had been ground down and large pieces had sloughed off over the millennia, they were not without power.

Seraina came to this place often to visit the Mythen, and in return for her company, they helped her listen to the wind. The wind guided her thoughts and through them, her actions. Without the voice of the wind she would be lost, her place in the Great Weave unknown.

But the messages were never clear, and today's bordered on cryptic. She had not yet seen thirty harvests, a child in the eyes of the elders. Seraina cursed her youth and lack of wisdom for not being able to discern the exact message, but just as quickly she thanked the Mythen for bringing her what they could. This day, laced together with the sound of human suffering, the warm wind whispered its message over and over. Her heart pounded in her ears.

The Catalyst's time was near.

Chapter 2

Salzburg

THE HABSBURG FOOL was a stringy gnome of a man, easily twice Leopold's twenty-four years but little more than half his height. He wore no hat but his purple hair was cut short and plastered to his head in a star pattern. His frilly tunic was black on the left and white on the right, while his tights were the opposite. Yellow, pointed, soft-leather shoes completed the ensemble. When Leopold approached, the Fool made a flourishing gesture with his arms and bowed to the young Duke before thrusting open the double doors to the council chambers. At the last second he stepped in front of Leopold and strutted ahead to escort him into the large room, the soft tinkling of bells on the Fool's pointed shoes marking every step.

The sound had infuriated Leopold since childhood, for somehow the Fool had complete control over the loudness and intensity of the bells and, Leopold felt, used them purposely to mock him. He could walk without making a sound when he wanted to, for despite being a garish entertainer, the Fool had always been by King Albrecht's side when he was alive and could in fact blend in when he so wished. Since the King's assassination the previous year, the Fool had attached himself to Frederick, Leopold's older brother by a year, and who now sat at the head of an ornate rectangular table in the council room.

Frederick smiled and held up a hand in greeting as his brother entered, relief etched deep in his face. Seated around him were eight older men, the advisors to his late father, but unlike Frederick, not one of them looked pleased at the entrance of the younger Habsburg Duke.

"The fool has arrived!" the jester announced.

Leopold shot him an angry glare and imagined what it would feel like to have his hands around the insufferable creature's throat, shaking him until the only sound that escaped was the tinkling of those cursed chimes.

"Welcome brother, we are happy you could join us on such short notice." Frederick 'the Handsome', as he was called, came around the table and the two brothers embraced. Only a year separated them but they looked nothing alike. Leopold was fair haired and willowy in build while Frederick was dark and stocky, like their father had been. Most women would not say Frederick was any more 'handsome' than Leopold, but there was a beatific honesty in his smile that made people feel comfortable. When under Leopold's bold stare on the other hand, people were never at ease. He had his mother's sharp features: glistening blue eyes and a high-bridged raptorial nose.

Six of the men were nobles of prestigious Austrian

houses, powerful members of the German Empire, but Leopold's sudden presence made many of them shift in their seats. His open disdain for his father's advisors was well known. He trusted none of them and felt sick when he thought of his brother in this room alone with these carrion eaters. He made a point of looking at each man and noting who met his eyes and who seemed surprised to see him here. The few who met his eyes quickly looked away, but that in and of itself was not a measure of guilt.

The Archbishop was seated to one side of Frederick along with a simpler dressed monk Leopold had never before seen. Though he wore the robe of a Dominican, his face had the smugness of a merchant.

"Forgive my lateness brother. I should have liked to be here sooner but the messenger bearing your summons was waylaid on the road some miles from Habsburg Castle." Leopold let his eyes wander over the nobles, openly accusing anyone who met his stare.

Count Henri of Hunenberg, a veteran knight in his late forties who was renowned for spending much of his family's fortune on several campaigns to the Holy Lands, shook his head and said, "This is further evidence of what I spoke—even the roads in the Aargau are no longer safe since so many of our soldiers were sent north. We must have more patrols to ensure the safety of messengers and merchants. And from what the Archbishop here tells us, the monks of Einsiedeln also require enforcers in their pastures near Schwyz."

"Ridiculous," Otto, the late King Albrecht's grey-haired military adviser grunted. "Louis the Bavarian openly defies Frederick's tutelage and is marshaling his forces as we speak. We must maintain a show of force in the north. Only war will decide the German kingship now. I must be granted direct control of the *Sturmritter* if Habsburg rule is to prevail."

Leopold looked at Otto, shocked by the old general's cunning. No one understood Otto better than Leopold, for Otto had been his principal tutor growing up. King Albrecht had recognized the natural gifts of his children; Frederick, with his easy smile, was the natural politician, but in Leopold he had seen the future Marshal of the Habsburg armies, and his father had seen to his education accordingly.

Otto had just made his play for control of the most fearsome fighting force in all of Europe. The Stormriders were a cavalry force created by Leopold's grandfather, the first Habsburger to become King of the Germans. He had assembled the top fighting men in Europe, provided them with the best horses and equipment, and granted them their own castle from which they would serve the Habsburg rulers. They were full-time warriors and the highest paid knights in the known world. Competition to join the Sturmritter was intense and every year men died during the fierce tournaments that served as auditions for young men seeking to earn fame and a place amongst the elite.

Otto openly stared at Frederick, demanding a response, but before Frederick could say anything, Leopold spoke up. "I am afraid that is impossible, Lord Otto. The Sturmritter are suppressing a revolt in Schwabia at the moment."

Otto eyed Leopold with an odd mix of loathing and pride. "A peasant revolt. Hardly a situation to warrant the use of the Sturmritter."

"But a strategic location that is crucial to Austria.

When they are finished their work in Schwabia I am sure my brother will make them available to your cause, if they are still required. In the meantime, surely all the soldiers of Austria, under your unfailing leadership, shall be sufficient to deal with Louis the Bavarian."

Leopold turned quickly from Otto before he could reply and addressed his brother directly. "Frederick, I need to speak with you on a topic of the utmost importance. *Family* matters."

Frederick caught Leopold's hidden meaning, and ignoring the frustrated looks of the nobles in the room, gestured for his brother to follow him out the door. "Of course. Let us take a recess. Gentlemen, excuse us if you would."

They walked down the stone corridor to a smaller receiving room at the end of the hall. Fresh rushes covered the stone floor and a fire burned in the hearth, while a thick layer of smoke hovered, trapped near the top of the twelve-foot ceiling. Leopold reached to close the heavy door behind them, and was startled to see the Fool about to follow them in.

Leopold held out his arm. "You can stay out there. I've seen enough of your painted face for one day," he said and threw the door shut before the smiling little man could set even one of his pointed shoes over the threshold.

"You have news of the assassin? Has he been found?" Frederick asked, unable to contain himself a second more.

"I do have news of our cousin's whereabouts, but it is only a tip—nothing more. I was on my way to investigate when I heard you were to meet with the nobles alone."

Frederick placed his hand on his brother's shoulder and let out a long breath. The tension in him eased somewhat.

"And I am thankful you are here. Word is the German Princes are favoring Louis for the throne and our supporters are calling for an immediate show of force. But how can I march on Louis? He has been our friend since childhood."

"It is not Louis, but the Princes who are behind this. They fear Habsburg power—it has always been so. It was the same when our father came to power. He was not given the kingship, but had to take it, and now brother, you must do the same."

Frederick dropped into one of the intricately carved wooden chairs in front of the fire. "How goes work on the Altdorf citadel?"

Leopold grunted. "It is little more than a mound of rubble at the moment. Certainly not a citadel. I need more workers. Speaking of which, I do not suppose…"

"If I had men to spare they would be readying for battle, I am afraid," Frederick said. "Not playing with stone and mallet."

Leopold's jaw clenched, starting a tremor in the muscles under his cheekbones.

"Traffic over the Gotthard Pass doubles every month with the recent improvements the Milanese have made on the Devil's bridge over the Reuss. The Gotthard is now the fastest way for all Mediterranean merchants to traverse the Alps and trade with the Hanseatic League. Both the King of France and the Duke of Milan are scheming for its control. Protecting Habsburg land from their hungry eyes is hardly *playing*, brother."

Frederick let out a sigh and pinched the bridge of his

nose between his fingers. He let his chin momentarily dip to his chest.

"Forgive me, Leo. I am tired. I do not have the patience for these games. You should have been born the elder."

Leopold forced a laugh, but in truth a chill went through him at the thought of being King of the Holy Roman Empire. Having to deal with advisers and petty petitions from nobles and commoners alike, always in the midst of the conniving German princes. No, that was not a position to covet. "Nonsense. I work better behind the lines. You know that."

"I wish father were still alive. I can understand our cousin for feeling slighted, deprived even, of his inheritance, but to go so far as to plan the assassination of the King? For the love of Christ I cannot see what drove him to it."

"Evil can be found in all men's hearts if you look deep enough," Leopold said.

"Father was a great man. Even the Jews would admit as much. But something in him changed when Rudolph died. I know you felt it too."

Leopold knew exactly what Frederick meant. King Albrecht had had three sons. The oldest was Rudolph and it had been no secret that he was the King's favorite. After many years of scheming and brilliant politics, Albrecht had secured the throne of Bohemia for his son Rudolph. Unfortunately, barely a year into his reign, Rudolph succumbed to a fever and died.

With the death of his eldest son, the aging Albrecht's mind had come unhinged. Not all at once, in an obvious way, but to those closest to him, especially his sons Frederick and Leopold, the changes were readily apparent. He became forgetful, drank wine in the evenings, something he had forbidden his own sons to do, and appeared less frequently at the local courts he had fought so hard to establish during his reign.

Near the end, he would not be seen for days, and when he did appear, he was frequently in his cups. And then, one afternoon while crossing the Reuss River, he was attacked and killed by his nephew John and three fellow conspirators. The bloated bodies of John's accomplices were found days later miles downstream but somehow John 'the Parricide' managed to escape the wrath of Albrecht's sons and fled into hiding. Claiming Frederick had enough to worry about with being the head of the Habsburg family, and potentially the new Emperor of the Germans, Leopold had declared he would take it upon himself to find John and bring him to justice.

"You must be strong in this hour," Leopold said. "All eyes are on you now, and if the princes see weakness you will never be elected to the throne. But more importantly, you cannot trust any of those nobles in the other room. They stand with you only because they need your strength to protect their lands. Not because of any past loyalty to our father. Never for a moment forget this." *Parasites,* he thought. *Every last one of them.*

Frederick looked up from his chair, his usually smiling eyes now dark and red-rimmed. It hurt Leopold to see him this way. His brother was a simple man, honorable and just, if not overly wise. He would make a good king. Too good—the German princes would flay him alive. It would be best for all if Frederick was not a candidate for the throne, but Leopold knew that was impossible.

Their father had built the German Empire up for one of his sons to rule, and Frederick would give his life to honor his father's ambitions, no matter the cost to himself. Everyone knew Frederick the Handsome's honor and sympathy for his subjects were his greatest strengths, but Leopold saw them as weaknesses that would eventually lead to his downfall. And when he fell, as he most surely would, it was Leopold's duty to ensure the Habsburg line survived. And the longer he kept Frederick alive, the longer he would have to increase the family's private holdings. In Leopold's mind, the acquisition of land and estates in the Habsburg name was the key to maintaining power.

That, and of course, the Stormriders.

"Promise me something," Leopold said.

Frederick stared into the fire. "If I can," he said.

"You will never relinquish control of the Sturmritter to another man. Not even your military advisors." *Especially them.*

"Then I would ask something of you," Frederick said.

Leopold's head cocked to one side. It was unlike his brother to barter with him. With a great effort Frederick pushed himself up from his warm chair like a drowning man kicking to the water's surface.

"Take the Fool with you to Aargau. It seems he has a history with many of our father's advisors and I fear for his life while he is here. I cannot possibly devote the time every day to keep him from harm's path."

Leopold took a deep breath before he spoke. "Surely no one could gain from killing the Fool. This is his home. He would not be happy, nor comfortable, in our rustic country estates."

"You and I know he is no threat. But some feel he

was too close to father and was privy to all types of sensitive information. Please, Leo, obey me on this one thing. Father would want to see our childhood playmate taken care of as he enters his twilight years."

Leopold forced his thin lips into something resembling a smile.

"Of course. But I have business to attend before returning to Habsburg. Have him ready his belongings and send him in a few days."

Even that much of a respite would be welcome. Frederick placed his hands on Leo's shoulders.

"Thank you brother. It may be a small thing to you, but knowing our Fool is safe in your care lessens much of the weight bearing on my mind."

He threw his arms around Leopold and they embraced.

Then holding him at arms length he looked at his brother and said, "Besides, you may find his advice intriguing. Sometimes I think he is my wisest advisor."

Frederick broke into honest, deep-belly laughter at this, which lifted years from his face. Leopold, grateful to see the change, echoed his brother's laughter, musing all the while whether God had a hand in inflicting this punishment.

***

The cheese hut stood alone high in the hills. To provide a level foundation in the mountainous terrain, it was built on legs of differing heights consisting of flat stones stacked upon one another. The top stone of each leg was smooth and twice the size of the others so as to create an overhang, an impossible barrier for field mice trying to climb up the legs and gain entry to the hut. A month from now, when the snow was completely gone and the grasses turned the hills green, the farmer and his wife would drive their animals up from the lowlands and live in the hut all summer long making cheese.

But for now, there was only one resident: a young man, once used to the silk and linen comforts of the noble class but now garbed in the coarse, itchy brown robe of a Dominican friar. His hair was disheveled, and dark, bloodshot eyes told of countless nights with little sleep.

As dusk approached, he stood inside the small hut with the door ajar, looking out over the hills as two riders approached. His first impulse was to flee, but he soon recognized the riders and willed himself to stay put.

Moments later, Leopold dismounted, while Klaus, a thick soldier who had been Leopold's man for many years, remained on his horse and kept a watchful eye on the surrounding slopes.

"Cousin, I thought you had broken your word and forsaken me in this damnable place," John said, his voice accusing and rough from lack of use.

Leopold untied a bag from his saddle and tossed it to John, who snatched it out of the air and immediately snaked his hand inside to retrieve a thin slice of dried meat and a crusty loaf. It had been three weeks since his last visit from Leopold and his desire to speak with another person was great, but so was his need to eat something other than the porridge and cheese he had been living on. He crammed the slice of meat into his mouth and bit into the loaf. Crumbs flaked off and clung to his shaggy beard.

Leopold screwed up his nose and shook his head. "I

do not recall you being so uncouth at our last encounter. Perhaps you tire of this peaceful retreat in the Alps and are ready to move on?"

John ripped off another piece of bread with his teeth and spoke around it. "You know I am. Do not play games with me Leo—what news have you?"

"Good news cousin. You are free to go wherever you like now."

John's eyes lit up and he lowered the bag of food. "The princes will grant clemency then? I can return to Salzburg?"

"Salzburg? I suppose you could, but keep in mind you are still Wolf's head in Austria and like the beast, your skin can be traded for coin."

"What do you mean? You said I had to but wait for the princes to assemble and vote. Surely they see what a madman the King had become. I have served the German Empire and yet I hide in these hills cowering like a common criminal! You swore to me—"

Leopold cut him off by grabbing the front of his robe and pulling him close. "You are far worse than a common criminal," he said, and then disgusted by the stench of the man, pushed him stumbling back into the cheese hut's wall.

"The Pope has placed you under the Holy Ban."

The effect of the words was instantaneous. Horrified, John's legs went slack and he slid down the wall to sit on the ground. Leopold rubbed his hands together and then wiped them on one of Klaus's legs. The veteran soldier kept his eyes locked on the horizon.

"Apparently I underestimated how much the Pope respected my father."

John sat on the ground hugging his knees. His mouth

opened and closed several times before he finally found his voice. "No, it cannot be. I will flee to Spain. No Italia. I must go to Rome and buy indulgence…"

"Fool. How far do you think you will get when every man, child, and woman has the right to beat, rob, and kill you on sight? Under threat of excommunication, no one is allowed to aid you. I have wasted the past few months of my life building discreet relations with your connections at court. And for what? Nothing. You are useless to me now."

John shook his head slowly from side to side. "No— this is not what you promised. You said I would be granted lands and titles when Frederick became King." He pointed his finger up at Leopold. "You gave your word!"

Leopold rolled his eyes and walked over to his horse. "My word was it?"

He pulled himself up into the saddle and said, "Sorry cousin. I can deal with princes and kings, but a Papal Ban is beyond even me."

John stood on shaky legs and stumbled over to the two mounted men. Klaus grabbed the pommel of his sword, but Leo held up a restraining hand as John wrapped himself around the young Duke's boot and pleaded.

"No, do not go Leo. Please, I am sorry I accused you. I have been alone too long…my mind is not right. Surely there is something we can do. I will stay in hiding and when Frederick becomes king he can beseech the Pope…"

Leopold gently placed his hand on John's head and leaned over him. "My dear cousin, can you not see I have no choice?" One corner of his thin lips turned up in a smirk. "And besides…you did kill my father. Why would I assist the likes of you?"

Leopold pushed John away by his head, turned his horse, and jammed his heels into its side. He held up a hand in parting and called out, "Good luck on the road cousin. Beware old ladies and children trying to kill you in your sleep."

He left John the Parricide, slack-legged and hunched in front of the age-blackened shack, a man with no country and no god.

Chapter 3

WHEN THEY CAME to Altdorf, a town near the southern end of the Great Lake, Ruedi abruptly announced he would separate from the party.

Altdorf was a thriving town for these parts. Almost a city, Thomas thought. Easily the largest settlement they had seen since coming over the Gotthard Pass. On a rise in the distance he could even see new construction under way. It appeared to be a large stone keep beginning to take shape.

"Heard a rumor about five years back I have a sister in these parts," Ruedi said. "Course it came from a drunken Norseman, and he was not sure if he was in Burglen or Altdorf at the time. Still, nothing better to do. Might as well check it out."

"Best of luck finding her. I swear, this town has tripled in size since I saw it last. It was nothing more than a few farmer's huts clustered together from what I remember," Anton said.

"Well that is no farmer's hut," Pirmin said pointing at

the keep on the hill.

Thomas remembered the Norseman Ruedi talked about. *The Wyvern* had been patrolling the waters off the coast of Turkey and they came across the remains of a burned out merchant knarr floating dead in the water. Only one man remained alive, though he hovered precariously close to death.

Thomas ordered him to be taken to the Hospital in Rhodes, where to everyone's amazement and thanks in no small part to the skill of the Order's doctors, the man had survived and spent almost two months amongst the Hospitallers. He was well traveled and a tireless storyteller, provided he was kept in his cups, and told endless tales of the far North and how most people there still believed not in one god, but in many, similar to the Greeks of old.

The seven men dismounted in front of a church, which, though small, was still the most impressive building in sight. Next to it was a recently constructed barracks, with three Austrian soldiers standing about eyeing the travelers. It was midday, the street quiet as most people were at work.

Each man said some parting words to Ruedi and embraced him in the quick emotional manner of men who had forged a bond of incredible strength over the years. As a parting gift Thomas gave him a dozen crossbow quarrels.

"You will make better use of these than I ever could," Thomas said.

"Aye. You never had much of an eye, Cap'n. I will come find you sometime—maybe take you hunting. Try not to starve before then." His voice broke slightly and the forks of his mahogany beard twitched as he clamped his mouth shut.

Thomas mounted up and the men rode out of Altdorf, leaving Ruedi standing alone in the middle of the road, the occasional townsman scurrying past, pretending not to stare.

***

It was already dark when they rode into Schwyz, but they had no trouble finding a large inn. The village was a common stopping point for travelers who had made it over the Alps and the inn's business seemed good. The high-ceilinged common room held a dozen tables, half of them filled with patrons, when Thomas's party entered. A staircase, with sturdy treads formed from split logs, led up to several rooms on the second floor.

Faces looked up but quickly turned away again when someone from Thomas's group met their gaze. Good things rarely came from prolonged eye contact with six heavily armed men weary from the road.

The owner, a thin, tight-lipped man with strong hands, watched the new arrivals suspiciously from behind a high counter, which separated the crowd from several tapped kegs. He seemed to relax slightly when Max paid some coins up front and negotiated for rooms and horse stabling.

Soon, heaping bowls of chamois stew and ceramic mugs of ale were placed before the six men. As the owner brought the food out of the kitchen, Thomas glanced an older woman and a younger pretty girl with sand-colored hair. She stared at Thomas and his companions with wide eyes, and then the door swung shut obscuring her from view.

Thomas surveyed the patrons. A few tables of traveling merchants, and another with two grizzled and grey men and a woman hunched over their drinks, talking in hushed tones. Then he looked at his own group of dirty, rough men-at-arms as an outsider might and did not blame the innkeeper for hiding the womenfolk away in the kitchen.

While with the Order, Thomas and his men had always worn brown cloaks and tunics with the white Hospitaller cross prominently displayed on the chest or shoulder. His friends looked different now in plain traveling garb, albeit their weapons and partially visible chainmail marked them as more than simple travelers.

"Our coin will go a long way in this land," Max said, obviously pleased with the outcomes of his negotiations.

"A good thing that is. Since you still owe me for re-shaping that sword you carry," Urs said. During his years of service to the Order of Saint John, in addition to being a sergeant-at-arms, Urs had been apprenticed to one of the Order's weapons-makers. A quiet perfectionist with forearms almost as large as Pirmin's, Urs was far happier handling hammer and anvil than using the quality weapons he forged.

"I told you. Once we get to Zug I will sell some of my spices at the market and buy you a new horse. A good mountain pony that will carry your bulk to Basel without balking at every slope."

Urs grunted—a noncommittal sound that meant he neither agreed nor disagreed with Max. For a moment it looked like he might say more but instead wrapped his thick fingers around the mug in front of him and drained it.

Since leaving Ruedi at Altdorf, the reality that their

journey together was at an end had finally sunk in, and Thomas had been debating with himself where his own path would finish. Max had family in Zug, Urs was from Basel, Gissler's father was a steward of land in the Aargau, Anton was headed to Appenzell, and Pirmin could not stop talking about the mountains of Wallis and his family's black-necked goat farm, although he seemed to be taking the long way home by going through Schwyz.

Schwyz. This was where their journey together had begun so many years ago. It was fitting that it should also end here.

"Max, I would collect my share here in the morning," Thomas said.

Conversation within the group ceased and as one they turned to look at Thomas. When they were on campaign, Max had always looked after the troop's money. He had a mind that never forgot a sum and he could write numbers. He knew a few letters, but the only one of the group who could truly read and write was Thomas.

Money had not played a large part in the sergeants' military lives, since their everyday needs were supplied by the Order, but they were given a small salarium every month to be spent how they chose. Before leaving Rhodes for the last time, Max had collected the meager life savings of his friends together and exchanged the coins for a letter of credit from the Order of Saint John, which was redeemable at any of the Order's hospices or estates scattered throughout Europe. Many merchants took advantage of this deposit and withdrawal system offered by both the Hospitallers and the Templars, since it was a safe way to conduct business in lands rife with thieves and highwaymen.

Max had redeemed the letter at a hospice they found in northern Italia a week ago, but since everyone trusted him, he still held all the coin himself, doling it out carefully when they needed to purchase meals or lodging.

"So you will be staying here in Schwyz then?" Max asked, looking over his half-eaten bowl of stew.

Thomas shrugged. "For awhile. Remember that old man and his ferry we passed on the lake close to Brunnen? It gave me an idea."

"You will be wasting yourself here in the poor country," Gissler said. "Come with me up north to the Aargau. My father has connections—I am sure he knows someone who could put our swords to use."

Thomas shook his head. "I appreciate the offer, Gissler, but I mean to try my hand at something different. It seems the Good Lord has more than hinted that my time as one of His sword bearers has come to an end, and frankly, I have no desire to see it put to another's use."

"Thomi, Thomi. Your days on the water are over. What would you be wanting with an old rotten barge I wonder?" Pirmin said, already drinking from his third mug of ale.

Thomas's eyes came to life. "She will not be rotten when I finish with her."

Pirmin stared at Thomas for a moment while he sopped up the juices of his stew with a chunk of crusty bread. He popped it into his mouth and spoke around it, which had the effect of lessening his Wallis accent, and curiously, made his speech easier to understand.

"Well I know as soon as I get back home to Tasch my family will want to marry me off to keep the

---

40

Schnidrig line going strong. And I admit I look forward to one part of that. Those Wallis women are easy on the eyes and know how to keep their men warm at night, I tell you that much."

"What do you know about Wallis women? You were eight the last time you saw one," Thomas said.

"Must be talking about his mother," Anton said.

"It is the air and the water," Pirmin said, ignoring them both. "Something about it produces the most handsome animals, and people. Similar to how the bitter water in Appenzell keeps all Anton's people small and stunted. Talk nice to me lads, and maybe I will bring some of that Wallis nectar and sell it to you. No reason your children need to be ugly—God knows you and your kin have suffered enough already."

Anton punched the giant man in the shoulder, while Gissler dipped his fingers in his ale and flicked them at Pirmin. Pirmin wiped his face and crossed himself and then held up a finger.

"But first, I think I will stay here for a time and help Thomi build his boat. Raise up gentlemen and let us drink to making ugly people better looking!"

"To new ventures," Max said, raising his mug.

They echoed Max's toast and clanked their mugs together, splashing ale over the table. They laughed hard and drank long into the night, reminiscing over thirty years of shared exploits. For the remainder of the evening, they peeled back the years until each man saw only the faces of boys before him, and the aches and pains inflicted by a lifetime of war dissolved into the night.

Chapter 4

NOLL MELCHTHAL SPRINTED up the treed slope, breathing through his nose and pacing himself carefully so the armored men cursing and shouting behind did not fall too far back. His powerful legs pumped with a rhythm all their own. These were his woods, his mountains. No foreign lapdog soldier could touch him here.

He stooped and picked up a good rock. Taking careful aim he wound up and launched it at the closest man. A boiled-leather breastplate emblazoned with the red fist insignia of Berenger von Landenberg, the Habsburg appointed Vogt of Unterwalden, protected the man's chest, but the stone hit him high in the shoulder and he let out a squeal of pain. Noll laughed and ducked behind a tree as a crossbow bolt flew past and skittered off the rock bluff behind him.

He pulled up the hood on his cloak, stepped out from behind his cover to make sure the soldiers got a good look at him, and started climbing again. A minute later he crested the rise and the path leveled out for a straight stretch through the forest.

Squatting against a tree was Aldo, a tall boy in his late teens wearing a cloak the same drab brown as Noll's. He stood up and grinned at Noll with a questioning look on his face. Noll slowed to a walk and counted slowly to ten, then he made a forward motion with his hand and the young man pulled up the hood of his cloak and ran away through the forest.

Noll veered off the path and sat down in the underbrush. He could hear the soldiers crashing up the slope for some time before they finally appeared at the top. They spotted the figure running through the trees in the distance and, heartened by the level ground, immediately gave chase with renewed vigor. They charged by so close to Noll's hiding spot he could see the sweat on their red faces and hear the bellows of their breathing.

Seconds later, Noll stood and watched the clumsy soldiers crashing through the underbrush in pursuit of their quarry. He shook his head, then turned and began walking back down the hill to the Austrian soldiers' deserted camp.

***

Trees were the most vocal beings in the forest. They were kind and generous souls and although Seraina rarely comprehended what they were saying to one another, she never tired of listening to their creaks and murmurs. Occasionally, she would even understand a reference to a creature or an upcoming storm, or experience a sense of emotion such as the joy of stretching out towards the morning sun or the cooling relief of a summer rain. It did not bother her that she understood so little of their language, for the sound of their voices was comforting enough.

She tended her garden behind the small cottage she had come to inhabit three years ago. It was in thick forest that allowed only sporadic beams of sunlight to pierce the canopy of trees, and perhaps that is why the previous owner deserted it. But she was no ordinary gardener. She knew how and where to plant vegetables and herbs so they flourished.

The foundation of the cottage and lower half were made from stone, upon which rough-hewn timber comprised the walls. It was a sturdy shelter and had been built with great skill many years ago, but when she found it, the thatched roof was mostly rotted away and needed to be replaced. A nearby farmer and his wife assisted her with the necessary repairs, and in return, she helped them when they needed a healer's skill.

It was three hours from the nearest village, and the village of Schwyz easily twice that, for to reach it, one must first cross an arm of the Great Lake or walk around. Seraina could not imagine why the original owner had chosen to live so far from the towns, but it suited her fine. It was far enough away that the townsfolk could pretend she did not exist, yet near enough to seek her out when they needed help.

She had not always lived so far from her people.

Like their trees, the people of these lands were capable of great kindness and looked after one another fiercely. Yet they were a private lot and devoted Christians. For a time she lived amongst them in the small village of Tellikon, near Zurich, where her skills with growing herbs and in the healing arts became well known. Even though she did not share their Christian faith, many people came to accept Seraina as a member of the community.

Until one night, with frozen rain pelting the village roofs, she assisted in a breached childbirth that left the mother dead and the baby a cripple. Death during childbirth was a common enough affair, and all would have been fine, but the baby had the misfortune of being born with misshapen feet. The parish priest called them hooves.

He tried to take the child but Seraina refused to give her up. The next night the priest appeared at her shack with a rabble of angry villagers and they tore the child from her arms. He named her a witch and a servant sent by the Devil to corrupt the people of Tellikon. Few believed his words but even fewer were foolish enough to take the chance that a demon lived amongst them.

She was driven from the town but managed to escape her pursuers and watch from the safety of the trees as they burnt her shack and the entirety of her few belongings. The torches set to her home were lit from the same bonfire used to burn the child.

Lost in her thoughts of the past, Seraina did not hear the young man approach until he spoke.

"Pretty girls should pay more attention when alone in the woods. You never know what beast might be lurking nearby."

Seraina started and stood from her garden. She cocked her head, her ears still picking up the voices of the trees, loud and unconcerned. Noll grunted as he dropped a large sack on the ground that clanged as it hit.

The trees were extremely sensitive and Seraina could

---

tell when people, and even some animals, approached by how they reacted. She used to think it strange that Noll's presence never disturbed them, but that was before she knew him. Before she had come to realize he was the Catalyst.

"The only dangerous beasts in this area are of the human variety," Seraina said. She nodded toward the bag on the ground. "What treasures have you liberated today?"

Noll shrugged. "Soldier provisions mostly. Bread, some cheese, a few cooking pots. Choose what you want and I will take the rest back with me to the men."

Noll walked over to a barrel of rainwater, splashed some on his face and ran his fingers back through his short dark hair. He removed his shirt and began splashing water under his arms and on his neck and chest, his wiry muscles tensing under the cold water. At least five years younger than Seraina, he was lean but wide at the shoulders. For one so young he had a rare self-confidence women found irresistible and men respected.

"Oh, and I need a refill on the ivy powder," Noll said, his blue eyes glinting as beads of water ran through his hair and down the stubble on his cheeks. She allowed herself to stare for a moment before responding.

"More? You must be using too much. Where did the last three vials go?"

Noll grinned and dried off his face with his shirt. "Been lots of bedrolls to attend. Our Habsburg lords seem to be sending more soldiers than usual out into the woods these days."

Seraina shook her head. "These are games you play Noll. Really, what good are they? You steal from soldiers, taunt them, make them angry. It does nothing for the people. It changes nothing."

"Ah, but it is entertaining. And who is to say it does nothing for the people? It shows them that if my men and me can stand up to Landenberg then they can too. Two more men joined us last month."

Seraina smiled and shook her head. "Aldo and Martin? They are boys. Boys that should be at home working farms, not running through the forest playing tricks on real soldiers."

"The boys of today make up the armies of tomorrow," Noll said.

"And what if you are caught and hung? What will your *men* do then?"

Noll laughed and pulled on his shirt. "They would have to find me first. These are my woods, Seraina. I refuse to bend to the will of a foreigner who thinks because he has soldiers and the blessing of some King I have never seen, he can take land my family has lived on for a thousand years."

Seraina felt a flutter in her breast. She liked it when Noll spoke with such conviction, but she also knew better than to encourage him. Once Noll got started he was an unstoppable force and she would rather see that energy directed somewhere that it would do some good.

"I hear you moved your camp again," Seraina said, changing the topic.

"You are well-informed," Noll said, surprised. "Spying on me are you? Jealous perhaps? No need to be, you know. We are so far away from civilization we cannot even get camp whores to come to our tents."

"So where are you now?"

Noll shook his head. "You know I cannot tell you,"

he said, then his eyes took on a mischievous glint. "But I could show you. Why not come with me? We could use someone with your talents and it is too dangerous for you to be out here on your own. Too lonely. Come with me and I promise you would want for nothing."

His smile was bold and tempting. The invitation was not subtle, for that was not Noll's way. He lived for the moment, and at the moment Seraina could sense his desire. As enjoyable as helping him sate that desire might be, Seraina knew she could not go with him. He was the Catalyst, and to share his bed would cloud her visions of the Weave.

He was right though. She was lonely at times. But the horrors of Tellikon had taught her that to serve her people she must maintain her distance.

Seraina shook her head. "I have responsibilities here. I cannot just leave."

Noll exhaled and held up his hands. "You have an overgrown garden and some birds that you feed. What is so important that you have to be here?"

Seraina laughed and took his arm.

"As I have told you before. I must be close enough to help you but far enough away that I can still listen to the wind. Come. Let us go get you some more ivy powder."

Noll shook his head and fixed her with a puzzled smile.

"You are the strangest woman I have ever known." And then he remembered something. "Seraina, a few miles from here I found wolf tracks—the biggest I have ever seen. He was all alone, so probably driven out of the pack and hungry. Keep an eye out and be careful, will you?"

48

Seraina's breath caught in her throat.

"Seraina, did you hear what I said?" Noll asked.

Her only response was a curt nod, for she was not sure her voice could be trusted.

Chapter 5

THE TWO ARMORED MEN, thronged by cheering spectators, circled each other. Both let their shields drop slightly to ease their aching arms and sucked in ragged breaths to prepare for the next assault. Then, one man charged forward to swing his hand-and-a-half sword down upon the other's shield.

"I never understood what the point is in hitting another man's shield," Leopold said, holding his goblet out to be refilled by a servant standing ready with a pitcher of honeyed wine. "Why not simply aim where the shield is not?"

"Intimidation," Berenger Von Landenberg, the Vogt of Unterwalden said, taking a pull off his own mead. "Shake a man's shield arm to the core and it takes the fight out of him."

He sat forward in his high-backed chair, but not because the match enthralled him. Landenberg was a large man with a rounded salt and pepper beard and the soft, blackened teeth of a noble who had eaten too much white bread. Though he wore no armor, squeezing his girth between the armrests of the wooden chair, if possible, would be far from comfortable. In his early fifties now, he watched the competitors with disdain and undisguised jealousy.

Count Henri of Hunenberg also sat on the raised platform with the young Habsburg Duke and the Vogt, albeit in a plain chair that lacked the intricate carvings of the other two men. The ever-present Klaus, Leopold's man, stood at the bottom of the platform's stairs, unmoving as an iron rod driven straight into hard-packed earth.

The crowd groaned as one of the competitors missed an overhead strike leaving himself open and his opponent brought his own blade crashing down across the man's back, knocking him to the ground and ending the match.

"Sweet Mary. Finally. This match should have been finished long ago," Landenberg said, standing to fart and stretch his joints. "Wine," he said thrusting out his mug. "I have a mind to send for my own armor."

Leopold was in no mood for Landenberg's blustering. Granted the man had his uses, especially when it came to keeping order in the backward villages and mountain settlements of Unterwalden. Violence and intimidation were all those people understood, so they deserved to be governed by a filthy boar of a man like Landenberg.

The ride back from Salzburg had been long and wearying, made even more so because Leopold had to suffer the company of the Fool. His eyes scanned the crowd and immediately picked out the little man's purple hair and white and black outfit doing a dance in front of some shabbily dressed peasants, who seemed to have forgotten their miserable lot in life and were enjoying his antics.

"Our tournament days are over, Berenger," Count Henri said, invading on Leopold's thoughts. "This is a young man's domain." Although much smaller than the hulking Landenberg, Henri still had the fit body of a knight. He had been fighting off and on in the Holy Lands for almost twenty years and had returned to the Aargau five years ago when his father died. He inherited his father's lands: three lucrative estates in the Aargau and one rocky tract of land at the head of the Gotthard Pass. Not exceptionally rich titles, but Leopold was in negotiations to acquire the Gotthard land to add to the Habsburg family's holdings. Henri's family connections with landowners in Uri, where Saint Gotthard's Pass was located, had proved valuable when Leopold had purchased land at the head of the pass last year. The same land where Leopold currently had fifty stone masons constructing a fortress that would be his new home. He needed some farmland to support the fortress, and poor though it was, Henri's small estate should do nicely. Henri's Connections would prove useful in the coming years if Leopold were to bring the pass under Habsburg control.

"Count Hunenberg is right. You have seen too many years to be playing the part of a ram so sit down and accept your place. I would wager there is not a man on this field who would not rather be one of my governors than chafing under sweaty armor."

Landenberg grunted at the rebuke. "If I had your youth, my lord, I would gladly be on that field winning my share of honors."

"Honor is a myth. The tourney was created to keep our warriors occupied in times of peace. To prevent the dogs from turning on their masters, if you will. A soldier is a tool of the nobility. One that must be stored with care, mind you, and sharpened regularly, but nothing more."

"And when that tool ages and shows signs of rust?" Count Henri asked. "What then?"

Leopold did not hesitate. "We throw it out. Or occasionally, the axe is melted down and reshaped into a hoe." He made a point in looking at Landenberg as he spoke.

Henri stood, smiling at Landenberg's discomfort, and said to Leopold, "All this talk of politics has stirred my bowels. If you will excuse me, my lord." He stepped down off the dais and moved between two merchant stalls, one selling fire-roasted sausages on a stick and the other small loaves of crusty dark bread.

Leopold motioned the next pair of combatants into the ring. Landenberg, scowling, wedged himself back down into his chair. His eyes lit up when he recognized one of the combatants, a thick young man with blonde hair and the neck of a bull whose shield bore the markings of several tourneys he had won.

"Ah. Now we shall see some sport," Landenberg said. "That is Sir Rolf of Nuremberg—saw him kill a man on this field last year. Damned fool's helm was too big and the force of Sir Rolf's blow shook his skull to pieces."

"He does appear capable," Leopold said, but his eyes were on Rolf's opponent.

He was a thin, unremarkable fellow with greying hair

at least fifteen years older than any competitor on the field. And unlike the other fighters, the only armor he wore was a light mail vest that was almost hidden beneath a faded black tunic. Leather bracers covered his wrists, but there were neither plates on his shoulders or legs, nor a gorget around his throat. The older man hefted several different swords from the weapons rack and tested them for balance, shifting each one carefully from hand to hand, before finally deciding on a smaller one-handed blade with a single cutting edge.

Leopold's lips turned up in a smirk. The young duke had been raised amongst men such as this. From an early age Leopold had been sent by his father to live for months at a time in soldier barracks throughout the German Empire, France, Denmark, and Italia. While his older brothers were kept at King Albrecht's side in Austria to learn how to rule, Leopold's father shipped him off to live with foreign tutors. Not so much to learn to be a soldier, but to learn how one thinks. To recognize what motivates them and what kind of discipline it takes to control them. He learned to read men's eyes, their postures, what body types made a good horseman, and which were better suited to infantry. Who would be loyal and who could be bribed. This was his education. From the ages of ten to fifteen, Leopold saw his father only three times, at public functions of state that demanded a show of Habsburg solidarity. Frederick had visited his younger brother regularly, but both Leopold's father and oldest brother were strangers who happened to share the same family name.

"One hundred silver says the old man makes your Sir Rolf yield like a pliant serving girl."

Landenberg's eyebrows arched and he looked at Sir

Rolf's opponent for the first time. He saw only an aging man with inferior equipment desperate to earn some prize money and perhaps, to hold onto a piece of his youth.

"Let us make it two hundred, and since you mentioned a serving girl, you arrange to have the innkeeper in Schwyz send his daughter to serve in my household."

Leopold had no idea who this innkeeper was, but it did not matter.

"Done," he said, waving his hand to a nearby servant. The aroma of the nearby roasted sausages had watered his mouth. He summoned a page and soon he had a hot, spitting sausage on a stick in one hand and a piece of dark bread in the other. He nibbled off a piece of the succulent meat and settled back into his chair to watch the match.

The master of the ring called the men to their marks.

"For the pleasure of our Lord Leopold, Prince of the august German Empire, Duke of Further Austria and Styria, Regent and heir—" Leopold made a cutting motion across his neck and waved impatiently at the man. He bowed stiffly and continued. "Lords and ladies, our next contest shall be between Sir Rolf of Nuremberg and..." He leaned close to the older man and asked him something. "...and...Gissler."

***

Gissler bore no shield or helm, but walked calmly to his starting position. He avoided looking at his opponent. Sir Rolf's face visor was raised and strands of blonde hair poked out from beneath his chain coif. A green silk

---

55

kerchief from some female admirer fluttered in the breeze at his belt.

"Fear not grandfather," Sir Rolf said to his older opponent in a clear tone that carried far into the ranks of spectators. "You will suffer no serious injury by my hand." Laughter rippled through the crowd.

Gissler looked up for the first time at his much larger adversary. His eyes narrowed and flitted casually over the young knight. He rolled his shoulders once and spit on the ground.

"Of that I am sure," Gissler said. He lifted his sword to a low guard.

Sir Rolf flinched at the impetuous attitude of his lowborn opponent. A few people close enough to hear Gissler's quiet response cheered. One boisterous man yelled, "Take him over your knee old man!"

"Begin," shouted the master of the ring and backpedaled away from between the two men. The crowd erupted.

Sir Rolf raised his shield and stalked forward without bothering to lower his visor. Gissler waited for him to close the distance and then changed to a high guard. He swung his sword at Sir Rolf's head and the young knight thrust his shield up to meet the blow and set up his counter. With surprising speed for such a large man in full armor, Sir Rolf took the blow on his shield and then dipped it to the side as he swung his hand and a half sword towards Gissler. But the older man was no longer in front of him.

The moment the knight's vision was blocked by his own shield, Gissler spun around his shield arm to Sir Rolf's back, lifted his foot and smashed it down into the back of the young man's knee, then thrust his shoulder into his back to topple the man forward. The knight hit the ground hard and he grunted with the impact. Gissler turned and whipped his sword down onto the back of Sir Rolf's helm so hard the blade shattered like an icicle dropping onto a winter-hardened flagstone floor. Sir Rolf's eyes jerked up into his head, the color all but disappearing and leaving only vacant whites staring into the crowd. He slowly pitched forward from his knees onto his face and did not move.

The crowd fell silent at the violent and excessive blow, but once it dawned on them the fight was over the cheering began. Sir Rolf's squires pushed forward and rolled their liege lord onto his side and carefully removed his helm. He was unconscious, but came to moaning when they sat him up, and the sudden movement caused him to retch. Vomit cascaded down his chin, while a squire frantically used his sleeve to wipe the unseemly mess off Sir Rolf's polished chest protector.

The ringmaster pushed his way forward and, his eyes wide with surprise, raised his arm in Gissler's direction. "The winner is...Gessel!"

Gissler was already moving out of the circle toward the weapon racks when he heard his name called.

"Gissler? By God, what land is this? Is that really you?" Count Henri stepped out of the crowd and clamped his hand on Gissler's shoulder. Gissler flinched, and he looked as though he might repel this new attacker, but then recognition flooded his face and he stared open-mouthed, unable to speak.

"But of course it is—I recognize your work," Henri said, nodding towards Sir Rolf's squires struggling to get their lord on his feet.

"Henri," Gissler said finally, shaking his head. "Look

57

at you." He stepped back and gestured at the Count's richly tailored clothes and plumed hat. "A lord of peacocks if ever there was one." The two men laughed and threw their arms around one another in a rough soldier embrace.

"What are you doing here? Why are you not with the Order on Rhodes? I have word the Turks are giving the black knights an awful time on that rock."

Gissler shrugged. "That no longer concerns us. The Grand Master released us from our oaths coming on a year now."

"Us? Who else is with you man?"

"Every Schwyzer crew member of *The Wyvern*." Gissler told Henri how he had traveled back with Thomas, Pirmin, Ruedi, Anton, Urs, and Max. A puzzled look crossed Henri's face.

"But what of the others? Thomas's crew had three score of you when I was last aboard. What of Lars and Gerhard? And that pug-faced fellow who fell in love with every Saracen whore he saw?"

Gissler nodded, but his smile turned grim. "Geoff. Turks captured him during one of our raids on the coast. He was known to them, so his passing was not easy, I have been told. Lars has been dead nigh ten years, about the time the Mohammedans stopped accepting ransom for Hospitallers. We lost Gerhard at Rhodes, and as for the others..." Gissler held up his hands and shrugged. "We have been fighting a long time."

Henri's grin faded and after a moment, he nodded.

"The mind tries hard to forget the wars in Outremer after leaving. Some memories are better left stored away, I suppose, but I shall make a point of remembering the Schwyzers in my prayers tonight. They were good lads.

Some, like your captain Thomas, a little pious and headstrong, but a more loyal core of soldiers I have never known."

He winked and put his hand on Gissler's shoulder again. "But enough. I am sure you wish to put all that behind you now, so welcome home. What are your plans?"

Gissler shrugged. "I arrived only yesterday," he said.

Out of the corner of his eye, Henri noticed Duke Leopold ascending from his dais and walking in their direction, his man Klaus hulking one step behind. Leopold was looking directly at Gissler, but pretending not to.

"Well, it seems fate is descending upon you as we speak. Let us make the most of it, shall we? Come, allow me to present you to the Duke."

***

"You were a soldier in the Holy Lands?" Leopold asked.

"Yes, my lord," Gissler said.

"He was no mere soldier. Gissler was with the Black Knights," Count Henri said.

Leopold's eyes widened and he looked a little harder at Gissler.

Ah, I see it now, he thought. The alert way the man carried himself hinted at a life of discipline, but the aloof mannerisms and impetuous eyes betrayed him. He was indeed used to being seen as more than a mere soldier. He was far above that. He was one of God's chosen warriors, a Gabriel here on Earth. These Black Knights answered to no one but the Pope and God himself, just as the Templars once did. The Church had decreed that not even kings could command these men, never mind a lowly Duke of the German Empire.

"Your Order has done a great service protecting Christendom from the infidels. You are a Hospitaller Knight then?"

Gissler's mouth twitched at the corner, and he paused before responding.

"Not a knight, your Grace. Merely a brother sergeant-at-arms. Or I was. I have recently been released from the Order."

Leopold nodded, noting the bitter edge to Gissler's voice. The Knights of Saint John were largely made up of nobles from France, Germany, England, Spain, and Italia. They were required to give up their noble rights and will their land and holdings to the Order upon their death. They also took vows of chastity and poverty, and swore to accept the poor and sick as their lords. But the title of "Knight" was reserved for those of noble blood. Despite the Order's disdain for secular titles, there existed a strict hierarchy within the Order itself, and no commoner could ever rise above the rank of brother-sergeant.

"Tell me Hospitaller. What do you think of the recent trial and condemnation of the Templar Knights by his Holiness the Pope? I understand they were rivals of your Order in a way."

Seven years previous, the Christian world had been shocked to hear the Church and King Philip of France accuse the Templar Knights of heresy. The charges included spitting upon the cross, permitting sodomy, idol worshipping, and denying Christ and treading upon his image. Templars throughout Europe were arrested, including the Grandmaster Jacques de Molay. Subsequently, Molay and many others were subjected to the inquisition and confessed their crimes under torture. They had been kept in the dungeons of France for the past seven years awaiting their fate.

"We were both working to carry out God's will. I never considered them rivals," Gissler said.

"I have read the charges against the Temple. Incredible. And the knights have confessed to many of them. Did you know they worshipped a skull with three faces?"

"I did not," Gissler said.

"And they rubbed small cords on this idol which they then wore wrapped around various parts of their bodies. The grandmaster himself confessed that the idol was responsible for imbuing the knights with great riches. Behavior more fitting a coven of witches than a holy order, do you not agree?"

"A man will confess to much under torture," Gissler said, shifting his weight.

"Would he? Does not God dull the pain of the righteous? The Church tells us the innocent have nothing to fear from the inquisitor's tools of truth. And in fact, the courts will not recognize a confession unless it has been obtained through torture. Is that not so?"

"It is my lord."

"Well, it is in the past now I suppose, since the Grandmaster of the Temple has been burned at the stake. Ah, I see you did not know this."

Gissler cleared his throat. "The last I heard Grandmaster Molay had been cleared of all charges."

"Apparently King Philip of France decided otherwise. It is no secret that he has coveted the Templars' holdings in France for many years, but his plan bore no fruit. The Pope transferred all Templar estates to the Hospitallers. How in the world your Grandmaster convinced the Pope to do that, I cannot imagine. What do you suppose he will do with all that wealth now? Continue fighting the infidel? After nearly two hundred years it seems pointless really."

"As I said, I have no knowledge of any of this, my lord. I have been on the road for the better part of a year."

Leopold could tell the conversation was making Gissler uncomfortable, but to his credit he held the Duke's intense gaze with his own look of defiance. If he had been a normal peasant, Leopold would have had him whipped. Or worse. But he was a Hospitaller man-at-arms. A soldier forged in the wars of the Levant, and there was no finer training ground for his kind. And now, much to Leopold's liking, he was without a master.

A murmur shot through the crowd as the next two competitors made their way to the clearing and readied themselves for battle.

"Where does the name Gissler hail from? It sounds familiar," Leopold asked.

Gissler's face brightened. "Here in the Aargau, my lord. My family is steward for one of the King's estates near Sursee. Perhaps you know of my father? Hubert Gissler? Or, I suppose it possible my older brother Hugo is now chief steward."

Leopold pursed his lips and turned to his man Klaus. The old soldier thought for a moment and then cleared his throat. When he finally spoke, his voice sounded like gravel sliding down a rock slope.

"King Albrecht granted that land to a French Count

years ago. Brought in his own people to run it. Man named Lafayette is steward now."

The light in Gissler's eyes faded as quickly as it had appeared.

"They may still be working the land," Count Henri said. "And if not, someone there would surely know where to find them."

Gissler nodded slowly.

The crowd cheered again as the ringmaster called the combatants to their marks.

"Come Klaus. We must be returning to Kussnacht," Leopold said.

"You will not stay and see the outcome of the tourney?" Count Henri asked.

Leopold waved his hand. "I have my wedding to prepare for, and besides, the outcome of the tourney was decided the moment our Hospitaller entered. For who can compete with someone who has God on his side?"

The young Duke held the trace of a smile in his eyes but did not wait for an answer as he turned to take his leave. At the last moment, seemingly as an afterthought, he turned back and said, "Gissler, once you have sorted out your family affairs, come to Habsburg castle. Perhaps I will have work for you."

Klaus strode a few steps ahead of Leopold, cutting a path through the crowd with wide sweeps of his tree-limb arms, as they made their way to a waiting carriage with an armed escort of a dozen mounted soldiers clothed in the Habsburg colors of black and red. Two flag-bearers, one carrying a standard with the red lion of Habsburg, and the other a black bird of prey on a field of yellow, the colors of the Holy Roman Empire, stood nearby. A lithe figure with purple hair twisted its way through the hundreds of spectators and was waiting at the carriage door seconds before Leopold arrived.

By late afternoon Leopold's predictions had materialized, for no knight at the country tourney could stand before Gissler's speed and skill. He dispatched his opponents with a ruthless efficiency, never taking longer than one or two minutes, except on those occasions when he decided a knight needed to be toyed with and publicly humiliated. Every man who faced him sustained injuries and limped, crawled, or was carried from the circle. By the final matches, Gissler's ferocious reputation did as much to defeat his opponents as his sword blows.

After the final match, while a young knight still lay on the ground, his feet twitching in unconsciousness, Gissler took his prize purse and walked away.

He left the championship cup and pennant sitting on the table.

Chapter 6

SPRING BURST UPON THE ALPS like God was determined to thaw the Devil's glaciers and drive the mighty stone crags back into the recesses of the earth once and for all. The green-covered slopes erupted in golden clusters of cowslips, interspersed with patches of blue grape hyacinths. Sparkling streams of the sweetest water trickled down every hill, and what seemed like an endless assortment of wild game suddenly appeared.

To Thomas and Pirmin, after having spent a lifetime campaigning in the deserts of the Levant, it seemed like a miracle. They welcomed the heat and worked better in it.

Thomas had convinced the old ferryman to sell his barge for twice what it was worth, making Thomas wish Max had been there to help him negotiate. During his life with the Order Thomas had very little experience with money and business dealings had always made him uncomfortable. It did not help matters when Pirmin finally saw the old barge Thomas had spent most of his savings on.

"Thomi, Thomi. I agreed to help you fix up a boat. Not build one from scratch."

It was really no more than a rectangular raft of log floats covered with thick decking, most of which was rotting and in need of repair. It was large enough to carry five or six horses and perhaps ten men. The ferryman had connected it to a come-along system of ropes and pulleys hitched to a team of oxen on land. He was able to transport people across a narrow arm of the lake, and though it proved a safe way to cut almost two hours off the trip around the outside of the lake via the road, it could only cross at the same point every time.

Thomas knew it was not much, but he had a weakness for boats of all shapes and sizes and in his mind he saw what they could be. He meant to unshackle this barge and sail her freely. To him anything still sitting above the water had a God-given right to sail.

He was well versed in the mechanical laws that made sailing possible, but he did not credit their development to the ingenuity of men. Standing on the high side of a boat with the sails reefed in tight while she sailed almost straight into the wind was as close as one could get to God, for without His assistance, how else could a boat move forward with the wind blowing in your face, striving to halt your progress and spin you off in the opposite direction?

"A little work never killed a man, but you never were one to understand that," Thomas said, shaking his head. "Do not look down on her. She's got good bones and once we fit her with a leeboard, mast and a lateen-rigged yard, she will cut through this lake fast enough."

"You mean to sail the beast? She will handle like what she is—a pile of logs held together with pitch! At least when she sinks and we have built up an appetite from our swim to shore, we will be able to eat the oxen."

"We could have..." Thomas said. "If I had the silver to buy them."

Pirmin groaned and held his head between his massive hands.

"And where are you going to get good planks if you already spent all your coin?"

Thomas picked up one of two old axes the ferryman had included in the deal. Holding it by the head, he pointed with the handle at the forest behind Pirmin.

"We have a shipbuilder's dream of resources. Have you ever in your life seen trees as tall and straight as that? Granted, it may take a little more effort than ready cut timber—"

"You always insist on doing it the hard way, eh Captain?"

"Ah, but the ability to work hard is God's gift to the common man," Thomas said smiling. The scar tightened on his skin, but under the hot sun and with only Pirmin standing before him, it felt good.

They worked on the barge and lived in a tent on the water's edge, rising before dawn and starting early to avoid the mid-day's heat. Every day, they would watch in silence as the sun rose above the Alps and infused the Great Lake with light, turning the deep water a glimmering emerald green. It became a breathless ritual with them; one which involved no conversation for they could find no words to express how utterly different this life was from the one they had been living only a year ago.

But they did not live in isolation. Every few days, whenever they tired of camp cooking, they would saddle up their horses and ride into Schwyz. They would buy supplies and take a meal at Sutter's Inn, the same inn and tavern that they had stopped at the first night they had spent in Schwyz those few weeks past. The inn had been in the Sutter family for generations, but with the recent traffic increase over Saint Gotthard's Pass, Sutter's business grew to be too much for his family alone and he found himself hiring on a cook and another widow to help his wife make the ale and honeyed mead.

"Sutter says he knows a man with a bitch that just had a new litter," Pirmin said one night as they rode back from the inn, their bellies swollen with stew and ale. A half-moon hung over the Great Lake, sharing its other half with the water's surface.

The comment snapped Thomas out of the hypnotic trance brought on by the rhythm of Anid's gait and he looked up at Pirmin's silhouette. The size of the big man's charger made Thomas feel like he was rowing a skiff alongside a war galley. Thomas's stallion, Anid, was a pure Egyptian, a breed many Franks would consider too light to carry a fully armored man into battle. But Thomas had found Anid to have the perfect combination of strength and fearlessness for the role. And like most Arabian horses, Anid's speed and endurance was far greater than any destrier Thomas had ever ridden.

"You remember Zora?" Pirmin asked, his features unreadable in the dim moonlight.

"Of course," Thomas said.

How could he forget? Every couple years Pirmin would bring up his childhood dog and talk about her. Usually when he was drunk. And once again, at the mention of Zora, a wave of exhaustion shot through Thomas's body as his muscles remembered the long march from Schwyz to the shores of the Mid-Earth Sea.

A blonde-haired, scowling boy walked beside Thomas and though his words were laced with an accent Thomas struggled to understand, the boy talked enough that Thomas soon grew accustomed to his speech.

He was older, perhaps eight, but already his stocky build hinted at the massive man he would become. At his side walked the biggest working dog Thomas had ever seen. She was shorthaired and largely black, with a powerful white chest and snout, and a square head with a mask of black surrounding even blacker eyes. She would have been terrifying if it were not for the rust-colored thumbprints above her eyes that softened her expressions. The draft dog was hitched to a cart that she pulled effortlessly with a nonchalant grace, as though trying to pretend it was not there.

After a grueling three-month journey by land and then sea, the army of children was marching on a dusty road, less than five hours from the gates of Acre, when slavers came for them.

An avalanche of boulders and smaller rocks careened down the steep hillside, crushing a knight and the handful of children in its path. A deafening rumble echoed all around them and dust billowed up and choked the gorge. Then, a hundred men appeared and swarmed down into the ravine like so many ants, yelling and screaming in various languages.

All around Thomas was chaos. Dust hung in the air like smoke and children were running, screaming, trying to escape the slavers who seemed to be everywhere with ropes and leather collars. Thomas saw one of the black knights pinned to the ground with a spear, and two more fighting in the distance, several bodies at their feet.

Thomas pressed his back up against the rock wall of the canyon, trying to disappear, as he watched Zora savage the throat of one of the slavers that moments before had been dragging Pirmin away by his hair. Pirmin snatched up the dead man's war axe and leveled it at a heavyset man with a full beard and dark, fleshy circles under his eyes who stalked warily towards the snarling dog.

The man raised a heavy crossbow and shot an iron bolt into Zora's side, lifting her up and throwing her away from the dead man. She yelped, her feet scrambling briefly to find purchase on the rocky ground before her strength gave out and she toppled over on her side.

Zora raised her head once weakly to bite at the shaft lodged deep between her ribs. Shaking with the effort, she was unable to reach it, and finally her head dropped hard to the ground, as though it were made of stone. She panted a few times. Then, with a whole-body shudder, she died.

Pirmin, eyes wide and chest heaving, charged the man with his axe while screaming something in his strange accent that Thomas could not comprehend. The heavy man dropped his crossbow, sidestepped, and caught the axe shaft twisting it out of the young boy's hands. Then he whipped the butt-end across Pirmin's face. To the man's surprise, the enraged boy took the blow, threw his arms around the slaver's upper legs and drove his head into his stomach, knocking them both to the ground. Pirmin straddled the man and rained blows down upon the man's face and chest.

Although big, Pirmin was still just a boy and his adversary outweighed him by at least a hundred and fifty pounds. His blows were ineffective and once the man recovered from the fall to the ground and the surprise of the boy's ferociousness, he rolled the boy over and beat him without mercy until Pirmin's hands fell limp at his side and blood flowed freely from his mouth and nose.

The slaver stood up quickly, as though embarrassed, and produced a rope from his belt with several leather collars strung along its length. He kicked the stunned Pirmin over on his stomach and kneeled to slip one over Pirmin's head, cinching the metal buckle in place at the back of his neck. The boy coughed into the dusty ground and moaned, but other than that did not try to fight back.

Thomas stared at the big dog's still form. Zora was dead, and already at that young age, Thomas knew well the consequences that went along with death. It meant that as soon as she was out of his sight, he would never see her again. And somehow he understood, without the smallest doubt that the man kneeling over Pirmin intended to take Thomas's friend far away, to a place Pirmin did not want to go.

"Good folk, the Sutters," Pirmin said, bringing Thomas back to the moment. These days, Thomas hardly noticed his singsong Wallis accent, but others did. Especially women.

"Their girl has a fondness for you," Thomas said. "Though she is not much more than a child."

Pirmin laughed, a deep, honest sound that bubbled up from his soul and would put at ease anyone within earshot.

"I have done nothing to encourage that. And even if I had, Mera will be of a marrying age in another season."

"Do not even think it. She is a child, and you older than her father." Though, Thomas admitted to himself, Pirmin looked ten years younger than his age and his boyish good looks had faded little over the years.

"Ah but she's a beauty that one. Might be just the woman to pluck me out of this monk's life I have been living all these years."

Thomas grunted. "I think you do not fully grasp the meaning of the word *monk*. Monks do not sleep through matins because they have been out all night whoring."

"Whoa. Easy now, Captain. I would appreciate it if you did not put me in the company of the common soldier. I do not have anything against whores, a necessary trade if you ask me, but one I prefer not to support. In fact, I have paid for a woman only twice in my life, once—"

Thomas interrupted. "Once before you knew you could get it for free, and another time when your lovemaking was so rigorous you were sure you left the woman with child. I have heard the story more times than you have told it."

"Ah, yes of course. I know how you and the rest of the lads would whisper about me in the dark of the barracks after I had snuck out."

Thomas shook his head in denial, but there was some truth to the big man's words. From a young age Pirmin had developed an appreciation for the fairer sex, and they for him, and so had a tendency to stray from the converted stables that had become the boys home in Acre's Hospitaller fortress.

By the time he was thirteen he was taller than most men and seemed to know every tavern and shopkeeper in the crowded city. How he managed to escape the fortress at night after the portcullis had been dropped, no one knew, but it was well known that he was the main supplier of goods sold by Max, who ran his own secret merchant stall in the barracks. For many boys, as well as some of the monks, who had lived most of their lives inside the Hospitaller fortress, Pirmin was their link to the outside world, and he played the part well.

A natural entertainer, he told stories of tavern brawls and wild women that few believed, but they hung on every word nonetheless. And when he was led into the courtyard and forced to make what the Abbot termed the *march of shame* to the whipping post, he did so with his head held high and shoulders thrown back, like some mythical hero, as boys laughed and cheered him on. He never cried out when the strap bit into his exposed flesh and when it was done he would limp away, but not without smiling or winking at a few of the other children, as if to say *you know it was worth it.*

The Schwyzers were inducted into the Order of Saint John as brother-sergeants; fighting men. They were required to take the Vow of Obediance, and the Vow of Poverty, but not the Vow of Chastity, and that Pirmin often said, was God's way of telling him that it was his duty to share himself with the female populace. Thomas knew, of course, it merely showed that the Schwyzers were meant to be an expendable military arm of the Order and, since their life expectancy was so very short, nothing more was expected of them.

Still, living amongst monks and priests had had its influence, and unlike Pirmin, Thomas had taken his studies seriously. Women were the origin of sin and Satan's ultimate instrument of temptation. One that Thomas had successfully resisted his entire life, though he saw little evidence of the Devil in most women.

"I wonder what he is doing now?" Pirmin said suddenly.

"Who?"

"You know, my son."

"You cannot be talking about the whore you imagined you planted your seed in?" Thomas said.

"Of course. A man can tell when he has sired offspring, you know. Wonder if he looks like me? Or his mother…cannot rightly recall what she looked like though. Comely I think."

Thomas shook his head. "If you left that woman with child she no doubt went to a witch and had it rooted out."

"No," Pirmin said, shaking his head. "I would have known. And why so negative brother? Jealous I have a son out there somewhere?"

"Probably a daughter. A seven-foot hulking brute of a daughter terrifying the countryside."

Pirmin grimaced and clenched his teeth. The possibility of a daughter had never entered his mind.

"Nah, not possible. Definitely a boy."

They rode on in silence for a while, the muted thudding of hooves on grass the only sound.

"You ever think about it Thomi? Having a family?"

"No," he said.

"You should think on it. This would be a nice place to raise one, and I do not know how much longer I will be around. Have to push on to Wallis soon, I suppose."

Thomas nodded, forgetting it was probably too dark for Pirmin to see the gesture. He would miss the man deeply when he left, though he would never let Pirmin know that. For over thirty years the Order had been his family, and it was strange to imagine being alone, truly alone. Strange, but not frightening, like he had once thought it would be.

A peace washed over him as he imagined living out the rest of his life as a ferryman on the shores of this lake, knowing he had served out his time as God's soldier to the best of his ability. Perhaps this stage of his life was his reward for faithful service. A taste of Heaven here on Earth.

"Why so quiet? What are you thinking about Thomi? You make me nervous when you get like that."

Thomas took a deep breath of the warm night air. He nudged Anid with his knees to pick up the pace. The stallion surged ahead.

They were both eager for home.

Chapter 7

GISSLER HOVERED AT THE EDGE of the trees looking at the small hovel in the distance. An aged man struggled across the muddy courtyard carrying a bucket of slop, each jerky step causing a foul splash down his leg. Finally, with a Herculean effort he upended the bucket into a pigpen's trough, and a half dozen dirty sows squealed with delight.

The man was gaunt, a fact even the full grey beard and baggy russet clothes could not conceal. Gissler recognized the man as his brother only on some primal, spiritual level, for there was nothing left of the proud older boy he had looked up to as a child. Hugo was only five years older than Gissler, but the bent, misshapen figure shuffling about the pigpen looked to be in his sixties. Gissler could not remember even his father looking as old, or broken, as his brother did now.

The Gisslers had been a family with stature. Being stewards of land for three generations had given them a position of respect within the community and the right to a share of the land's crops and animals. His father always talked about the peasant class as *those* people. He knew the Gisslers did not have any blue blood, but in his heart he felt they were much closer to the noble class than that of peasants.

He had been wrong. When King Albrecht awarded the family estate to a French count, the Gisslers were unceremoniously forced to leave the land they had faithfully managed for more than fifty years. It must have been a devastating transition for his father to learn to rut in the mud as just another peasant, Gissler thought, and upon seeing the sorry living conditions of his elder brother, one that his father could not have survived.

"You come to talk with my papa?"

Gissler whirled at the sound of the voice to see a small girl no older than seven years old. Dirty bare feet stuck out the bottom of her grey, threadbare dress, which may have been pale blue at one time. She had a small mountain flower pinned in her hair and a few more clutched in one tiny hand. In the other she cupped a baby bird close to her chest.

"He is just over there, if you want to talk to him," she said pointing with her chin.

"What is your name?" Gissler asked, surprised at the little girl's fearlessness.

"Sara," she said.

She had her father's large brown eyes. They were the eyes Gissler remembered from his boyhood.

"Actually, I came to see you," Gissler said.

Sara's eyes narrowed. "Why do you want to see me? I am just a kid."

Gissler laughed and the sound made Sara smile.

"A friend of your father's asked me to give him

something, but I am in a hurry. I was hoping you could give it to him for me. Would you do that?"

Sara shrugged. "I guess so. But I have to put this bird back in his nest first. I saved him from a cat, you know."

"Fair enough. I will help you and then you help me. Agreed?"

"You said you were in a hurry."

"I make time for worthy causes. And I can think of no purpose higher right now than returning your friend to his home."

With only a slight hesitation, she led Gissler to the bird's tree and pointed out the nest. He asked about her family and learned her mother and brother died and she never had any grandparents. Only a papa.

After the bird was tucked safely back in its nest, Gissler hung the coin purse that he had won at the tourney around Sara's neck.

"Take this to your father right away," he said. "I think he may be waiting for it."

She promised she would and started walking back towards the cabin.

Then she turned abruptly. She ran back and handed Gissler one of the little white flowers she still held in her hand.

"Here. Take this. It will protect you from the bad elves."

Without a moment's pause, she was off again running full speed towards the house.

Hugo looked up in alarm at the sound of his daughter's calls. She ran up to him and he listened to her words stumble over one another in an excited recounting of the man she had met in the forest. His eyes went wide when he opened the purse. He looked up and scanned the woods, searching for any sign of the man.

A soft wind stirred the trees, but nothing more.

Chapter 8

THE FIRST HEAT OF SUMMER was upon them by the time Thomas and Pirmin finished work on the ferry. Thomas had his first customer the same day they completed rigging the sail; a goat herder moving his herd to new pasture. He paid with a bag of green apples, and the goats left their own payment all over the ferry deck. It took Thomas and Pirmin the rest of the day to scrub down the wooden planking.

That was enough of the ferry business for Pirmin. He began hanging out more often at Sutter's inn doing odd jobs for the family. Sutter would usually pay him with food and ale, which suited Pirmin just fine. But Thomas knew Pirmin would have done the work for nothing, so long as he could sit in the evenings drinking and talking with the inn's patrons. It did not matter whether they were traveling merchants or the local regulars.

Thomas had never seen another man like him. So huge and terrifying on one level, but if left in a room for an hour with total strangers, they would part as the closest friends, slapping each other on the back, and swearing to get together soon.

Pirmin set up a bed in Sutter's hayloft and Thomas saw him less and less. At first Thomas would go to the inn every other day, but lately his trips had grown less frequent. Unlike Pirmin, Thomas found little pleasure in the company of strangers. Where Pirmin saw the good in people, Thomas was deeply suspicious of almost everyone, and he found being in large groups of strangers exhausting. So he spent more time alone working on a cabin near his ferry, seeing one or two people a day, many of the locals as wary of the new ferryman as he was of them.

Thomas stood on the wharf originally built by a ferryman long before the time of the one he had bought the barge from. He wrapped the ends of a rope, making a mental note that he should replace it the first chance he had enough coin, and stowed it on the bottom of the barge.

His eye caught something moving up the road. Whoever was coming, was not moving fast. He continued with his inspection of every sheet and halyard on his ferry, and when he next looked down the road, the lone figure began to take shape.

It was an old woman, hunched over by the years and rail thin. Her threadbare cloak flapped around her bones in the breeze like a flour sack snagged on scrub brush. Slung across her back, threatening to topple her with every step, was something heavy. Her eyes were fixed on Thomas as she stepped onto the dock and made her way to the side of the ferry. Thomas picked up another rope and began running the length through his hands.

The old woman halted in front of Thomas and

pushed back the hood of her cloak, letting much-needed light into eyes whitened with age. She kinked her neck up at an awkward angle to look at Thomas and stared at him, her eyes scrutinizing his face and coming to rest on the pale jagged line running down the left side. For all her physical ailments, her voice was surprisingly strong and clear.

"You would be the one they call the ferryman. They said I could tell by the scar."

"Or the ferry," Thomas said, nodding at the barge he stood on. "You looking to go to the other side old woman?"

"Not yet," she said, offended. "I have a few more years in me."

She continued to stare at the scar on Thomas's face and did not say anything else. The silence was uncomfortable. Thomas leaned over and tucked away his coil of rope, then stepped onto the wharf. When he faced the woman again he had his left side angled away.

"Something I can do for you then, grandmother?"

"Came to give you something," she said.

"Oh? And what might that be?"

The woman reached to her shoulder and struggled briefly to duck her head under the shoulder strap. She held out the pack with both hands.

"Take it," she said. Her arms were starting to shake. "Take it! Cannot hold this thing all day."

He reached out, not because he wanted anything from her, but he thought she might fall over if he did not relieve her of the weight. He took the bag and helped the old woman sit on the edge of his barge. The bag was heavy; the woman was stronger than she looked to have carried it from who knew where. He peered inside cautiously.

"It is a wheel of cheese. One of our better ones. Me and my daughter made it. Her son helped some, but mostly he is useless that one."

Within the pack, the cheese was carefully wrapped in a clean white cloth, which did little to keep the enticing aroma contained.

"It smells delicious. But why give this to me if you have no need to cross?"

She gave no indication that she had heard his question. "When my daughter was born, we did not have animals. Very few people in these parts did. Were grain farmers for years, then finally we came together as a community and got some pigs." She paused and looked out over the water for a time.

Thomas nodded and glanced helplessly around. The woman was old and had no one to talk to. But then again, neither did he.

"Pigs are good, I suppose," he said.

The woman shook her head, the movement more a quiver. "We knew nothing about animals then. Not how cruel they could be, or how a sow will deny the runts of her litter her milk."

Thomas knew little of animals himself. To keep up their strength during campaigns, the fighting men of the Hospitallers were permitted to eat meat. But since the monks and priests of the order were forbidden to consume flesh, the Order did not raise its own animals, save for a few chickens and maybe the odd goat for milk. Any meat that ended up on the trenchers of the brother-sergeants was bought at market.

The woman seemed to recognize his confusion, and explained.

"You see, she has only got so much milk and if she let the little weak ones drink, the others, well, they might not get enough to grow up strong. Some of them might even die. Better to let the little ones starve than end up with a whole litter of runts."

She was not looking at Thomas now. Her white eyes were gazing out across the greenish blue waters again.

"Me and my husband never cared much about that. We were just happy to have some animals. Life had been much harder before we got those pigs. But every time we had to pull dead piglets out of the pen, our daughter would cry and ask us why. Every time. It is God's will, we would tell her. Every time."

"Children can get attached to farm animals," Thomas said. He remembered Zora from all those years ago and how hard Pirmin had cried when his dog was killed. He cringed inwardly at the memory.

The old woman had not seemed to hear him. She was lost in a different time. "Eventually, we got rid of those pigs, when we could afford to. Sold them and bought a cow, couple of goats."

"And now you make cheese. Fine cheese by the smell of it," Thomas said.

There was something about the woman that was beginning to grow on him. She was a survivor and he sensed an inner strength about her. She heard him this time and when she turned to look at him, he felt her eyes probing. She wanted something from him. Something she would never ask for.

"Still, I cannot look at my daughter today and not see that poor little thing of yesteryear crying her eyes out. I wonder if she blames me. Sometimes I think I should have given those first pigs back. Kept to grain farming."

Her thin shoulders fell and she seemed to be trapped in her memories of the past. Finally, she spoke. "But the truth is, we would have all starved. We needed those pigs."

The old woman looked at Thomas, her jaw set firmly. She motioned for him to help her up. He did so and she put the hood of her cloak back up. Then, without another word, she turned and began to walk back the way she had come.

"Are you sure you do not need me to help you go somewhere?" Thomas asked, puzzled by her sudden departure.

Without stopping or even turning to look back, the old woman said, "You have done more than your bit. Enjoy the cheese ferryman."

Thomas shook his head. *Crazy old woman.*

He picked up another rope and began working it through practiced hands, squeezing and pulling, testing for weaknesses. He watched the old woman until she eventually receded into the distance and disappeared amongst the green slopes.

He heard the heavy breathing of the two men before he saw them. Unlike the hard-packed desert ground in Outremer, the grassy slopes in this country muffled the sounds of approaching footsteps. Thomas turned to see two men struggling down the hill toward him, one leaning heavily on the other for support.

Even though one man was obviously injured, they moved quickly and were at Thomas's ferry moments later. Thomas helped the one man lower his companion, a boy in his late teens, to the deck. When he took his hand away from the boy's back it was covered in blood.

"We were hunting in the woods and my friend fell off

his horse," the man said, speaking quickly. "I need to get him to the healer in the woods fast."

He was only a handful of years older than the injured teen, but he spoke with the commanding confidence of one much more senior. He was used to giving orders.

"What happened to your horses?" Thomas asked.

"Bolted when I got off to help him. Somewhere in the woods yonder," the young man said without hesitation. But when he looked in the direction of the woods his eyes flicked over the landscape nervously, as though searching for something. Thomas got the impression he was not looking for his own horses.

"We better stop that bleeding first, or your friend will not make it to the other side."

The man looked at Thomas and said, "You get this ferry moving and I will see to him. The sooner we get him to the healer the better. I have double your payment here, if that concerns you." He patted the pouch at his belt, next to a short sword in a well-oiled leather scabbard. His eyes were hard, determined, but fear danced at their edges.

A soft groan escaped from the boy on the deck and Thomas turned to see him squirm onto his side.

"Get some pressure on his wound. I will cast off."

The wind was up and they were well out into the deep waters when a dozen horsemen rode into view. They sat atop a hill and watched the ferry make its way across the Great Lake. They were too far away for Thomas to make out the details of their crests, but the way they rode in formation told him they were soldiers. He shook his head as he pondered the ramifications of helping fugitives escape the local authorities. Well, he would worry about that later, he told himself. Right now a man was dying on his deck.

He trimmed the sail and lashed the rudder in place, then went to where the man dabbed at the wound with a dirty rag attempting to staunch the steady flow of blood coming from the boy's back. His ministrations were clumsy and reckless.

Thomas grabbed the man by the wrist.

"Give me that," he said. "You do not know what you are doing."

The young man snarled and pulled his arm free. He dropped the rag and grabbed the handle of his sword.

Thomas ignored him and ripped open the boy's shirt to expose the wound. "You will not be needing to use that on me. But if you insist on cutting your own throat for almost killing this boy, I will not stop you."

"Watch your tongue ferryman. I saved his life."

"I have seen many things, but never a man who can pull a crossbow bolt out of the middle of his own back. Some unthinking fool pulled it out cutting open every blood vessel around and leaving a jagged hole bigger than some men's brains."

The young man clenched his teeth and glared at Thomas.

"Careful. We are off the bank—out of reach of Landenberg's men. I do not need you anymore to sail this raft."

Thomas pulled out his curved belt knife in one quick motion. The young man jumped to his feet, his hand starting to pull his own blade. Without paying the man even a sidelong glance, Thomas sliced a relatively clean piece of cloth off his own shirt and then pushed it hard against the boy's wound.

"Since you are up, reach in that saddle bag at your

feet and hand me some of that clotting moss," Thomas said.

The man glowered, but he relaxed his grip on his sword and did as Thomas asked. Thomas pushed a handful of the moss into the wound and held it for a minute; until he was satisfied the bleeding had slowed. Then he had the man take over and keep pressure on while he went back to helm the ferry and bring her into shore.

Once on shore he cut some clean bandages and produced a moldy piece of bread from his bag along with some more moss. He put them over the wound and wrapped it tightly with the bandages. The young man watched quietly.

"You learn that in the Holy Lands?"

Thomas looked up, his eyebrows knit together. "What makes you so sure you know anything about me?"

The man laughed. "I know more about you Thomas Schwyzer than you know about yourself. I know you have returned to Schwyz after thirty years of fighting in the Holy Lands. These are my mountains. I have eyes and ears everywhere. If I did not, the Habsburgs would have hung me years ago."

"You are the outlaw Noll Melchthal." The realization came fast. He was a favorite topic between Pirmin and Sutter at the inn, but Thomas had imagined him as a much older man. Apparently this Noll was a brigand wanted by the Habsburgs but was looked on fondly by many of the locals. They saw him as some kind of freedom fighter. The thought of turning him over to the Austrians for a reward crossed Thomas's mind.

"I am no outlaw. I recognize no Habsburg judge and refuse to be ruled by oafs such as Landenberg. He may be the Vogt of Unterwalden, but he has no authority in Schwyz or Uri. We are a free people."

Thomas nodded at the boy lying on the ground. "Talk like that gets people hurt. I know your type. You are a rebel by nature and live only to disrupt the natural order ordained by God."

"Only a fool would believe God wants these lands ruled by Austrian blue-bloods."

"What would you do? Overthrow the noble class? And replace it with what?"

"Do you find it so hard to believe that common people can rule themselves? We need no royalty, or foreign judges enforcing corrupt laws. The Habsburgs get rich from our pain and suffering. It is not right and I have a hundred men under my command that agree. We do not only want to drive the Austrians from our lands, we want justice."

Thomas blinked at the force of Noll's convictions, but then shook his head. One did not simply tamper with the divine natural order. The King and Church worked together to protect the common man from the devil and himself, not subjugate him. God had granted the peasant class the ability to work in the fields, perhaps learn a trade. They had no capacity for politics, and thrust into that arena would prove incapable of ruling themselves. Politicking was the domain of the noble class, which in turn was under direct control of the King. Together they saw to all matters secular while the Church protected the spiritual souls of all devout Christians.

"True justice can only be dispensed by God. A hundred men is nothing but mouths to feed, for the Habsburgs could have a thousand soldiers on your doorstep tomorrow. Do not be in a hurry to throw your life away in war."

Noll shook his head. "God does not concern himself with justice. I have seen enough of this world to know that."

Thomas crossed himself and leveled a finger at Noll. "Still your tongue. I will have none of your blasphemy on my boat."

"Why not join us, ferryman? You have been back long enough to see the poverty, the corrupt soldiers that reap our lands. Help us drive out the Habsburg blue-bloods."

Thomas shook his head. "You swim in black waters, boy. This will end badly. Mark my words."

Noll scowled at Thomas and then shrugged. He bent low and scooped up his wounded friend, hoisting him across his shoulders. He stood up easily, as though he carried no more than a sack of grain. He was not a large man, but lean and efficient, and his powerful legs did not tremble in the least at the added weight.

"When you are shut up safe in your hut, in front of a warm fire, and the screams of dying country men can be heard beyond your walls, I trust you will say a prayer for them, ferryman."

"I am no priest," Thomas said.

"You talk like one."

Noll turned away. He stepped slowly but took long strides so as not to jostle his precious load. From up the path, without turning his head, he called out, "If you should change your mind and want to meet with me, mention it to Sutter. The right words travel easily in these mountains."

Thomas watched until Noll disappeared in the trees. The Devil had a purchase on that one, he thought, and at the same moment, he realized Noll had neglected to pay him for the ferry trip.

Chapter 9

"SERAINA!"

She looked up from trimming one of her plants in the direction from which Noll's voice carried. The cry was desperate and the trees marked his coming with incessant whispers, which Seraina followed with her eyes. Seconds later Noll burst into her clearing with Aldo hanging limp across his back.

"Lay him here—in the sunlight," she said.

Together they eased him down onto his side and Seraina began examining the wound on his back, fearing the worst. She peeled back the bandage and was surprised to see the moldy bread and moss covering the wound. She did not move them, but held a hand to Aldo's cheek. He was pale from loss of blood, yet not feverish, as he should be. She placed her other hand on his chest and listened to his heart rhythms while Noll fidgeted at her side. *Deep, but strong and regular.* She leaned back and looked at Noll.

"He will live," she said. "But not by my craft."

Noll, who was still standing, fell down on the ground and wiped the sweat off his brow with the back of his arm. He took in a deep breath.

"Who saw to his wound?" Seraina asked. "It was not you. That much I know."

Noll still labored over his breathing. He had carried the boy far, and up a steep slope as well. "What? Oh, the new ferryman applied a simple poultice. A pox on his hide, he is a stubborn man that one."

"The ferryman?" Seraina's eyes widened in surprise. The dressing had been wrapped with precision and skill. The use of birch mane to stem the flow of blood and clean the wound was not well known.

She continued to quiz Noll about the man until he threw up his arms and said he knew nothing more, and if she wanted to know more about the ferryman she was going to have to ask him herself.

Noll walked to the rain barrel and ladled some water into one hand and then rubbed them together to wash off the dried blood.

"Can I leave Aldo with you until the morrow? The Eidgenossen are meeting tonight and if I am to reach the meadow in time I had best be on my way."

Ah, Seraina thought. That explained Noll's foul mood.

"Has the council finally invited you?" she asked. When the leaders of Uri, Schwyz, and Unterwalden met it was always in secret and strictly by invitation, for they feared reprisals by their Austrian overlords.

"What need do I have for an invitation? I merely assume my father's position, since he cannot be there himself." Noll shook the bloody water off his hands and wiped them on his breeches. "And if Walter Furst, or old

Stauffacher try to deny my right to speak, I am prepared to make them listen."

Seraina met Noll's icy stare and felt her heart skip a beat. Behind her, the trees murmured their approval.

A short time later Noll said farewell and she watched him wind his way up the slope above the tree line until he disappeared over the grassy ridge.

"He is an exceptional young man. And as headstrong as all you Helvetii seem to be."

Seraina jumped at the sound of the voice behind her. *Gildas!*

She turned to see the old man sitting on a boulder, a blade of grass between his straight teeth. The green stood in stark contrast to the downy white of his beard, which in turn, blended into the white hooded robe of the druids. She was aware of another white form, but this one as insubstantial as mist, padding through the trees to her right. Remembering her manners, she fought off the urge to run into the trees, chase after Oppid, and nuzzle his fur. Instead she held up her hand in a ritual greeting.

"Blessed be the knowledge of the Weave as passed through the Elders." She bowed her head and held her right palm over her womb, her center and link to the natural world.

The old man stood and held out his arms.

"Come now child. It is just you and I—leave the formalities of another age in the past where they belong. Give me a hug, for nothing would gladden this old heart more."

Seraina laughed, ran to Gildas and threw her arms around his neck. She was a little girl again, and words bubbled out of her before they were thoughts.

"I was so excited when I heard of your arrival. Then,

when you did not show, I thought I was mistaken, and was only hearing the empty echoes of my heart. It has been so long…I thought I was alone."

"And I am sorry for that child. Truly sorry. I wanted to come to you after your ordeal with the villagers of Tellikon but—"

Seraina stepped back. "You know of that? Then why did you not come? I was so lost. And angry. What purpose could the burning of an innocent child have in the Weave? I wandered, desolate and alone for weeks, waiting for a sign from the Elders. But nothing. I thought something happened to you all. I had just about given up hope when the Mythen called and led me to this grove."

Gildas nodded, his face pale and taut. "And you have done well. The trees are strong here, and ancient. And a great number of these people are of the old world, although few remember. They will have need of you, before their end."

He took Seraina's hands in his. It had been six years since she had seen him, but he looked far older than Seraina remembered.

"It pained me greatly to not seek you out when you were betrayed by those under your care. But I could not. There are so few elders left, and fewer talented ones seem to be born each year. I have not found a single adept in the last ten years, though I have searched every valley and mountain village from the lands of the *Menapi* to those of the *Ausci.*"

He used the ancient names of the tribes. Names kept alive only through the oral traditions of druids like Gildas. The regret in his eyes placated Seraina's anger, and she found herself feeling sorry for the man who had been like a father to her. Or what she imagined having a father would be like.

"Cease your worry Gildas. The Weave is only changing her colors. The adepts will appear again, you will see."

He smiled, and his face softened, on the surface.

"You were my greatest find Seraina and I have missed you terribly, child. Now. Tell me of this Arnold of Melchthal. You believe him to be a true Catalyst of the Weave?"

Seraina nodded and her green eyes lit up like poplar leaves backlit with the sun's early morning rays.

"It is no accident the Weave led me here. Noll was the first person I met. He stepped out of the trees, with not a sound from them, mind you. And from that first encounter I knew he was something special."

Gildas nodded. "I have no doubt he is of the old blood. In different times, he may even have been trained to serve the Weave as we do. But he was not discovered early enough I am afraid."

Seraina became excited at the observation and started to pace. "You feel it too? But of course you do! That is why you are here. Is it not, Gildas?"

"Your instincts have always been keen, my child. You will make a fine Elder one day. We have agreed the Weave is creating a powerful nexus in this area. And with every nexus there must be a Catalyst—one capable of nudging the Weave in the direction of change."

Seraina's eyebrows furrowed. "There has been something bothering me," she said. "How do we know this change will be good for our people?"

Gildas sighed. "Seraina, you are a priestess of the Old Religion. It is your place to be concerned for the well being of the people. But never forget that the patterns of the Great Weave can never be fully known. Even by us. All we can do is be vigilant and do what we think right, for both the people and the land. Now, about this Arnold, or Noll as you call him. Why do you feel he is the one?"

"The people love him. Even though he is an outlaw hunted by the Austrians. Or, perhaps that is why they love him. I have seen how the Habsburgs have come into these lands and stripped them bare. The best crops, animals, even tradespeople, are taken north and east to support the great Austrian cities. And for years they have been granting tracts of our people's land to foreign lords who send men and soldiers to desecrate it. They have no respect for the old ways, and neither the people nor the land can hope to endure much longer. They plant the same crops year after year on the same land, never allowing it to rest. They cut down our ancient groves and float the trees down the river to faraway places I have never heard of, they—"

Gildas held up his hand. Seraina's voice had been growing louder and her hand movements more vigorous, but looking into the old man's peaceful eyes gave her pause, and she took a deep breath, regaining some measure of control.

"Forgive me," she said. "It has been some time since I have had anyone to speak of these things with."

"Other tribes of our people have suffered much worse. Most in fact are no longer with us at all. But you must remember that strong emotions will only cloud your view of the Weave, and that in turn will greatly hinder your ability to help the land or those who call it home," Gildas said.

"I am sorry. It is just that this is *my* tribe. The last of the Helvetii. And they have already suffered so much. But I think Noll could change that. He could be as great as Vercingetorix, if only I knew how to help him," Seraina said.

The impatience and despair that had been building within her these last few months, as she watched Noll and his army of boys and beggars play with Austrian soldiers, finally overwhelmed her. Seraina's eyes glistened as they welled with the first sign of tears.

"Vercingetorix had the benefit of a full druidic counsel. He had access to all the wisdom we could offer, yet he still failed to turn aside the armies of the Romans. Do not be so hard on yourself," the old druid said.

"Please, Gildas. I beg you—tell me what I must do."

He looked like he would speak, but instead placed his hand on her shoulder. Its warmth spread into her. They stood in silence, listening to the trees together as they used to when Seraina was a little girl. In time, the feelings of despair shriveled and withered, then blossomed into something else entirely.

Hope.

Finally, when Seraina had settled and nothing could be heard but the murmurs of the forest, Gildas spoke.

"Do not worry yourself too much, my child. The Helvetii are a resilient people, and I believe they still have a place in the Great Weave. Unlike my own tribe, your people's time is yet to come."

Seraina kept her eyes closed and wrapped herself in the strength of his words. His voice was deep and resonated with power amongst the trees. She felt at peace.

As he spoke, the old man's own eyes roved slowly

over the grove, drinking in every moss-coated stone and sun-dappled plant, logging the memory. Tucking it away somewhere deep enough that it would stay with him for the rest of this life, and into the next. When his gaze came to rest, finally, on the young woman at his side, his lips trembled and a single tear fled from the corner of his eye. In one swift motion he wiped it away and turned Seraina towards him. She opened her eyes and Gildas nodded towards the forest.

"Now, go and say hello to Oppid. He has missed you more than you know."

Seraina beamed and an unstoppable grin spread across her face. With a shriek of delight she ran off into the trees calling out the wolf's name.

Chapter 10

THE SLIVERED MOON offered little light to guide Seraina's climb up the path from the water's edge. Being careful to stay well back of torchlight and the harsh whispers of men's voices, she avoided the main route and made her way in darkness through the forest of straight pines towards the Ruetli meadow. She took her time to enjoy the clear night air, stooping occasionally to pick star lilies, a red-petaled plant with flowers that only revealed themselves at night and was the base for many of her fever suppressing remedies. Slipping silently through the woods, Seraina caressed saplings, spoke in soft tones to the old growth, and skirted around areas with new shoots poking up from the forest floor. Finally, she reached the edge of the Ruetli, a clearing nestled in a thick copse of trees overlooking the eastern shores of the Great Lake of the four forest regions.

In the meadow's center, a low fire burned, illuminating the faces of a dozen men in flickering light. Walter Furst, the Justice from Altdorf, was there, as was old Werner Stauffacher of Schwyz. She recognized a guild man from Zurich named Studer, and although she did not know some of the other men, she saw the bear crest of Berne on one of their shoulders.

"Torches coming up the path," called out one of the two guards standing at the entrance to the meadow.

The men at the fire cast questioning looks at one another.

Walter Furst held out his hands. "We are expecting no others," he said.

"How many?" Studer, the guild man from Zurich asked.

"Six torches. At least that many men."

Werner Stauffacher walked over and peered down the path into the darkness. He was tall and very old, but he still had the loose-limbed gait of one who spent countless hours walking up and down mountain trails. "Arnold of Melchthal, and his band," he said, shaking his head.

Studer cursed. "Outlaws," he said to the man from Berne. "Stauffacher, if this is some ploy of your doing, I swear I will bring the wrath of the guilds down on you and all of Schwyz."

"No need to get excited Master Studer. Werner had no idea the young Melchthal would be joining us. None of us did, but I must admit I am not so surprised," Judge Furst said. A head shorter than old Stauffacher, Walter Furst was round in the face and had grey, wispy hair that seemed to float above his head.

Studer and the men around them had their hands on their swords. "What do you mean not surprised?"

"Arnold's father is a member of the Oathbound Council," Furst said.

"I am not sure I want to deal with the Eidgenossen if their members include murderers and highwaymen," the man from Berne said. He was a squat hairy man that Seraina did not know but who, she thought with a wry smile, resembled the bear his city had been named after.

Studer nodded. "The guilds of Zurich feel the same. We are here to discuss how we can legally benefit our towns. We have no interest in rebelling against the German Empire. And where is Henri Melchthal? Why is he not here but sends his outlaw son in his stead?"

There was a commotion at the head of the path as Noll and his men approached the guards. The two guards looked at Stauffacher for guidance on how to treat the newcomer, and when he shook his head they stood down.

Noll strode into the clearing looking as unconcerned as a man coming home from the fields for dinner. He nodded to Stauffacher as he passed. His men spread out and took up positions on the outer ring of firelight, and their torches bathed the clearing in a bright light.

"Evening Furst," Noll said, pleasantly enough. Then his voice took on a hard edge. "I believe I heard my father's name mentioned? By all means, tell the guild man why he cannot be present."

Walter Furst grimaced at Noll's tone.

"Your father paid a terrible price for his pride. We all wish it had turned out differently," Furst said.

"The charges were false. You knew it and did nothing," Noll said.

"I tried to help your father, but you know how stubborn he can be."

"You did nothing!" Noll stepped forward and grabbed Furst's cloak with both fists. "You failed to act then just as you sit in the woods now like frightened rabbits while the Austrians take our homes and our land." The guards moved towards Noll but Furst waved them off.

Stauffacher moved in and laid a hand on Noll's shoulder. "Easy lad. Henri is a friend of many a man here, as well as a father."

"Believe me Arnold, I tried everything within my power to have your father tried in my court. But Landenberg would have none of it. He has since accused me of sympathizing with rebels against the German Empire and I fear it is only a matter of time before he finds a way to remove me from my seat."

Seraina slid forward through the brush. She had no fear of being seen. The trees embraced her and accepted her presence amongst them as one of their own. A cool breeze stirred the leaves of a low hanging willow branch, rustling at her in warning, but she parted them and peered out like a curious child half hiding in her mother's skirts.

She faced Noll's back and saw his shoulders bunch up, tensing under Stauffacher's touch. Noll released Furst and stepped away from the two old men and turned towards Seraina's hiding spot, his face bathed in the wavering glow of torchlight. The pain she saw there made her cringe.

She had tried to talk to Noll about his father, tell him it was not his fault. But what Furst had said about the elder Melchthal being stubborn was equally true of his son. These men of the Alps had a willful streak to them that was at once their curse and their greatest strength.

Henri Melchthal had been accused of not meeting his annual grain quota, so Landenberg gave orders to his tax collector to seize a team of Henri's prized oxen. Noll argued with the man and ended up rapping his hand with an ax handle when he tried to take the oxen by force. The collector fled the young Melchthal's wrath with several broken fingers. A few days later Landenberg himself came with an escort of soldiers. While Noll hid in the woods and watched, Landenberg allowed his collector to burn out Henri Melchthal's eyes with the very same ax handle Noll had struck him with.

Perhaps Noll felt Seraina's presence, knew she stood only paces away and had caught him in a vulnerable moment, for suddenly he dragged a hand across his face and gave the woods a long, blank stare. She leaned back and held her breath, feeling guilty for having experienced Noll's pain without his knowing.

Noll turned back to the group of men. He stared hard at Furst and let out a slow breath before he spoke.

"I am sorry for my words Walter. I know you did what you could. It would do our people little good to have the last non-Austrian Judge removed from office."

Noll whirled to face the other men and raised his voice. "One territory cannot stand against the might of the Habsburgs, but if the guilds of Zurich and Berne joined with the Eidgenossen we could drive the Austrian dogs from our doorsteps for good."

"You are a fool," the leader of the men from Berne said. "The Habsburgs have the might of the German Princes at their command. This is nonsense. I will not listen to any more of this."

"And when will you listen? You think you are safe behind your city walls? For the time being perhaps. But what will happen once the Habsburg fortress is complete at Altdorf? They will control all trade that flows through

Italia to the Hanseatic League of the North Sea. Altdorf will be the new Habsburg center of commerce and they will choke the flow of goods to your cities and tax your caravans like you have never known."

Studer, the Zurich guild leader, crossed his arms and laughed.

"And what would an outlaw hiding in the hills know of commerce, boy? What information are you privy to that the guilds of Zurich and Berne are not? We have given the Altdorf fortress much thought and when it is completed, we will survive. We will pay our tithes when they come due, but in the meantime, our guilds profit nicely at Duke Leopold's expense. One of the first rules of business is do not bite the hand that feeds you."

Noll opened his mouth to respond, but an old woman's voice rang out across the clearing before he could speak.

"Some hands you would be wise to snap at Master Studer."

Gertrude of Iberg stood at the path, leaning on an ancient walking stick, and since she carried no torch, the guards there jumped at her words, surprised as anyone at her sudden appearance.

Of course, Seraina had been hearing whispers of Gertrude's approach for some time and was relieved the woman had made the climb safely. She put her hand over her mouth lest the glint of her smile give her away to those around the fire.

"Is there anyone who does not know of this secret meeting?" one of the Berne men asked.

Furst threw up his hands. "Werner, what is your wife doing here?" Stauffacher cast him an apologetic look and shrugged.

"Werner, do not answer him. Come help me get these old bones over to the fire. And Walter keep quiet. I am sure you have said enough already tonight."

Stauffacher scurried over to take her arm and the men made room for the old woman around the fire. Few people did not know Gertrude of Iberg, but she had retreated from actual council work in recent years, so her appearance at the secret meeting of the Oathbound was unusual.

Studer bowed his head stiffly. "You look well Gertrude. The years favor you more than most."

"Time has no favorites, but I appreciate any show of civility I can get from a merchant," she said.

She bent down and grasped a piece of firewood larger than a woman her age should be attempting to lift, and flicked it onto the fire, sending a plume of sparks drifting up to rival the stars.

"Zurich and Berne would do well to listen to the likes of Arnold Melchthal. What the boy says is true. Leopold has designs for these lands and I fear none of us will prosper by the likes of him."

The man from Berne spoke up. "Berne is a free city state, granted the right to rule herself by the German Emperor before my father's time. We have no quarrel with the Habsburgs."

Noll turned on him. "As was Schwyz, and the free men of Uri. But look around and count the Austrian soldiers that patrol our towns, and the corrupt judges that sentence our people. Walter, how many of our countrymen have been sentenced to work on the Altdorf fortress now? Fifty? A hundred? How many have died? Just last week the Menznau boy was found thrown out like so much garbage. Leopold keeps that fortress clouded in secrecy so we have no way of knowing how many of our sons and daughters have suffered similar fates."

Seraina's smile left her face at the mention of the Menznaus. She wrapped her arms around herself and was suddenly aware of the coolness of the night. She imagined herself standing amongst everyone near the fire, and although the thought warmed her, her smile did not return.

"And if *you* controlled the Gotthard, just how much would you charge my caravan to pass?" Studer said, a contemptuous smile on his lips.

"Nothing," Noll said. "I would welcome every merchant at the top of the pass with open arms. Provide a warm, safe refuge to water and feed his animals, let him rest, and send him on his way when, and only when, he wished."

The men around the fire laughed. Noll raised his voice to be heard.

"Word would soon spread and merchant caravans would be lining up to use the *free* Gotthard Pass. And as they descended into Andermatt, the villagers there would also welcome them. Of course their services would not be free, but they would be appreciated nonetheless. The innkeepers would feed the travelers, the smiths would shoe their mules, apothecaries would heal them, and the resources to accomplish all this would come from the farms and trades people surrounding the town. The coin from these foreigners would travel far into the countryside. And it would be the same for every town and village the merchant caravans passed through."

The men no longer talked amongst themselves as Noll's words took hold.

"Merchants and locals alike would prosper," the man from Berne said.

"Everyone except the Habsburgs," Studer said. "Therein lies the flaw in your plan. Leopold would never allow free passage through the Gotthard."

Noll grinned. "Consider it a redistribution of wealth."

"Well this is a first. A highwayman waving folks through without charging for safe passage," the Berne man said. "But all fantasy aside, the Habsburgs are not going to pack up their Altdorf fortress and leave."

Noll nodded. "They will need persuading. And that is why we have to act soon. The Holy Roman Empire has been torn apart since King Albrecht died, and the Habsburgs are fighting to get one of their own crowned again. I hear rumors of war between Frederick and Louis the Bavarian, which means Leopold will have no money, and no soldiers to send against us." He looked at Furst and said, "But we have to move before the fortress is finished, and Leopold cocoons himself up in it."

For a few moments the only sound was the popping and sizzling of sap boiling in burning logs. Finally the Zurich and Berne leaders agreed to take the matter back to their respective cities and hold council with their guild associations. They left the clearing before the darkest hours of the night to begin the long journey home.

"I hope you know what you have set in motion," Gertrude said to Noll when the guildsmen had left.

Seraina did not hear his reply, but she could hardly contain the excitement she felt. At last, the Catalyst had awakened.

Chapter 11

"**D**ID THE WITCH'S brothers give you any trouble?" Leopold asked.

Gissler shrugged, and his hand went to the fresh scratch marks on his cheek, just now beginning to scab over. "Not as much as she did, my lord."

Leopold leaned back in his upholstered chair and looked at the motley group forced to their knees before him. The three brothers were chained to one another at the neck, and their wrists and ankles were likewise shackled. All of them had black eyes or bloodied faces. One could barely walk and was helped along by the other two.

Gissler had done well, Leopold thought. It may be time to put some men under his command.

He turned his attention to the woman. She lay curled up on her side on the flagstone floor. Her right thumb was shackled to her right big toe, as was her left thumb to her left toe, making it impossible for her to walk. A necessary precaution, for if the witch's hands were left free, she would be able to cast spells and carry out the Devil's mischief. The guards had carried her into the throne room suspended from a thick pole, and slid her off onto the cold floor at Leopold's feet.

The young Duke let out a breath, and with it, some of the tension of the last few days. Constructing the new fortress at Altdorf was moving far too slowly. Mid-winter was when many merchant caravans set out over the Gotthard Pass. It was crossable once the heavy snows had fallen and crusted over, but when spring came its trails became too soft for carts, and the threat of avalanches of melting snow was constant. The footing would remain too treacherous for most travelers until the first day of summer. This meant that if Leopold did not have his tollgates active before winter, he would have no revenues from the pass until well into next summer, almost a year from now. With Frederick's campaign already eating up most of the Habsburg coffers, Leopold knew he could not wait that long. The Altdorf fortress must be finished before the first snows fell.

There was still time, but he needed more workers. He had sent a messenger to his brother requesting fifty more laborers (he knew Frederick could not spare soldiers) and was confident they would arrive any day now.

Added to these worries was the pressure of his upcoming marriage only two weeks away. Lady Catherine and her entourage would arrive on the morrow and the thought of having to don his courtly mask of manners twisted his lips in a grimace. Originally set for next year, Leopold had pushed for his betrothal to take place earlier. The dowry was needed now, not in a year's time.

A moan came from the witch as she tried to shift herself into a position that eased the pressure on her thumbs and toes. She was young, with an angelic face. How did the Devil manage to recruit one so full of innocence? Yes, this was just the diversion he needed. There was nothing like the battle of good versus evil to take one's mind off matters of state.

"Shall I remove the witch and her servants to the dungeon to await trial your lordship?" Leopold's secretary asked.

The young duke nodded.

"Take the men away but leave the woman. And summon the judge. I would try her within the hour."

"Today? But my lord, may I remind you that you have other appointments to make preparations for the arrival of Lady Catherine—"

Leopold waved his hand and brushed the comment aside. He looked at the girl and caught her eye briefly. She trembled and looked away, apparently not finding any comfort under Leopold's intense gaze. Few ever did.

"Cancel all my appointments," he said. "Keeping my people safe from the Devil's spawn must take all precedence. Now get me that judge. And summon my scribe. There may be useful information gained here today for my manuscript."

The secretary bowed and hurried from the room. A short, black and white clad fool followed closely behind imitating the secretary's hasty shuffle, the soft tinkling of bells punctuating every step.

But for once, Leopold did not notice.

***

"What do you know of witches, Gissler?" Leopold asked, squinting beneath a hand raised to block out the

111

bright sun. He strained his eyes to keep track of the naked body of the girl as she bobbed in the slow-flowing river.

A guard on either bank held her in the middle with ropes tied around her waist. Her thumbs and toes still clamped together, she struggled to float on her back, gasping for air. Then the current rolled her over in slow motion like a piece of driftwood. There was a series of frantic splashes beneath the surface of the water before a guard righted her by pulling on one of the ropes. She broke the surface coughing and gasping for breath, her eyes bulging with terror. A judge, a wizened man in a black and yellow ceremonial cloak, stood at the riverbank, staring intently at the proceedings.

"I have no experience with witches, my lord," Gissler said.

Leopold's eyebrows arched and he cast a sidelong glance at Gissler. "A cautious answer. But I suppose it would not do for one of God's soldiers to admit to keeping company with Satan's kin." He focused again on the dunking, anxious to not miss any outward displays of devilry.

"Fascinating creatures, really. But this one is not as clever as some I have seen tested. Perhaps she is too young. Her craft has not matured properly."

He may be right, Gissler thought. She had indeed failed the very first test.

Once the judge arrived in the receiving hall, he had the guards strip the girl bare, and while she screamed and then sobbed quietly, he examined her body carefully looking for non-human marks. When he found something suspect, a freckle that was too large, or a swollen lump of tissue, he would poke it with a needle to see if it bled. After testing spots on her thighs, buttocks, and neck, which all bled, he finally inserted the needle into the lower part of her left breast. He pulled it out, looked at the needle, then roughly lifted her breast up and examined the location. He passed sentence immediately.

"No blood my lord. The Devil protects this one, there can be no doubt." The judge was convinced, and that should have finished it, but Leopold had insisted they perform a dunking trial as well. His scribe was to carefully record the results for Leopold's witchcraft manuscript he had been working on for the past several years.

"There! Did you see that? She floats with no aid from the ropes," Leopold said. Wonder filled his voice as he pointed at the girl whose struggles were growing less with every moment.

"I saw it too your grace," the judge shouted. He shook his head. "There can be no doubt."

"I am not King, so call me 'grace' again and I will have you flogged."

"Forgive me, your...*lordship*. I served your father for too many years and my tongue has grown careless. But I am sure it will not be long before another Habsburg sits upon the German throne."

Leopold waved the man to silence.

"Did you see that Gissler? It makes one's blood run cold does it not?"

Leopold craned his neck to get a better look at the Devil's handiwork. He walked to where the judge stood and signaled the soldiers to let go of the rope. As they did so, the girl who had now been facedown in the water for several minutes and was no longer struggling, continued to float, and drifted a short distance on the river's almost imperceptible current. The judge gasped, and both he and Leopold made the sign of the cross in front of their faces. Leopold barked at the soldiers to take up their rope again quickly.

Gissler saw nothing but a young girl drowned to death.

When Leopold turned back to Gissler, his face was alight. "You did a good thing bringing me this creature," he said.

Gissler bowed. "I am here to serve, my lord. But one question if I may..."

"Of course."

"The witch's guilt was proven beyond all doubt, because even shackled, she could float?"

Leopold nodded. "Even now, though she is most likely dead and her stomach filled with water, she still floats."

Gissler nodded. "I see. And if she sank to the bottom of the river, it would have proven her innocence?"

"Of course," Leopold said.

"But in all likelihood, she would be just as dead," Gissler said.

"Yes, and God would have received her into his Kingdom," Leopold said, looking perturbed.

Gissler nodded, masking his thoughts. Having been part of the Hospitaller navy for twenty years, he knew very well what dead bodies did in open water. Some floated, some sank, a few drifted between the bottom and the surface. The only way to guarantee a body would sink to the ocean floor, was to cut the air from its lungs and weight it with a bag of rocks.

He searched the Duke's eyes for some sign of

insanity, a glint of madness, but found nothing. They were clear, focused, and fiercely intelligent. And yet, somehow, he was convinced that by ridding the world of this beautiful young girl he had promoted himself in the eyes of God.

"Come Gissler. Time to celebrate. Tonight you dine at my table. Ah—I almost forgot," Leopold said and reached into his vestment and pulled out a purse that he tossed to Gissler. "Your payment. Stand by me and you will rise high, Hermann Gissler."

Hearing his full name spoken by a duke, and a Prince of the German Empire no less, made Gissler forget about the witch and stand a little taller.

He caught the purse in one hand and then almost dropped it because of its weight. It was easily double what he had won at the tourney.

All his life Gissler had followed orders. And what had the Knights of Saint John ever given him in return? Food, a place to sleep, and two sets of clothing. His rank in the brotherhood had never changed from brother-sergeant. He could never have been a true Hospitaller Knight, for only those of noble blood were permitted to rise past the rank of sergeant. He had given them everything; his obedience, his loyalty, his youth, even his name.

He would never again be merely a *Schwyzer*, and that thought gave him great satisfaction. For to be a *Schwyzer* in the brotherhood was to be a slave. A front line soldier sent to test the strength of the enemy, to look after the Knights' mounts and muck out the stables.

Tonight he would sit at a duke's table. Yes, he was still following orders, but he was being rewarded for his talents. And, once again, he owned his name. His true name. His throat tightened as he thought of his mother and father. If only his father were still alive to see him return the Gissler name to its past glory, all would be perfect. But his brother, Hugo yet lived.

Gissler tightened his hand around the heavy purse. Soon, he would go back to his brother's dismal hog farm and take him and his daughter away from their wretched life of poverty.

***

Leopold stood above his scribe in the Habsburg castle library and watched him carefully transcribe his notes into the leather-bound volume Leopold had titled *Malleus Maleficarum*, 'The Hammer of Witches'. Once finished, Leopold was confident it would be the Church's greatest weapon against witchcraft ever assembled.

"Be sure you list all who were present this day," Leopold said. Reading in Latin had never been his strong point, but he could recognize names easily enough.

There was a commotion at the door to the small library and Leopold looked to see Landenberg push through, snarling harsh words at a young scribe who trailed behind him. The scribe froze when he saw Leopold look up.

"I am sorry my lord. The Vogt demanded entry and I…"

"I had him!" Landenberg shouted. "He and one of his boys walked out of the trees right in front of us. I was—"

Leopold held up a hand and cut him off. "Gather your quills, Bernard. It would seem Vogt Landenberg has some pressing matter to discuss."

Even in this place could he not find a moment's peace?

The scribe hastily blotted the page he had been working on, and keeping the manuscript open, carefully carried it from the room. He was not foolish enough to let the book out of his sight. Bernard was the only one permitted to touch Leopold's tome, and he knew his life was forfeit should anything happen to it.

"From the enthusiasm in your words, I can only assume you had another encounter with Arnold Melchthal."

"We crested a rise outside Brunnen and there he was. Him and one of his men just stood there. We stared at one another like startled cats, unsure what to do. They ran, we gave chase, and I put a bolt into his man's back. That one's thieving days have come to an end, I tell you that much. Beautiful shot. From horseback too, I might add."

"So Melchthal eluded you again? Is that why you have burst into my study? To bring news of such a noteworthy event?" Leopold said the words softly, with only the slightest trace of sarcasm. In truth, there were few things in this world he enjoyed more than seeing Landenberg squirm after being played for a fool.

Landenberg threw up his hands. "He is more rabbit than man, that one. We lost him for a bit in the trees and when next we saw him he was half way across the lake on a ferry."

"What ferry?"

"Some peasants set up a barge that crosses the waters near Brunnen."

"Who uses this ferry? Merchants?"

"No, only locals I should think. The road runs along the water's edge and merchants tend to be a distrusting sort. They would not risk their goods on those unpredictable waters."

Leopold sat in the chair Bernard had been in moments before and steepled his fingers in front of his face as he thought through what Landenberg told him.

"Then burn it," he said.

"What?"

"Burn the ferry. As it stands now, Melchthal has beaten you. He escaped. By removing the method of his escape, you ensure that this particular tactic of his will never work again. Also, you send a message, a warning, to both Melchthal and, more importantly, to those who would harbor him."

Landenberg nodded. His thick lips spread into a grin clearly visible even through his shaggy, greying beard.

"Consider it done. My lord."

Chapter 12

ONCE EVERY MONTH Seraina would load up her mule and make the daylong journey into Schwyz. Once there, she would set up in the market, and sell fresh herbs from her garden, or ground up ingredients with her granite mortar and pestle to relieve people's ailments. After, she would go to the homes of anyone that was too sick or injured to come to her stall in the market. Invariably, someone would offer her a bed or at least a barn full of straw to sleep in for the night. Early the next morning she would begin the trek home to her grove.

But that was not the only time she had contact with the villagers. A few times every month someone would turn up on her doorstep looking for healing, or advice. These were usually men and women whose positions or circumstances made it difficult to seek her out in the public space of the market. Once, even a priest came all the way from Altdorf to see her when a stubborn lesion on his arm refused to scab over and heal. Seraina never refused anyone treatment, and that included Austrian soldiers that came to her stall in the market, although she was careful never to mention this to Noll.

On this day, it was already noon when she set out from Schwyz for home, which meant it would be well past dark by the time she arrived at her cabin. Unless, of course, she took the Brunnen ferry. She smiled, knowing all too well this had been the plan of her private weave all along. She had slept late and tarried at the farm, helping Gertie and her infant daughter feed the chickens and then broke her fast with them before she finally took to the road.

When she reached the crossing, she was disappointed to see no sign of the ferry. But just as she was about to go back to the road, a white sail peeked through the trees, moving steadily towards a small wharf jetting out into the green waters. The long, rectangular barge drifted up to the makeshift dock and a tall man holding a rope leapt gracefully from the ferry and tied it up to a post worn smooth and black. Unfortunately, he was not alone.

Seraina bit her lip as she recognized his passengers, old man Menznau and his wife. The wind was up and the lake simmered with small waves as the couple stepped down gingerly, their legs unaccustomed to fighting the swells.

Seraina pulled the hood of her cloak up and watched from the water's edge as the old man reached into a sack and pulled out a loaf of dark bread. He handed it to the ferryman and they exchanged a few words, then Menznau and his wife wobbled down the dock. As they came towards her, the old couple made it a point not to look at Seraina, and she felt that if she had been standing on the dock, they may very well have pushed her into the water.

Their son had died recently from the lung sickness. He had been caught stealing and was sentenced to do hard labor on the Altdorf fortress. Seraina had tried to see him, but the soldiers would not let her anywhere near the prisoners. They assured her their own doctor would look after him. He did not, and the only reason the Menznaus learned of the fate of their son, was because a relative found his body mixed with the ever-growing pile of refuse heaped against an outer wall of the fortress.

As the couple passed, she felt their grief surface and flare. Seraina watched their backs, hoping they might turn around and let her try and soothe their pain.

"You wishing to go across? If so we leave now, as I would be back at this dock before nightfall."

She turned to see the ferryman running his hands along the mooring rope, head down and focused on it like his question had been directed to it instead of Seraina. But as she stepped down onto the ferry he held out his hand and she took it.

Just then the barge lurched on the waves and she leaned into his grip to right herself. She laughed and not so much saw, but felt him smile at the sound. She looked up into his face and his eyes made her gasp. They were large and brown, with amber flecks, and would have been beautiful, but Seraina could see deeper than most people. Beneath the calm, swirled unfathomable darkness, and pain. There could be no doubt that his spirit had brushed up against evil.

She blinked hard from the intensity of the man's life. He immediately turned away, and as he did so Seraina noticed a long scar that stretched from beneath his eye to the bottom of his jaw.

Oh you fool, she said to herself. He thought she had been staring at the old wound. He kept his back to her and prepared to cast off.

"Best hold onto something. Wind has been unpredictable all day," he said. His voice scratched in his throat, like he was not used to speaking.

He pushed away from the dock with an ancient oar as scarred as his face, and then busied himself with adjusting the sail until it filled with wind. The ponderous barge plowed through the water at a slow, but steady pace. He rested one hand on the steerboard, making slight corrections now and again to keep the sail from spilling the wind, and asked where she would like to go.

"The hanging rocks south of Seelisberg, if the waters permit."

"Ah. Going to see the old hag are you?"

"Old hag?"

He shrugged. "The only reason anyone goes to the hanging rocks is because some old pagan woman lives in those woods. Trades coin for magic potions some say."

Seraina laughed and the ferryman looked at her, his dark eyebrows arched upwards.

"Magic," she said, "is the name people give to something they do not understand. Some might say what you did for Noll's young friend the other day was magic."

He gave her a dark look and crossed himself at the suggestion he might use magic.

"So, you are one of the outlaw's band, are you? One of his women?"

"Are you asking if I am a whore that passes herself amongst Noll Melchthal and his men?" Seraina's tone was light and sweet.

The ferryman's face reddened and he looked down at his hand on the tiller.

"It was not my intention to compare you to that kind of woman," he said, after a long pause.

Seraina caught his eye and tipped her head to show she was not insulted. It had the desired effect of putting the man at ease.

"Well, I am not a whore, but if I were, I would not be afraid to admit it. For a woman who sells herself is a survivor. Most often she has simply run out of options and is doing what she can to live."

He frowned at this. "There is always the nunnery," he said. "She would be better off giving herself to God, rather than some sour-breathed drunk in an alley."

Seraina put a finger to the corner of her mouth and cocked her head. "I suppose she would be safe in a nunnery. For 'sour-breathed drunks' are never found within a House of God." One side of her mouth turned up in a smile that the ferryman could not help but match with one of his own.

"You do have a point," he said.

"You would know much better than I about Houses of God, for Noll tells me you were with the Hospitallers?"

He nodded. "My whole life. What I can remember, that is."

"Do all Hospitallers study the healer's craft?"

He shrugged. "We are all required to spend time in the Hospitals. But some take to it more than others. I suppose I was one of those."

"Your teachers were Christian monks then?"

"Some. But many of the Order's physiks were Mohammedans."

Ah, that makes sense, Seraina thought.

The Arabs were an old people with a culture stretching back thousands of years. They would have much knowledge to offer.

"Do you miss your life across the sea?"

"Do you always ask so many questions?"

Seraina laughed and said, "I have been told that I do. We all have more questions than answers, but here is one answer I give to you freely, with no question attached. My name is Seraina." She performed a mock curtsy. "You might say I am the gardener for this old hag you mentioned."

The ferryman grimaced and once again looked down at the tiller.

"My apologies. I meant no disrespect to you or your mistress. I am Thomas," he said. "Thomas Schwyzer."

He said his last name quietly, like a boy admitting to a theft.

***

It was Thomas's favorite time to be on the water. The sun was beginning its descent behind the Alps and soon the bright ball would disappear, yet enough light would remain to sail by for some time. So different from the saltwater-scented evenings of the Mid-Earth Sea, where few high mountains encroached on the coastline. There, once the sun had fled, the whole world went dark.

Curious woman, this Seraina, Thomas thought. He remembered the sound of her innocent laughter and how her green eyes opened wide and flashed when she spoke, like the world was filled solely with beauty and wonder. He envied her that.

Do all Hospitallers study the healer's craft?

All people experience a turning point in their lives. A precipice, where on one side lies the innocence of youth, and the other a sheer drop into the darkness that is life. For Thomas, that moment came when he learned to read.

It had been during the waning days of Christian power in the Holy Lands. All the great Templar and Hospitaller fortresses had fallen. Beaufort, Akkar, Safed, even the once impregnable Krak des Chevaliers.

The year was 1290 and the port city of Acre was the last Christian foothold in the Levant. Thomas was called into a meeting with the Knight Marshal of the Hospitaller forces, Brother Foulques de Villaret.

Foulques had been raised within the Order in Outremer and was something of a legend amongst the other knights and sergeants, both for his skill at arms and his unwavering dedication. A Knight Justice at the age of eighteen, and a Knight Commander in his early twenties, he was recently appointed as Knight Marshal in the Holy Lands, the chief military adviser to the Grand Master. He had earned even the monks' respect because he was one of the few fighting men who was able to read and write.

So, in the summer of Thomas's fourteenth year, it was with some trepidation that he answered a summons to meet with Foulques de Villaret in the Marshal's keep office. Thomas had grown into a tall, lanky boy who may have been awkward if not for the physical rigors of his everyday training. Even so, he almost tripped as his foot snagged the edge of a lush Turkish carpet when he entered de Villaret's office.

He was used to the stone floor of his own dormitory, and the only place he had seen carpets, such as the one he stood upon, was hanging from one of the Arab merchant stalls in the city marketplace. In fact, the entire room reminded him of the eastern area of the bazaar. Sheer fabrics draped from the windows, allowing in ample light but diffusing it in a way that softened the grey stone room, and tapestries hung on every wall with multicolored motifs that matched those of the carpets. Elaborate candelabras were placed throughout the room and numerous feather pillows covered a seating area in one corner.

Seated behind an ornately carved desk, even de Villaret himself looked like he had just stepped out of the bazaar. His usual black Hospitaller tunic was replaced by the loose-fitting silks and linens that the Arabs preferred, but his head was uncovered, leaving his mass of black hair to float unfettered around his head. He saw Thomas's surprise at the room's décor and his own mode of dress.

"The East has much to offer," de Villaret said, sweeping his arm across the room. "Why else would so many Franks come to these lands?"

There was an uncomfortable silence as Thomas considered how to answer the knight, or if indeed it had even been a question. De Villaret stood, walked to the window, and looked out. "Your studies go well?"

"Yes, Marshal," Thomas said, finding his voice.

"Weapons master Glynn speaks highly of your abilities," de Villaret said, turning back to face Thom, his eyes probing. "Especially, with the dagger. Not the most noble of weapons though, I must say."

Thomas did not know what to say. He had no distinctive talent that made him stand out, like Pirmin's great strength, Gissler's uncanny speed with a sword, or

Ruedi, who could hit figs with a crossbow from across the training ground.

"I have been told you requested extra hours working in the hospital. Do you seek to replace your martial training with something you see as less strenuous?"

"No, Marshal. I would use the hours I have free in the evening after Vespers."

De Villaret nodded. "It is good you have an interest in medicine, for that is the founding vocation of our order. However, God has willed you should become a soldier, not a physician. Do you understand this?"

Thomas looked down at the ground. "Yes."

"How many patrols have you ridden out on?"

"One a week for the past year."

"Have you taken the lives of any of the enemy?"

Thomas looked up and one of his dark eyes twitched.

"I have killed a boy," he said finally. "Though I thought him a man at the time."

A month earlier his patrol had ridden to the rescue of an Italian caravan under attack by Bedouin raiders. His horse took an arrow in the lung and threw Thomas in front of the archer. He recovered, and without thinking thrust his sword into the raider's guts, mortally wounding him. As the figure writhed in pain on the ground, his face covering came away, and Thomas saw his attacker was a young boy, no more than twelve years of age.

Both the horse and the boy took a long time to die.

"Boys grow into men. Men who would undermine the one true faith. You carried out God's will and that is the end of it. Think no more on it, for there will be more. Many more."

De Villaret turned back to the window and gazed out. "If I grant you permission to work extra hours in the hospital, then you must do something for me. You will learn to read and write. First in Latin, then Arabic."

Thomas perked up, hardly believing his ears. He was going to learn to read! But he was not sure he had heard the knight correctly.

"Arabic, Commander?"

"Of course. Latin may be the word of God, but Arabic is the language of medicine. Although Frankish doctors are loath to admit it, the Arabian *hakim* are vastly superior. The works of the great Greek and Roman physicians have been lost to the West for centuries, but not to the East."

"But the writings of Galen and Hippocrates have been translated to Latin," Thomas said. "One of the monks showed us copies."

"Copies, yes. Copies of Arabic texts. The originals are long lost, so the Latin versions are translations of Arabic works. I feel the Latin copies possess a sometimes diluting layer of interpretation that the Arabic texts never intended."

"You have read them?"

"Yes, and so should you, provided it does not interfere with your military training. But not only the works of Galen and Hippocrates. Arabic medicine is the medicine of the Islamic world, not just the Arabs. That means that the Persians and Nestorians in the east and even the Spanish and Jews in the west have all contributed to Arabic medicine. You will become familiar with these works as well."

Thomas was shocked. What de Villaret suggested was blasphemy. "Even the Jews? But they are the enemy of Christ."

"So we are told. But as His soldiers, then is it not our

duty to learn from the enemy? The truth is, as Hospitallers we owe the Jews and Moslems a great deal for keeping the knowledge of the ancients alive. Knowledge long ago lost in the west, due in no small part to the Church's fear of the common man exploring the divine mysteries of the human body. The Church is content to have us refuse medical treatment and pray while sickness ravages our body, leaving our lives in the hands of God alone."

There was a hard edge to de Villaret's voice. Thomas glanced around the room, looking for any place that may conceal an eavesdropper. The talk made him nervous.

"But surely the Church's position has changed. We are, after all, an exempt Order subject only to the Pope himself. If the Church was truly against the study of medicine, why would they have allowed the Hospitallers to form in the first place?"

De Villaret's eyes narrowed as he looked at the youth before him and he shook his head. "Although both the Templars and the Hospitallers are sworn to poverty, we control vast fortunes that rival that of many monarchs. In fact, a good deal of that fortune has been earned by lending money to Kings. But often wealth is merely the illusion of power. For the moment only the Pope himself has the power to command us, but that will not always be so. Change is the only certainty in life."

He turned to look out the window, and spoke quietly. "We tread softly here. Much softer than you can possibly imagine. Especially now. The Mohammedans are not the only wolf baying at our door."

There was silence for a moment, and then de Villaret wheeled around. "But I did not summon you here to lecture. In return for me allowing you to study in the hospital, I have a task that you are to complete for me. But it is for me alone. No one is to know of our conversation today. Is that clear?"

"Yes, Marshal." Thomas's eyes darted around the room once before answering.

De Villaret reached down to his desk and lifted a rolled up scroll.

"First you must learn to read the three hundred names on this list. Then you will learn to write well enough to prepare your own list of the one hundred young men you think are the most suitable. They must be strong of arm and skilled in combat. But above all, loyal. Select only those you would trust with your life, and make no mistake on it, for that is precisely what you will be doing. You have sixty days to complete your task before we depart."

Thomas's head spun. "Depart Marshal? Where are we going?"

"Our hospice on the island of Cypress," de Villaret said. His intense blue eyes dimmed and when he looked at Thomas he had a sad, faraway look. "Ready all your possessions to take with you, Thomas, for once we leave, Acre will no longer be your home."

The Alpine wind suddenly changed direction and the ferry's sail luffed, fluttering uselessly for a moment until the boom started a slow swing to the other side of the barge. So lost in thought of the past, Thomas did not see it until the last moment. He ducked, and the long beam, crafted from a young tree as thick as his leg, swung harmlessly overhead and the sail once again filled with wind.

Thomas cursed the ever-changing winds on the lake. The influence of the Alps could send breezes whistling in from any direction. He would have to pay more attention. The emerald waters were as unpredictable as they were beautiful.

With his hand clutched around the steerboard, Thomas stared out over the dark waters, but all he could really see was his quill tracing the names of one hundred Schwyzer youths onto parchment. They would become members of the newly created Hospitaller Navy, under the direction of the Order's first Admiral, Foulques de Villaret.

The other two hundred Schwyzers would perish defending the walls of Acre less than a year later.

Chapter 13

HABSBURG CASTLE lay a half-day's ride from the easternmost inlet of the Great Lake. 'Castle' was a generous term, for it was more a stone mansion surrounded with a low fence to keep the animals out of the courtyard. Servants and farmers that looked after the estate lived in a dozen hovels that extended beyond the grounds and were scattered throughout the surrounding woods. Leopold's father had used the estate as a hunting lodge and referred to it as his summer castle. He came here to escape court life in Vienna, however, it was not a place he had shared with his family. Neither Frederick nor Leopold had ever visited the estate while their father was alive.

Immediately upon his father's death, Leopold had masons and carpenters from Berne construct a soldier's barracks, courtroom and prison cells just far enough outside the walls to be hardly visible from the main keep. He burned most of his father's furniture and stuffed boars from countless hunting expeditions and made the castle his new, albeit temporary, home. He intended to relocate to Altdorf once the fortress was complete.

The remoteness of Habsburg suited Leopold and he could understand why his father spent so much time here. However, the past week had been anything but peaceful. French and Austrian nobles had invaded Habsburg Castle, along with their baggage trains of servants and guards, and the odd Italian or Spanish popinjay flitted about as well. They had all come to see Catherine of Savoy marry Prince Leopold. A union that Leopold had opposed for years, but after spending everything he had on construction of the Altdorf fortress, he began to develop an appreciation for Catherine's charms, along with the dowry her father Amadeus, the wealthy Count of Savoy was offering.

It was a match ordained in heaven, Leopold had assured the Count. Amadeus had agreed and blessed the marriage wholeheartedly, contributing generously towards their new life together. He knew full well Leopold planned to control the Gotthard Pass from his fortress at Altdorf, but he also knew the French King had been showing expansionistic tendencies towards the pass as well, and he had no love for the French Crown. Having his own son-in-law overseeing the Gotthard would be far more advantageous.

The Archbishop of Savoy performed the ceremony in the largest church the Kussnacht area had to offer, which was not saying much. The local clergy were awed to have His Eminence conducting a royal wedding in their humble House of God, and so they fretted to make it a raucous event to be remembered by all. For Leopold, it had been the longest day of his life. After being subjected to the insufferable pomp and ceremony of the Catholic

Church for hours on end, he and his new wife had to endure the feast at Habsburg Castle with foreign crowds of fickle well-wishers and bawdy entertainers. His own jester, the Habsburg Fool, reveled in it, and performed several times throughout the day to the cheers of the spectators. Leopold swore he would slit the throat of the next man who told him how fortunate he was to have such a talented entertainer in his court.

Strange, Leopold thought, how a man with hundreds of people listening to his every word and watching his every movement could feel so alone. He had been disappointed to hear his brother Frederick would not be able to attend his wedding because war had finally broken out between him and Louis over the German crown. Frederick's presence could have made this entire farce bearable.

When he finally entered the wedding chamber and left the world outside, the last thing he felt like doing was breaking in some plain in the face, skinny virgin. But the bones had been cast and the moons read. This day had been chosen for the wedding because it was the most auspicious time for a successful consummation, and Leopold's physicians assured him it was the perfect time for his seed to take root.

So, as his new wife waited dutifully under the sheets of his four-poster oak bed, he had his servants remove his own clothes and then dismissed them. The girl was nervous, as to be expected, so he took his time. One of his two principal physicians recommended a gentle approach to intercourse to avoid loosening the tenuous purchase of his seed in her virgin womb. She cried out when he penetrated her, but quickly bit her lip and remained quiet until the Duke was spent. Afterward, he propped himself up on his elbow and caressed the young girl's hair and spoke soft, reassuring words.

"I hope to give you many children my lord, if God wills it," she said.

Leopold leaned over and kissed her forehead, noting how her eyes were spaced too far apart. Leopold hoped that trait would not show in his children.

"Nothing would make me happier, my sweet. But we have a responsibility to more than just one another now."

"My lord?"

"Our families depend on us as much as you and I depend on one another. Your father needs a grandchild and I need an heir."

And with Frederick at war, the sooner the better.

Her brows furrowed, accentuating the division between her eyes. Leopold forced himself to not look away.

"But my father has several grandchildren already. My three sisters are all married, and father had eight children with his first wife before she died."

"But how many of those grandchildren are heirs to the Holy Roman Empire? Your son stands to be King of the largest empire in the world. You must hold a special place in your father's heart for him to entrust you with this union." Leopold stroked her cheek once with the back of his hand. "And I for one, will be eternally grateful to him."

Catherine beamed at his words. He kissed her once on the mouth, and tasted the willingness to please on her lips. Leopold got up from the bed and pulled the servant chord as he shrugged into a nightshirt. Catherine sat up.

"Are you leaving my lord?"

"I leave for Altdorf at first light. I am afraid sleep will not find me if I stay within reach of your loveliness," Leopold said. He gave her a coy smile and kissed her hand. "I will not be gone more than a fortnight."

Leopold opened the door and the hulking figure of Klaus, his faithful man at arms, entered holding a lit lantern. Gone were his usual armor and weapons, and instead, the bearded man wore a knee-length, simple woolen tunic, which hung unbelted and loose at the waist. He looked at Catherine on the bed with no emotion in his face. Unruly tufts of hair, more grey than black, poked out the top of the v-shaped neckline that extended deep down his massive chest, and with his hooded eyes, he looked like a great eagle scouring a field for mice.

Catherine gasped and pulled the sheets up to her neck to cover her nakedness.

"Our family has a tradition, my sweet. One that I must honor, though it breaks my heart. But now that you are a Habsburg, I know you will understand."

"My lord?" she said.

"Klaus is a virile man, my sweet. He has served my family for many years and has been selected for his impeccable breeding. He is a Kingmaker. Remember that."

Her eyes widened and seemed to overtake her entire face.

"My lord, no, please."

Leopold took the lantern from Klaus, and the man bowed his head. He smiled revealing a mouth full of yellowed teeth, but all seemed intact. Admirable for someone as old as Klaus, Leopold thought.

Leopold exited the room. He stood in the hall and

listened at the door. He heard the bolt being slid into place, and the sound of the oak bed creaking as a ponderous weight fell into it. A muffled scream followed soon after, followed by some frenzied thrashing about and more protests from the wooden bed.

Leopold's second physician favored vigorous sexual intercourse because it made for a stronger, more robust fetus. One that would be more likely to survive a difficult birthing.

Leopold had ordered Klaus to be rough. Being a Habsburg was a dangerous business these days, and when it came to family planning, it was best to play it safe.

Chapter 14

HARVEST CAME QUICKLY that year, and once the crops were in, farmers rounded up their cows, sheep, and goats from the higher meadows where they had spent the summer, and marched them into town. There, they were placed in holding pens to await the festivities and fall market.

The town of Schwyz tripled in population over the course of the week as inhabitants of nearby smaller villages came in to celebrate the end of harvest. It was the biggest gala of the year, and for many, it was the one chance they would get to see relatives and friends from some of the more remote settlements.

Pirmin stayed in town all week of course, not wanting to miss a single day of the celebrations. But Thomas had remained at his cabin on the lake, using the busy ferry business as an excuse to avoid coming to town. The week of celebrations had indeed been good for business with a vast number of travelers seeking passage across the water. Thomas saw many new faces on his barge during the week, and almost every one looked at him with suspicion in their eyes and asked what happened to the old ferryman.

As the week came to an end, the number of people on the road lessened and things quieted down. Just when Thomas was sure he had avoided the festivities, Pirmin showed up at dawn on the last day.

"You drunk?" Thomas said.

"Drunk on the love of a good woman," Pirmin said slapping Thomas on the arm with one of his huge hands.

"Found out her name yet? Perhaps she had time to shout it at your back while you were riding away in the dark."

"Why so negative brother? I know just what you need to fix that sour song of yours. Breakfast. In fact, that is precisely why I have come. To break fast with my brother and thank God for all our fortunes."

"You have come all the way out here to make me breakfast?"

"Aye, Thomi. And after that, I mean to drag you kicking and screaming into town where I will revel in your discomfort."

True to his word, Pirmin did make them a hot breakfast of boiled oats with a handful of blackberries thrown in, and several thin slices of dried meat. Of course, he used Thomas's stores, and ate enough himself for three men.

***

Thomas did not recognize Schwyz. Brightly painted flower boxes hung from every window, overflowing with even brighter red and purple autumn blossoms of every shape and size. Freshly cut spruce and fir boughs adorned doors and hung from poles, filling the air with their scent. And people were everywhere: in the street, hanging off balconies, waving and calling from open windows, clustered in small groups on the ground, drinking mead and ale, or sharing bread and sausages smeared with spicy mustard. Children chased each other in and out of the crowd of people, screaming as loud as possible, but no one seemed to mind.

It was a time of celebration, the calm before the storms of winter set in. Women revealed dresses they had worked on in private all year and spent hours braiding and tying ribbons in their friends' and daughters' hair. Men donned short, colorful vests and put fresh feathers in their well-worn forester caps. But the real stars of the festival were the cows. Adorned in towering headdresses of pine boughs decorated with gentians, carnations, and edelweiss, their owners marched them through the main street of Schwyz like heroes returning from war.

Thomas and Pirmin watched a dozen cows saunter past, the bells at their necks announcing their passage. A group of proud farmers followed closely behind, waving at friends in the crowd lining both sides of the hard-packed earthen street.

"These beasts are pretty, I will give them that. But the cows of Wallis, now those are fine animals."

"More beautiful than the finest Arabian mares, I am sure," Thomas said.

"Beautiful? Naw, Thomi. Ugly as the Devil's arse. But strong, mean, and black as sin. Every spring we have a festival similar to this, but our farmers do not dress them up in girly headdresses and sweet smelling oils. We watch them fight."

Thomas smiled. "Fighting cows."

This was a new tale on the superiority of Wallis, the land of the Matterhorn; where the water was pure, the men brave, women descended from goddesses, and now, apparently, the cows ferocious.

"Do you doubt me?" Pirmin shook his head and wagged a finger in Thomas's face. "You are too mistrusting. I bet you only drank milk from one of your mother's teets."

"I have known you too long to start believing everything you say, my friend."

"Well, you can believe this. We would put all our cows in a big field and watch them fight all afternoon. Eventually the herd would declare a winner. That would be the one to lead them all up into the Alps, where they would dine on the sweet grasses all summer long. Of course the Queen, as we named her, would get her choice of the bulls."

"Of course," Thomas said.

Pirmin kept speaking, extolling the virtues of being nobility but Thomas only heard every other word. Standing beyond the line of parading cows and their handlers, stood the auburn-haired woman from his ferry, Seraina. He had learned soon after that day that she was in fact the 'old hag' in the woods, and not just a gardener. But, Thomas noted, there was absolutely nothing 'old hag' about Seraina.

Today she wore a sea-green dress, belted high, with a neckline low enough to make Thomas blush. She looked up and caught him staring, then smiled and Thomas marveled that he could make out the brilliance of her emerald eyes even at this distance.

Seraina stepped light-footed into the street, amongst

the rush of cows and bulls, and for a moment Thomas worried for her safety. But she paid them no mind and the throng of men and animals parted around her like water flowing around a boulder in a swift-flowing river. Smiling, she made her way towards the two men, occasionally reaching out a hand to caress an animal as it passed.

Pirmin had stopped talking. He elbowed Thomas in the shoulder. "What have we got here?" he said in a low voice as Seraina approached.

Seraina stopped in front of Thomas, to Primin's surprise, and said, "Hello again ferryman. Enjoying the parade?"

Thomas introduced her to Pirmin, who could not stop staring at Thomas with undisguised amazement.

"Thomi, when did you manage to meet such an enchanting creature?" Seraina laughed and color came to her cheeks, but she did not resist when Pirmin took her hand and kissed it.

The sight of Pirmin holding Seraina's hand and making her laugh, bothered Thomas at some level he did not understand. He brushed the thought aside. A few moments later Pirmin excused himself to chase after someone he spotted in the crowd, leaving Thomas alone with Seraina.

As she watched Pirmin leave, Seraina said, "Your friend is a charmer. I suspect he does quite well with the women."

"You have no idea," Thomas said.

She turned back to Thomas, her eyes flashing. "And you, ferryman? Are you also a man of many conquests?"

Thomas's head became hot and he was suddenly conscious of his scar. In the guise of looking at the last of the cows marching past, he angled the marred side of his face away from her.

He was saved from responding by a cow passing a few feet in front of them with a towering headdress of pine branches interspersed with brilliant yellow flowers. Seraina pointed and cooed with delight. But Thomas found himself more interested in how her eyes lit up at the sight. She stood close enough for him to smell the sunlight on her bronzed skin, and when she leaned forward to get a better view, her breast pressed lightly against his arm. He marveled at her softness and found himself rooted to the spot, afraid to move.

"That is my favorite flower in the world," Seraina said, turning to Thomas. He edged back a step and for the first time looked closely at the colorfully adorned cow.

"It is an autumn crocus," he said.

Seraina raised an eyebrow. "Some in these parts also call it a meadow saffron. But I prefer its older name," she said looking at Thomas with an impish grin.

"*Colchicum autumnale?*" Thomas recited its Latin name. In the right doses, he had seen it used to treat some types of fever. But it was more often used as a deadly poison.

"There are many languages older than that of your Church, Thomas," she said, using his name for the first time, he noted. He decided he enjoyed the sound of it on her lips.

"The name I was thinking of," Seraina continued, "is 'naked lady'." She smiled and held Thomas's eyes with her own until he looked away.

"I am sorry. I did not realize an ex-soldier would redden so easily," Seraina said with more amusement than sincerity.

Thomas cleared his throat. "I was a Hospitaller. Not a common soldier. Most of us...did not have occasion to speak with women."

"You mean it was discouraged because all women are sinful? Is that not how your priests see us?"

"Women are not all necessarily sinful, but they do tend to be more susceptible to certain temptations than men," Thomas said, realizing too late how much he sounded like one of his monk teachers.

"Ah, that would be lust? Temptations of the flesh?"

If Thomas's face was glowing before when Seraina mentioned the 'naked lady', it felt ablaze now.

"Perhaps..." he began, searching for the words that would make him look like lesser a fool than he had already proven himself.

"Strange, but I have known more than a few men to be just as lustful as any woman. And what of it? Lust is as essential as water in living a healthy life. Do you not agree?"

As Thomas wracked his mind to think of a response, Pirmin appeared out of the crowd. Thomas's relief vanished, however, when Pirmin stepped aside and revealed a man who had been eclipsed by his bulk.

"My lady, I apologize for interrupting," he flashed a smile down at Seraina, who returned it with a shake of her head. "Thomi, this here is the fellow I told you about."

The lithe figure of Noll Melchthal stepped from behind Pirmin and held out his hand. "Good to see you again, ferryman. Have you put thought to my offer?" His blue eyes sparkled like a melting glacier, and although he smiled, it came across as warm as his eyes.

Thomas gave Pirmin a withering glare. He did not

take Noll's hand.

"You two know each other then?" Pirmin said. "Good."

Seraina cut in and put a hand on Noll's shoulder. "Leave the man alone. This is a festive day, and not one for recruiting. Come, let us go sample some of Gertrude's cheeses."

She performed an elaborate curtsy to Thomas and Pirmin, looking every bit a little girl playing at being a lady, then took Noll by the hand and led him away to the food vendor stalls.

***

After the parade was over the games began. Enormous logs were rolled into the town square and men and women of all ages clambered over one another to take part in competitions devised around chopping or cutting through trees in all manners imaginable.

Pirmin lived for competition and when the ax-men lined up in front of the crowd he was standing amongst them, towering over them all. When his name was called he hefted his eight-foot war ax with one arm over his head and the crowd went crazy, cheering louder for the big man than any of the others.

The sight made Thomas smile. They had been in Schwyz for only a few months and Pirmin was already the hometown favorite.

Pirmin's first match saw him pitted against a young lad with thick forearms but the otherwise lean build of a boy stuck on the cusp of manhood. They each stood on top a log at either end, with their feet spread shoulder-width apart. The log rested across two other logs so it was lifted off the ground, effectively elevating the competitors above the crowd and providing them with a stage. Someone blew a horn and they were off.

The young man's ax glided into the wood at a slight angle, first from one side then the other. After each pair of strokes, a large chunk of wood sailed through the air. Pirmin on the other hand, at the sound of the horn, hefted his ax high into the air with one hand and looked out into the crowd. He egged them on with his other hand and they whistled and cheered. A group of young girls stood at the front and chanted "Pirmin! Pirmin!"

Only after he'd worked them into a frenzy did he grab hold of his ax with both hands. He let out a deafening bellow and brought the wide-bladed weapon thundering down to strike the log between his feet. The entire length of the log shook and wobbled, and both Pirmin and his opponent had to fight to regain their balance.

Pirmin's ax blade was embedded up to the handle in the wood. He tugged frantically but the log refused to give it up. His youthful opponent looked over and shook his head then went back to chopping. He was halfway through the log.

Pirmin cursed and jumped off the log. After several grunts and jerks from different angles, he managed to finally free the ax by heaving and pushing against the log with his foot. Red-faced he hoisted himself back on top, but before he could swing again there was a thump, as the young man's end of the log broke off and fell to the ground.

Pirmin lowered his ax, looked up to the sky and grinned. The crowd clapped and cheered as the two competitors met in the middle of the log and clasped arms. The young girls were still calling Pirmin's name long after the two men got down.

"That did not go so well," Thomas said when Pirmin found him in the crowd.

"Bah, that was a warm-up for the two man crosscutting round. That will be where we shine."

"We?"

"You and me Thomi. Entered us already. And after all that practice this spring cutting timber for your bleeding ferry, I expect to win. So drink some water and let us be off."

Thomas protested of course, but by the time they got to the crosscutting station Pirmin's enthusiasm had infected him as well. Of course, to a much lesser degree. It had always been that way when you were with Pirmin. He not only knew how to live life to the fullest, but somehow he also managed to bring life to those around him.

As Pirmin had said it would, the crosscutting went much better than the ax event. Laboring on either end of a long flexible saw, they managed to win their first four matches and had become a crowd favorite. Thomas knew it was not due to their skill, but he did not care. It felt good to hear strangers call out his name. Children ran up to give him and Pirmin drinks of water between rounds.

Eventually they lost to Sutter and his daughter Mera, but that came as no surprise, because they were last year's champions. Apparently innkeepers cut a lot of wood, and Thomas later learned that Sutter had been a forester for years before taking over the family inn, so he did not feel bad about losing.

Pirmin began complaining over and over how they

started before the horn, but when Mera jumped up and kissed him on the cheek, then ran off with her friends, he smiled and went silent enough. Of course, not as silent as Sutter.

Schwingen would prove to be Pirmin's event. A local form of wrestling, it had its own unique set of rules. The combatants each donned a sturdy pair of leather shorts over their breeches. Then by only holding the leather, they attempted to throw one another to the ground.

Pirmin had no technique but he was simply too big and strong for most of the men. He was the true hero of the crowd in this event, easily winning his way to the finals. He was to meet Gruber; a barrel-chested young dairy farmer from Seelisberg, who was shorter than Pirmin by a hand span, but almost as strong. And, despite his age, he was experienced in *Schwingen*.

Thomas stood by Pirmin as he struggled into his leather garment. On the other side of the ring, Gruber's father was helping his son get into his. His mother stood nearby, casting occasional worried glances in Pirmin's direction.

"The boy's mother thinks you aim to eat her boy," Thomas said.

"And I do," Pirmin said. "As soon as I can get these leathers on. Worse than our war kit. How many bleeding straps do these things need?"

Thomas watched Pirmin's huge fingers fumble with the fastenings on the leather shorts for a few seconds more. Finally, he had enough, and slapped his hands away.

"Give me those," Thomas said. "You never could put on your own armor."

Pirmin cursed but he let Thomas take over. He

crossed his arms and looked over at his opponent.

"You ever miss wearing your kit Thomi?"

"Never thought on it one way or the other."

"Well, I do. Especially the reds. I think I looked pretty fine in those reds."

A Hospitaller brother-sergeant wore brown with a white cross on the chest, or the shoulder, in his daily activities. Only the knights were permitted to wear black. But in times of war, everyone, brother-knights and brother-sergeants alike, would don vivid red tunics over their armor. On top of this blood-red background of war, a large white cross of peace was emblazoned on the chest.

Pirmin caught his opponent's mother looking at him. He screwed up his face and gnashed his teeth at her. She quickly looked away, wringing her hands.

"There you are," Thomas said stepping back.

Pirmin twisted a few times at the waist and raised each leg once. "Feels good. You still have the touch. Maybe I should have you dress me every day."

"They will stay on for exactly half the match," Thomas said.

The wrestlers were called into the circle and the match began.

It was an intense back and forth competition, but in the end, Gruber's youth and experience won out over Pirmin's strength. Both men were drenched in sweat and their breath came in labored gasps when Gruber finally won with a dramatic hip throw.

Pirmin pushed himself up off the ground and the two men embraced, after which Pirmin raised the victor's hand into the air. The crowd screamed and the boy's mother had tears in her eyes.

***

The meal that evening was both simple and decadent. Teams of oxen dragged the pieces of logs away from the town's streets and stacked them to dry for a year after which they would be turned into firewood. Hundreds of brooms appeared and for the next hour festivalgoers of every age and sex took turns sweeping sawdust, wood chips and dirt from the cobble-stoned square. Chatting with friends as they worked, many sweeping with one hand and holding a cup of mead in the other.

Then a hundred trestle tables appeared in the center of the square. Lids were removed from huge vats of chamois stew that had been simmering since morning and a delicious aroma blanketed the square. There was a sudden, unannounced flurry of activity as people realized it was time to feast and they began to pile lengths of sausages and slabs of dried meats on tables, followed by freshly baked loaves of dark bread and huge wheels of cheese and pickled vegetables. As the sun began to set, a group of women lit torches and placed them around the perimeter.

Pirmin and Thomas sat on upright log ends and watched as Sutter and his wife tapped a fresh keg each of ale and mead. Sutter collected cups from the two men and filled them with mead. He raised his own mug to Thomas and Pirmin and toasted Pirmin on his day's performance, and then scurried off to help his wife.

Thomas sipped the mead, detecting the tartness of plums within the honeyed alcohol. It was delicious and he was about to say so when Pirmin beat him to it.

"By God's hand, Vreni! This is the finest mead I have set my tongue to. Sutter, how did an ornery scarecrow like you, win the heart of such an angel?"

Vreni rolled her eyes and waved away the compliment. Sutter, with an amazing display of accuracy, picked up a keg stopper and tossed it at Pirmin, hitting him dead center in the forehead. Thomas thought he caught the faintest trace of a smile in Sutter's eyes as he turned away to fill someone else's mug, but he may have been wrong.

Pirmin scoured the ground for a moment, looking for the projectile, probably intending to throw it back, but his mug distracted him and he took another sip. His eyes rolled heavenward and he smacked his lips.

"Ah, this is the life, eh Thomi? Tell me you are not glad I dragged you out of your shack today."

Thomas took a satisfying pull off the mead. He knew the answer to Pirmin's question but he would never admit it. "At least it looks like we will eat well tonight. I will give you that."

"You should go into the innkeeping business. I have it on good authority the miserable sort can make a good living at it," Pirmin said.

This got a grudging smile out of Thomas. "And what would you know about making a living at anything?"

They settled into the easy, mocking banter they had known since childhood, but Thomas could sense uneasiness in his friend. He was working around to asking Thomas something. A favor perhaps. Maybe Pirmin needed money, which would not be unlike him. Finally, his curiosity won out over his patience.

"Pirmin, if you need a loan I can help. The ferry has been crowded with passengers as of late, thanks in no small part to you."

"Loan? No Thomi," Pirmin said, shaking his head.

"Sutter pays me more coin than I am worth, that I know. And more importantly, all the free food and drink I can stomach."

"He must be a very rich man," Thomas said. "Well, if it is not coin you are after, out with it then. Something is on your mind. I can see as much."

Pirmin chuckled and squinted down at Thomas. "You always could get up inside my head."

He quaffed his drink and looked out over the square at the hundreds of people milling about the tables filled with food. His eyes stopped scanning and rested on one table in particular. He nodded in that direction.

"That one," he said.

Thomas followed his gaze. Noll Melchthal sat on top of a table, deep in conversation with two young men standing near one end. But Thomas only gave them a cursory glance, and found his eyes settling instead on Seraina, who sat amongst a group of children at the far end of the table. She was helping them carve lanterns out of giant beets, which the children would later parade through the nearby woods to chase away bad spirits.

"He has been talking a lot of sense lately. 'Specially for one so young."

"Who?"

"The Melchthal lad. You hearing me, Thomi?"

Thomas turned his head towards Pirmin and his eyes followed, eventually.

"He is a good talker all right," Thomas said. "I will give him that. But Noll Melchthal is nothing more than a rabble-rouser. Men will die at his feet if they walk with him. Almost saw it happen last week." He remembered the young boy with the crossbow bolt in his back. Shaking his head he raised his mug to his lips.

"I know. He told me."

Thomas lowered his mug without drinking. "Just how much time have you and Noll been spending together?"

Pirmin's face was shadowed in the low light of early evening, but Thomas saw a familiar glint in his eyes. "Ever been to Einsiedeln, Thomi?"

"The monastery? What cause do I have to go there?"

He did not know much about the large order of monks living near the Mythen mountains, only that they raised horses and were especially respected as breeders of war mounts for the German Empire. They did not deal in mules or oxen, so the locals never had much to say about them.

"Quite a place they have there. Must be a hundred monks. They built a town within their cathedral grounds. Got farriers, blacksmiths, sheep, some cows, and an awful lot of nice pasture land."

"And you tell me this because you have decided to join their ranks, I suppose."

"Not if the Lord Jesus himself begged me to. But, I think I will consider visiting them again sometime before our next feast day."

Thomas followed his eyes and they stopped on a nearby table laden with roasted lamb shoulders, dried sausages, stacks of freshly baked trenchers, and a small keg of wine. He stared at Pirmin. The big man was grinning.

"Pirmin...what have you done?" Thomas was aghast.

"You know me. When I come to a feast I feel the need to contribute."

"You stole from followers of Saint Benedict! They live in austerity—how could you do that?"

"Bah! Those monks are better off than Templars.

They had mountains of foodstuffs in their cellars. They will hardly miss the morsels we took."

Thomas's eyes narrowed. There was more to this story, yet. "Who are *we*?"

"Well, you could say I asked Noll and his men to help me out on this one." Pirmin shrugged. "There was a lot to carry."

Thomas stood, sloshing half the contents of his mug onto the ground. "Are you touched? Raiding a monastery with a known outlaw could get you the noose. And if you avoid that, there is the small thing of blasphemy!"

Pirmin stared at the wet spot on the ground left by Thomas's mead. "That was Sutter's brew, not the monks'. Who are you to call me touched?"

"You have gone too far this time. Einsiedeln is under protection of the Habsburgs."

"And that is exactly why we raided it," Pirmin said. "How much do you know of the troubles Schwyz and the monks have been having?"

Thomas held his tongue and glowered at the big man sitting on his stump; he hardly needed to look down to be at eye level.

"They have been fighting over pasture land for years. Until ten months ago, when Habsburg soldiers started slaughtering any animal grazing within a day's march of Einsiedeln that did not bear the monks' brand." He waved his hand toward the nearby tables heavy with meat. "More than a few of these haunches never belonged to those cursed monks in the first place."

Pirmin had no love for monks, Thomas knew that. He suspected it was because monks always administered the beatings when they were children. And Pirmin, being the type of headstrong boy he was, received far more lashes than any other boy in the Acre hospice.

"Did you kill anyone?"

Pirmin's eyes went wide. "Of course not. We redistributed some foodstuffs, as Noll likes to call it. Nothing more. We left them with their lives and valuables, I swear. Oh, except for a few kegs of ale and cider that, as we speak, are on their way to Noll's camp for his men."

"They will petition the Duke, and the Habsburgs will have no choice but to retaliate. You realize this?"

Pirmin's grin widened. "Now Thomi, do not go all mother on me. It is a little meat, some wine, nothing more. Come—let us go fill that mug of yours."

The celebrations carried on into the night and hours later Thomas found himself helping Sutter pile empty barrel kegs onto the back of a wagon. On the other side of the road, laughter erupted from a group of revelers, and when Thomas looked up he saw Pirmin amongst the crowd. He bent low, almost in half, so a woman could whisper in his ear. As she stood on her tiptoes and placed her slender fingers on Pirmin's shoulder, Thomas realized it was Seraina.

He watched them for a moment, wondering what it was Pirmin was saying to make her smile and laugh so. He felt the scar on his face tighten as he forced a smile of his own. Pirmin was a force of nature when it came to women. Thomas had never known one to be immune to his charms. Why should Seraina be any different?

"Vreni made up a bed for you at the inn, if you want it," Sutter said.

It took Thomas a moment before he understood what the innkeeper was talking about. "No, but tell her thank you. I need to go back home tonight," Thomas said.

Sutter shrugged. "Suits me. It would just be another mouth eating my bread in the morning anyway."

The two men finished loading the wagon and Sutter dropped the end board into place. Thomas turned to see Pirmin and Seraina walking towards him, her hand lost in the huge crook of his arm.

"Ah, Thomi! Good. You have not slunk off into the night as of yet."

"As of yet," Thomas said.

"Seraina is insisting on going back to her cabin tonight, and while I offered to escort her to the end of the world if need be, she refused. Wanted me to ask you to take her. Imagine that, ferryman."

"Pirmin," Seraina said and hit his arm with her open hand. "That is not what I said."

"Oh I think it was."

"I told you I had no need of an escort," she said.

"And then you asked if Thomas was going back to the ferry tonight, and when I said 'I am sure he is'—"

Seraina cut Pirmin off. "I merely thought, since we were both going in the same direction, some company would be nice," She cast Thomas a sheepish, sidelong glance. "If you do not mind, that is."

Thomas shook his head and said, "No, of course not."

"I believe what he means to say is the thought of it horrifies him," Pirmin said grinning from ear to ear.

Chapter 15

THOMAS SADDLED UP ANID and they rode out of Schwyz an hour past midnight. The stars hid beneath fast-moving clouds, but enough moonlight reflected through the billowing forms that they did not need a lantern.

Thomas could tell Seraina was an inexperienced rider, but once mounted behind him, she settled into Anid's rhythm like she had been born a horse nomad of the desert steppes. Anid walked as though she was not even there.

But Thomas knew Seraina was there. Her hands rested lightly on his hips, and every so often when she leaned forward to say something, she would press against his back and he would feel the warmth of her breath on his neck.

For most of the trip they spoke of herbs and healing remedies. Quizzing each other on the different names of frequently used concoctions and compresses. They compared the medicine of the Greeks and Arabs to that of the druids, marveling at the similarities and laughed at some of history's more ridiculous treatments.

As the night wore on and they closed in on Thomas's cabin, their conversation slowed until it died off altogether, leaving only the creaks of Anid's saddle carrying on the night air. They rode in a silence that neither of them seemed to find uncomfortable and Thomas found himself wishing he lived further from town.

"Why do you dislike Noll so much?" Seraina said after clearing her throat.

Thomas stiffened.

"I do not dislike the man. I only worry what will happen to those closest to him," he said. "The fairer question might be, why is it that you have so much faith in him?" He felt her hands tighten on his hips. She was silent for some time before she spoke.

"I do not expect you to understand, but Noll is special. Every so often in history a person comes along with the potential to make a great difference in the lives of his people. The old religion would call him a Catalyst."

"And how exactly is Noll so different?"

"The Catalyst is a thread of the Great Weave, like every one of us. But most people's lives have very little effect on the Weave. Whether we live or die makes little difference. A few will mourn our passing, perhaps some will be relieved, but life goes on. The Catalyst, however, is the rarest of threads. If pulled in the right manner, it is capable of completely unraveling the Great Weave, and reworking it into something entirely different."

"Your talk hovers on the edge of blasphemy, Seraina. No man can change the world as you speak of it."

Seraina sighed. "I apologize. I did not wish to put you

in such a foul mood on one of the last nights of summer. Let us talk of something else." She leaned in close as she spoke, and Thomas felt his anger towards Noll dissipate with the warmth of her pressed against his back.

Then he felt Seraina tense and she pulled away from him, snatching away that wonderful heat. Anid threw back his head and skitted one step sideways.

"What is it? What do you see, boy?" Thomas leaned over the horse's head and spoke softly. He had long ago learned to trust his mount's senses over his own.

Seraina leapt to the ground and stood next to Anid's head. She stroked his velvet nostrils and said something in a language Thomas did not understand. When Seraina looked up at Thomas she had tears in her eyes.

"I am so sorry Thomas. Please. Stay here with me."

The sky had begun to lighten, or so Thomas had thought. The smell of smoke brought back his sense of reason. Dawn was yet another hour away.

His cabin was over the next rise, and when he looked in that direction he saw a flickering orange and red glow playing along the underbellies of the clouds overhead.

The ferry.

He pulled up on Anid's reins and commanded him backwards with his knees, away from Seraina. The stallion snorted in protest but complied immediately. Thomas was dimly aware of Seraina calling out his name as he forced Anid into a gallop. They pounded up the hill and when they reached the crest, Anid whinnied and reared up on two legs, startled by the sudden bright lights coming from his home below.

Everything was engulfed in flames. The cabin, the ferry, even the wharf. Thomas's hand went to his knife handle and he spun Anid in a circle, scouring the lit up countryside for some sign of who had done this.

He saw nothing but sparks whirling in the cool night air, and everywhere, reddish grey clouds. They hung over the lake and blocked out the forest bordering the road.

He was alone.

Chapter 16

"IT IS A FOOL'S HOPE. The fortress will never be completed before the first snows."

"Be careful who you call a fool, Landenberg."

Leopold glanced around him, wondering where that *other* Fool had gotten to. Leopold had arrived in Altdorf an hour before, and as he stood on top of the main gate surveying the masons and their teams of oxen and peasant labor milling about the main keep, he despised the fact that Landenberg was right.

While the living quarters in the main keep were almost finished, the outer walls were nothing more than a hole encircling the grounds. Extending the wall below the ground level was necessary both to prevent its buckling from frost heaves and to deter sappers from tunneling under in the event of a siege. The main gate was finished. However, what good was a gate with no walls?

"How is the tollgate on the road coming?"

"Good. Or fair I should say. We have no portcullis

for it as of yet. The iron workers had a fire in the forge and it has put them behind by weeks," Landenberg said.

Leopold squinted his eyes against the mid-day sun. He leaned over the edge of the gatehouse they stood upon. He could make out the top of the massive iron gate suspended with heavy ropes waiting to be dropped at a moment's notice.

"Yet there is one here," Leopold said.

Landenberg nodded. "You said to focus all work on the fortress."

Leopold closed his eyes. Unfortunately, Landenberg was still there when he opened them.

"Look around you. Why would we need a portcullis when we have no walls?"

The tollgate stood between Altdorf and the Gotthard Pass, and was located on a section of road that squeezed between two massive granite faces. It had a guard tower flanking either side, and could hold back an army if need be. That is, *if* it had a portcullis.

Leopold fixed Landenberg with a cold stare, and willed understanding into the dim man. Just when he thought he might have to resort to drawing a picture in the dirt with a stick, Landenberg's eyes lit up and a sheepish look crossed his face.

"We should remove this portcullis and fix it to the tollgate. That would allow us to begin collecting tolls immediately," Landenberg said.

Just then, the Habsburg Fool's green hair appeared at the top of the stairs, quiet as a snake.

"What a splendid idea! Is that not a splendid idea, my Duke? I wish I had thought of that one," the Fool said. He held his chin and muttered to himself as he stomped up and down the first three stairs several times. The chimes on his pointed shoes sounding more like church bells as they echoed off the stone walls of the narrow staircase.

Leopold clamped his teeth and did his best to ignore the little man. He turned to Landenberg. "Get the iron out of this gate today. Now, did you summon the local judge as I told you?"

"He waits in the hall, my lord."

"Good. Come with me. I would have both you and the judge there to listen. Then if there is some confusion, perhaps you can assist each other in understanding my wishes."

***

"This is most unexpected my lord. To be summoned before the Duke of Styria and Further Austria is an honor an old country judge like myself rarely sees."

"The honor is mine, Judge..." Leopold glanced at Landenberg.

"This is Judge Furst, my Duke. The Crown appointed Magistrate for both Uri and Schwyz," Landenberg said.

Furst bowed and his hands unconsciously smoothed the front of his black magistrate's robe. Faded and frayed around the hemlines, it matched the old man perfectly Leopold thought. He also could not help noticing the man's robe bore none of the red or yellow markings found on the clothing of Judges of other Habsburg territories.

Leopold moved to sit down on a chair behind an ornate desk, the only pieces of furniture in the recently constructed room, when Landenberg suddenly jerked and let out a howling sneeze, showering the desk with a fine mist. There was an awkward moment while the sound reverberated off the walls of the large, but bare, room.

"Cursed dust everywhere. These stonemasons must have lungs full of the stuff. Probably piss white mud," Landenberg said.

Leopold backed away from the desk, wondering how he had become so desperate to need men such as these.

"Let us walk to the balcony, gentlemen. A little fresh air will do us all some good."

They passed through an open doorway that led to a balcony overlooking the courtyard. Although the stonework was mostly complete, no doors or window shutters were yet in place. Apparently, the same ironworkers responsible for the portcullis delay were also behind in the production of hinges and latches. There were only two locations that the doors were fully operational: Leopold's bedchambers, and the prisons, which the men could now see from the balcony. The prisons were located across the courtyard from the keep, in a low rectangular building that extended two floors below ground.

"Vogt Landenberg has told me of the fine work you do for the Crown," Leopold said, resting his hands on the stone railing and looking over some workers in the courtyard.

"Thank you, my lord. I am flattered the Vogt of Unterwalden should concern himself with the governance of Uri and Schwyz at all."

Furst obviously resented Landenberg's presence in his district. And Leopold could not blame him.

"I have asked the Vogt to assist us with a troubling matter that has come to light."

"Oh? What might that be, my lord?"

Leopold could see by Landenberg's face that he was just as puzzled, but he managed to keep quiet.

"Recently, the Abbot of Einsiedeln sent me a most urgent, and if truth be told, disconcerting message concerning some of your Schwyz countrymen."

Furst looked up. His eyes narrowed, but he said nothing. A wise man fears his own words more than those of his betters.

"It seems a band of men led by Arnold Melchthal raided the monastery. They stole a great deal of their larder, and desecrated their place of worship. The Abbot said many of the brothers feared for their very lives."

Furst began to roll his eyes but quickly caught himself, remembering whom he addressed.

"Did you know of this attack?" Leopold asked.

"I heard a rumor, my lord. But no arrests have been made. I hear Melchthal is very difficult to find."

"Bleeding ghost he is, that one," Landenberg said. "But when I catch him, the Devil will not even find use for what I leave of him."

"Bold talk," Leopold said. "For one who has chased the man for what, three years?"

Landenberg's face grew as red as the fist emblazoned on his breastplate. "He cannot run forever."

"Since Melchthal is so difficult to find, perhaps you would have better fortune hunting one of his men. The Abbot described a huge man, fair in hair color and complexion, who was instrumental in the attack. He thought the man may even be Melchthal's lieutenant. He wielded a long-handled ax."

At the mention of the ax, Furst's eyes betrayed his thoughts.

"You know of this man," Leopold said.

Furst paused for a moment before answering. "I know of a big man like that. He does some work for Sutter on occasion."

Leopold gave Landenberg a questioning look.

"Sutter. The innkeeper in Schwyz. Has a fine daughter," Landenberg said.

Leopold nodded. "Very well. Take a few men and visit the inn. Find the big man and arrest him and anyone he is associating with. But not the innkeeper. Travelers and merchants need inns."

Landenberg bowed his head but not before Leopold saw his face light up like a candle in a prison cell.

He turned to Furst. "Judge, there will be some small changes to your sentencing system. From this day forward, all who are found guilty of even the smallest crimes will be sentenced to work on the fortress. They will be housed in the dungeons and divided equally among the masons. Is that understood?"

Furst's mouth twitched. "Of course my lord."

"This brazen attack on the defenseless monks of Einsiedeln, is a sign of just how widespread banditry has become in this area. We must make a strong stand, and I cannot expect you to rise to the occasion without help. That is why I have sent for three of my best judges from the Aargau to assist you. This is not the time for leniency."

"I will do my best, my lord."

"That is all I can ask of any man of rank and privilege, Judge Furst."

Leopold turned to send Landenberg on his way, but he was already gone.

Chapter 17

"THEY BURNED YOUR FERRY, Thomi. By the Devil's black arse, of course I am angry!" Vex, Pirmin's new puppy, barked twice and squatted low to the ground, distressed at his master's emotional outburst.

Thomas stood waist-deep in the lake. He had removed his boots but wore all his clothes, hoping they would retain some of his body heat. They did little to keep out the chill of the autumn water.

He finished lashing what remained of the blackened ferry deck to a mooring post on the wharf. The railings, mast, and sail had been completely consumed in the blaze, and most of the floorboards were ruined beyond repair, but the members closer to the water had been spared. At least most of the wharf remained.

"Noll says it was Landenberg. His cousin's boy saw him and a dozen red-fisters on the north road that night," Pirmin said, leaning on his ax and shaking his head.

Pirmin stood well back from the water lapping gently at the fine-pebbled shoreline. He had never enjoyed water. In fact, Thomas believed, it was the only thing in this world the big man feared. Curious that a man who served on a war galley for twenty years should be so cursed. But then again, with time, water could bring down mountains.

Thinking Thomas was not listening, Pirmin hefted his ax and shouted from the shore. "Did you hear that Thomi? Landenberg did this! I say we go visit him in his sleep tonight. You and me. With all the love we can muster." He smiled grimly and ran a thumb as thick as a broom handle over the blade of his ax, testing its edge.

Thomas had been furious the night he and Seraina had come upon his burning home. If someone had been there, Austrian soldier or not, he had no doubt he would have made them pay dearly. But now he was once more under control, and thinking straight.

"Noll would have you believe it was Landenberg. That suits his purpose fine. For all we know Noll burnt all this himself just to sway us to his cause."

Pirmin's face went from red to purple. "By God, you are a stubborn worm!" He lifted his ax and strode towards Thomas, but stopped instantly when his foot splashed into the water. He danced back, as did Vex, but not before snapping at the water's edge.

Pirmin cursed Thomas in his native Wallis dialect, and although Thomas could not understand the words, he was glad ten feet of water separated him from the enraged giant.

"I cannot understand what it is you have against Noll. He talks more sense than you do recently."

"You had best stay away from that one Pirmin. I have

told you as much already."

"Or what?"

When Thomas did not reply, Pirmin threw up his hands in disgust. "This country has turned you into a cowering Dominican. Or worse, if there is such a creature."

Thomas shrugged. "If it is as you say, and the Vogt's men burned my home, he did it because he thinks I helped Noll escape his men. The boy is playing you Pirmin. Any way I look at it, this whole mess is Noll Melchthal's fault."

Pirmin shook his head. "I have said it before, and will not shy from saying it again. You are a stubborn worm, and you get more so every day. I need a drink and a woman. And the order is not important. When you finally crawl out of your monk's cell, you come find me and I will talk reason into you."

Thomas watched Pirmin swing into the saddle of his war mount with the grace of a much smaller man. He looked around for Vex, and found him at the shoreline, gingerly testing the water with a paw disproportionately huge compared to the rest of his growing body.

"Vex! Get away from there! We are going home."

Without waiting for the dog, Pirmin nudged his horse into a gallop over the green-covered slopes. Vex cast one last look at the water, whined, and then bolted after Pirmin.

Thomas stood in the water, and shivered.

Chapter 18

PIRMIN AND NOLL STOOD completely still, hardly daring to breathe. The forest too had gone quiet, as though it sensed what was to come.

Noll sighted down the length of the crossbow bolt with both eyes open. He was an instinctive shooter and never used sights. He preferred to look at a small point on his target and will his bolt to that very spot.

A hairy mass exploded from the thicket with a squeal and charged directly at the two men. Noll flinched but then controlled his breath and waited.

"Shoot!" Pirmin said, stepping away from Noll and reaching for his knife.

Noll picked his spot and eased up on the tickler until the crossbow jumped in his hand and the bolt sprang forward. Noll followed it with his breath and saw it penetrate deep into the boar's chest. The animal veered off course, snorted, and took several steps towards the underbrush. Then it dropped.

"Fine shot!" Pirmin said standing upright and

releasing his grip on his knife. "That would have made any Genoese crossbowman proud. Thought for sure we were going to be wrestling pig."

"Pray that never happens. I have seen boar smaller than this one rip men up pretty bad," Noll said.

He walked over to the boar and touched it with his foot to make sure it was dead, then leaned over and removed his bolt.

"Did you know any Genoese bowmen?" Noll asked.

"Know any? The Levant was full of them. Highest paid mercenaries in the Holy Lands. We used them when we could afford them. I do not recall ever losing a fight when we had the green and red of Genoa with us. Except for Acre...but that fight was lost before it was ever started."

"Perhaps that is what we need—more crossbowmen. If I could get my hands on more of these," Noll held up his crossbow, "we could take the fight to Landenberg. Maybe even Habsburg castle."

Pirmin grinned and shook his head. "I admire your spirit, Noll. I really do. But that crossbow you have is a hunter's weapon. A bolt from that would bounce back from chainmail and stick you in your own eye. A true war bow capable of skewering a man at two hundred paces in full kit is what you would need. But a weapon like that costs more coin than I can drink in a year."

"A full year? By God, Pirmin, you know how to squash a man's dreams."

Pirmin leaned against a tree and plucked a long blade of grass. He chewed on it thoughtfully. "No, what we need are more men. What have you got now? A hundred?"

"I could have a hundred fifty in two days," Noll said.

Pirmin laughed at how proud Noll looked.

"A hundred fifty? Come talk to me when you have a thousand. We could work with that. In the meantime, I suppose we will have to stick to fighting monks."

Noll went silent. He pulled out his knife and cut two lengths of twine, then thrust his knife into the dirt. He began tying the forelegs of the boar together.

"You must know others that would fight for our cause. Do you have any connections?"

Pirmin shook his head. "Lost track of them all. All save Thomi."

Noll groaned. "Do not mention the ferryman again. We have no need of cowards like him."

"Watch your tongue boy. His kind is exactly what you need."

Noll grunted and Pirmin could tell by his face he was not convinced.

"He is a different sort that one. I know it, and the Grandmaster of our order knew it. That is why he made him captain of the Schwyzers."

"What do you mean by 'a different sort'? I've seen plenty of soldiers in my time and they all take to killing much the same in my eyes."

Pirmin shook his head as he stared off into the trees. How could he explain to someone who had never faced the true horrors of war?

"Not that one," he began. "The battle furies have no hold over Thomi. You see, most men survive in war by letting their animal side loose. Fear and anger rise up and give a man strength. They allow him to survive the loss of a limb or fight like a madman long past total exhaustion. Warriors of old called this being possessed by the battle furies."

"I know of the furies," Noll said.

Pirmin looked at the young man's eyes and could see a hard glint there that made him think Noll was perhaps not as green as he thought.

"Well our Thomi does not. You see he has never been visited by the furies. When the killing starts, his pulse never quickens, his guts do not boil up in the back of his throat. He might as well be at home eating soup as caving in a man's head with his mace."

"And why is that useful? You just said rage lends a man strength when he most needs it," Noll said.

"Let me tell you a story," Pirmin said, shaking his head. "We were boys and the Hospitallers had marched us out of Schwyz weeks earlier. Our ship finally put ashore in Outremer, a days march from Acre. A few hours after leaving the port, slavers set upon us. Ripe we were for their kind, what with five hundred children and only a handful of guards. The black knights fought like devils and managed to beat them off, but not before the slavers made off with near two hundred of the young ones."

Pirmin paused. He had not thought on that day for a long time. But he could still smell the sun-baked earth at his feet as they marched, and feel the cool relief as they entered a canyon, the stone walls providing shade from the relentless sun. Then the rockslide came, and relief changed to confusion and terror as dust blotted out the light and made breathing difficult. Screams followed. And soon a new scent for Pirmin, one he would never get used to: the smell of blood spilling onto hot sand and stone.

"Me and Thomi should have been amongst those taken. Fighting was all around us, and a fat-jowled man tried to grab us. Thomi was only five at the time. I was eight." Pirmin grinned at Noll. "But I was big for my age."

"You are still big for your age. What did you do?"

"I jumped on the whoreson and fought for all I was worth. I had a dog too, and she helped some. Before the bastard put her down."

Pirmin was silent for a moment. Thinking of Zora was never easy for him.

He quickly pressed on. "The slaver thrashed me good. I lay on the ground bleeding and hurting everywhere and he was about to tie my hands and drag me away when Thomi threw a rock at him. The slaver looked up and started laughing. And I tell you, I almost did too." Pirmin shook his head and chuckled at the memory.

"What was so funny? What was he doing?"

Pirmin wiped some moisture from one eye and continued. "That skinny little waif was using every muscle in his feeble body to point a crossbow at the slaver as he tried to haul me away. Not a toy like yours, mind you. It was a real war bow like I was talking about earlier. It weighed as much as him, I am sure. But you want to know the best part?"

Noll smiled. "He shot the man through the stomach?"

Pirmin laughed. "No, that he could not do. He had no bolt. The string was not even stretched. Thomi might as well have been pointing a stick at the bastard."

Noll shook his head. "Stupid boy."

"Ah, was he now?"

Pirmin grinned and took a drink from his wineskin before continuing with his story.

174

"He held that crossbow on the man, but his eyes were looking into my own. The slaver was laughing so hard as he walked over to Thomi, he had trouble drawing his knife, but what he did not see was Thomi leading me with his eyes to the man's axe lying in the sand behind him. The whoreson slapped the crossbow out of Thomi's hands and, just to teach him a lesson, slashed Thomi across the face."

Pirmin dragged two fingers down the entire length of his face. He was no longer smiling.

"He just stood there? Why did he not run?"

Pirmin used the same two fingers to tap the side of his head. "The plan. With Thomi it is always about the plan. Always has been. You see, Thomi lay on the ground crying and bleeding like a half-slaughtered goat. And when the man leaned over to slip a tether around the boy's neck, I drove the bugger's own ax between his shoulder blades, right through his spine. He died right then, no doubt, but his leg twitched for ten minutes. I will never forget that."

He took another pull off his wineskin and held it out to Noll, who did not seem to notice.

"You killed a man when you were eight?" There was awe in Noll's voice.

Pirmin shook his head. "This is what I have been trying to tell you, boy. I swung the ax, but truth be told, it was Thomi that killed his first man that day. If not for that skinny little boy, I would have spent my life rowing in the bowels of a Turkish slave galley."

Chapter 19

BERENGER VON LANDENBERG and seven of his men thrust open the heavy double doors to Sutter's inn shortly after mid-day. While Landenberg sat down in the middle of the room and put his booted feet on the table in front of him, his men forced the few patrons out and then rounded up Sutter and his family. Sutter, his wife Vreni, and daughter Mera, stood in front of Landenberg, displayed in single file.

"Fine place you have here," Landenberg said, waving his hand over the simple room. Behind him a stairway led up to several guest rooms. "I suppose you serve ale?"

"Yes, my lord," Sutter said, wiping his damp hands on the white apron tied about his waist. "And mead as well."

"It is a dusty trip from Altdorf, and I find the honeyed wine…unsatisfying. Perhaps I could bother you for a flagon of ale?"

"Of course," Sutter said, turning towards the bar.

"No, not you. I would have your daughter fetch it."

Sutter was tense before, but now his back jerked upright like a cold iron rod had been laid alongside his spine. He turned to his daughter. Her pale blue eyes looked at him for guidance. He nodded once and tried to smile.

Landenberg watched Mera with hooded eyes as she stepped behind the bar, and tipped a clay mug under the spout of the oaken keg. She looked up once and something in Landenberg's stare caused her to tremble. Frothy, warm ale flowed onto her hand. She carried the sticky mug over and placed it before Landenberg on the table. Without taking his eyes off her he raised the ale and drained off half, then set it down and dragged the back of his arm across his face to remove the foam from his heavy beard and moustache.

"Very nice," he said. Mera inched closer to her mother and stared at the floor.

Landenberg turned back to Sutter. "Tell me innkeeper. How is business these days?"

"Fair my lord. Could be better, but you will not hear me complain."

"And when was Arnold of Melchthal last here?"

"The outlaw? Surely my lord, we would not—"

"Oh shut up Sutter. I know he and his men frequent this place. Do not fret. I can hardly blame you if a band of outlaws choose your inn to quench their needs. But I would be remiss in my duties as your lord if I were to allow your innocent daughter to be exposed to such unscrupulous men."

Sutter opened his mouth to say something, but Landenberg held up his hand and continued speaking. "Fortunately, so to speak, a member of my own household's serving staff has recently left this world and must be replaced. Your daughter seems capable. What say you my child? Would you have the honor of attending to your lord's household?"

"You are not our lord," Sutter's wife spoke up. "Schwyz is not part of Unterwalden and you are not our Vogt. You have no right to—"

Landenberg nodded to one of his men and he stepped forward and backhanded the woman hard across the face. She fell back into some chairs and another soldier yanked her to her feet.

"Vreni!" Sutter tried to go to his wife but two men grabbed him and another held Mera, who began to shake and sob quietly.

Landenberg stood up. "I may not be Vogt to Schwyz or Uri, yet, but Duke Leopold charged me with keeping the peace in all lands north of the Gotthard. And you, woman, have been harboring outlaw scum in your inn."

He grabbed Mera from the soldier holding her and said, "Show the innkeeper's wife what could happen when one gets too close to outlaws."

The soldier's lips parted into a gap-toothed grin and he nodded to the two men holding Sutter's wife. They lifted her by the arms and slammed her back onto one of the tables, its trestle legs swayed unsteadily but held. The soldier drew his belt knife and starting at the bodice, sliced open the woman's dress. She fought and shouted obscenities at the men, surprising them with the crudity of her curses, and they laughed.

"Right bit of dirt in this one's mouth," one of the men said as he removed his sword belt. "Time to take the fight out of her."

Landenberg held Mera tightly around the neck from behind, as he watched his men take turns at the girl's mother. When Mera called out and tried to struggle free he clamped down, cutting off her air. Her struggles lessened and he eased off the pressure, but kept the soft skin of her face pressed up against his own. He leaned himself into the young girl and felt his loins stir.

His intention had been to get the girl back to his estate and have his way with her then, after she spent some time as a servant in his household. But as she squirmed against him and cried out again and again, he found himself becoming hard and knew he could not wait any longer.

Chapter 20

WITH THE FRESHLY KILLED BOAR at their feet, Noll and Pirmin crouched in the trees outside Sutter's inn looking at the two soldiers standing on guard outside the main doors.

"What are they doing here?" Pirmin said.

"Looking for me," Noll said. Over their armor, the men wore tunics bearing Landenberg's crest. He fingered the pommel of his sword wondering how many men were inside, and cursed himself. He should never have frequented Sutter's inn, but who would have thought Landenberg would send his soldiers this far from Unterwalden in search of a common outlaw? He must be getting to Landenberg. And while that thought pleased him to no end, it was not right that Sutter should pay the price. Or his family.

Lord God, please let Mera not be inside.

"We have to go in. Sutter is in trouble."

"What do you mean? He does not know where your camp is so there is precious little he can tell them. They will kick around the chairs, ask some questions, maybe drink some of Sutter's mead, and then be on their way."

"Vreni and Mera are in there."

Pirmin was oddly quiet for a moment. "Point taken," he said, and then gritted his teeth and blew air from between them. "This is turning out to be one hunting trip I wish I had lugged my ax along for."

The big man grabbed the dead boar by the scruff of its neck and dragged it close with one hand. "I will go first and you come when you have a mind to. I will not begrudge doing the lion's share of the work, but I will be right pissed if I need to do it all."

"What? That is your plan? You have no idea how many men are in there," Noll said.

"Bah, you sound like Thomi," a scowl crossed Pirmin's face. "Sometimes you just got to have at 'er. Do something, anything, and push your way through until the job is done."

Pirmin hefted the boar onto his shoulders, stepped out of the bush, and walked straight towards the two guards at the main door to the inn.

"Inn would be closed," one of the soldiers called out to Pirmin when he spotted him. The other one had his hand up inside his chainmail, scratching at something under his arm with a tortured look on his scrunched up face.

"Oh? For how long?" Pirmin said, stopping at the bottom of the steps leading up to the front doors. He shifted the boar on his shoulders and grunted, bending low under the weight.

"Go get your swill somewhere else, man. This tavern is closed until the Vogt decides otherwise."

"That so? Suppose I will leave Sutter's meat on his

---

porch then. Which one of you has my payment?"

The soldier laughed and turned to his companion. "This one is either funny or daft as a stone. Do not know what smells more, him or his pig." Smiling he turned back to Pirmin. "Take your pig and your own stinking hide away from here, now."

"All right, all right. No need for a tongue-lashing. But I would leave this boar here."

"Put it downwind on the far side of the porch," the second man said. His hand was still under his armor but was now raking at the area near the small of his back.

Pirmin nodded and climbed the stairs on unsteady legs, and when he got to the top he bounced once and hefted the boar over his head in an incredible show of strength. Then, he launched it at the furthest soldier, the one with the rash. It hit him square in the chest, knocking him into the guardrail. His legs flipped out from under him, and he tumbled clear over the railing. He hit the dirt hard and a split second later the dead animal landed on top of him.

Noll sprinted out of the bushes and stood over the man in an instant, but there was no need. The man was unconscious.

Meanwhile, the other guard snarled and reached for his sword. Pirmin grabbed his wrist with one hand and his throat with the other. He lifted the man three feet off the deck and slammed him against one of the log posts supporting the porch roof. He grunted and his eyes glossed over. Pirmin let him slide down the post and then used it to pull himself into the man, and delivered a bone-jarring knee to the man's sternum. Chainmail was designed to turn aside the points of blades. It did nothing against the full strength and momentum of a three hundred pound giant. The breath rushed out of the man and his ribs crackled like dry kindling. Pirmin held the man up long enough to take his sword and then tossed him away.

He glanced at Noll to make sure he was coming and then charged through the doors to the inn, screaming in a voice that froze Noll in place and chilled his blood. It was a wail filled with the anguish, hatred, and fear of war. It was the most terrifying thing Noll had ever heard, and it took a moment for its paralyzing effect to release its hold. God only knew the effect it had on the men Pirmin attacked.

By the time he made it through the door, one soldier was on the ground unmoving and Pirmin was exchanging sword blows with two others. Across the room was a flurry of movement as two more soldiers were struggling with Sutter, one of the men had his breeches down around his ankles, and Vreni, Sutter's wife, lay behind them curled up on top of a table, her dress torn and tattered. Sutter had his hands around the breech-less man's throat, while the other one had a handful of Sutter's hair and was punching him in the back of the head. Then he stepped back and drew his sword.

Noll jumped over a chair and knocked the man's blade aside before he could skewer Sutter. He slashed at the soldier's side but his armor protected him. In his peripheral vision Noll caught movement and risked a glance to his left. To his surprise, he saw Berenger Von Landenberg himself holding Mera from behind, and at that moment, the Duke's Vogt also saw Noll. His eyes went wide.

Landenberg's face reddened and twisted. He looked like he was going to charge Noll, but he saw Pirmin swatting his men aside like gnats and he hesitated.

Noll yelled out Landenberg's name in rage, but was forced to parry an attack and he lost track of the Vogt. All he could think of was how he had to get to Mera. Fury lent Noll strength and he sent a flurry of blows against his opponent. The soldier's face blurred and was replaced with that of Landenberg. He heard the Vogt's voice saying the same thing over and over.

His boy broke your fingers, so have your justice. Take the old man's eyes.

He heard his father scream and men's laughter.

His father's cry turned into a wet gurgle and Noll realized his sword was stuck in the throat of the soldier he was fighting. He pulled it free and scanned the room for Landenberg. He was nowhere to be seen, but Noll offered up a silent prayer when he saw Mera embracing with her parents. A dead soldier, his face blue, lay crumpled at Sutter's feet as the innkeeper held his sobbing daughter and wife.

Another man was dead on the floor near Pirmin, and the last soldier was on his knees begging for his life. Noll dashed through the kitchen to the back door. The stable gate was open and several horses were moving about some distance away in the woods. Landenberg had scattered them before taking flight himself. Far away up the road Noll saw a lone horseman receding into the distance. He kicked an empty milk can next to the door, grimacing as he felt the hard metal against his toes.

God had granted him a rare opportunity for justice today, but Noll had missed his chance. He had failed his father three years ago on the family farm, and he had let him down yet again here today.

Take the old man's eyes.

Noll kicked the pail one more time and screamed.

Chapter 21

SERAINA EASED THE DOOR to Vreni's room closed and made her way softly down the stairs to the inn's common room. Sutter, Mera, Pirmin and Noll sat around a table. They all looked up with pained, expectant faces and awaited her news.

"She will be fine. In time," she said.

The relief on everyone's face told Seraina she had chosen her words well. Vreni was a strong woman, but Seraina doubted she would ever be truly fine. Seraina had seen too many scars left on women by men to ignore the truth. The physical healed quickly, but those of the spirit ran deep, and in most cases, could only be concealed. Wounds of the spirit may scab over, but they never fully heal.

When Seraina had arrived at the inn, she had found Vreni on her knees praying to her god, thanking him over and over again for sparing her daughter the rape she had suffered. The sight had infuriated Seraina, but she allowed the woman her prayers, while inside she seethed at the uselessness of worshipping a god who would subject his faithful subjects to such torture.

Sutter stared at her, his eyes dull and the sockets around them black with exhaustion. The usually taciturn man could not conceal his gratitude.

"Thank you Seraina. I know your presence means a lot to Vreni. And to me. You have always been a friend to this family."

Seraina's vision clouded briefly with the beginnings of tears, but she blinked them back. She would be strong for them. She had suffered nothing, after all, and had no right to subject them to her own childish tears. She forced her lips into what she hoped was a smile, and stalled until her emotions were under control, and she was sure her voice would not quaver when she spoke. She handed Sutter a vial.

"Give her five drops in tea every night. It will help with the dreams." She wanted to say 'nightmares'. "Mera, your mother will need more help with her work than usual for the next few days."

"Of course." The young girl's eyes were still glossy with her own tears. "She spoke against the Vogt on my behalf. Perhaps if I had agreed to what he wanted none of this would have happened."

Noll stood up from the table, banging it with his hand. "Mera! Do not even think on that."

Mera flinched and Pirmin shot Noll an angry glare. He placed his hand lightly on her shoulder. "What Noll means to say is this is not your fault. Nothing you could have done would have changed this."

Chastened, Noll eased himself back onto the bench.

"Yes, forgive my abruptness, Mera," Noll said. He flashed her a weak smile.

"Please, Noll. Do not apologize. If you and Pirmin had not risked your lives to help us…" Mera could not bring herself to finish the thought.

"My daughter is right. I owe you more than I can ever pay, but I swear to damn well try my best," Sutter said.

Mera placed her hand over her father's for a moment and then stood slowly from the table. "I had best put something on the stove for our customers tonight. People need to eat," she said. The men watched in awe as she left them.

"Brave girl, that one," Pirmin said.

Seraina took Mera's seat at the table. She sensed anger rolling off the men in waves. Pirmin and Sutter both looked at Noll, their faces grim.

Noll said, "We live in Landenberg's shadow, cowering behind his back where his arms cannot reach. Where we pray he will not find us."

Noll stood from the table and drew out his bone-handled hunting knife.

"I, for one, am ready to once again feel the sun on my face." He drove his knife into the center of the table. It continued to quiver after he removed his hand.

"And I can see by your eyes, that your thoughts echo mine."

Seraina's breast swelled with both fear and hope for what Noll had in mind.

Chapter 22

GISSLER STOOD in the antechamber to the main hall in Altdorf.

A runner had come for him in Habsburg yesterday morning. Leopold requested his appearance in Altdorf immediately. He had made the trip with all due haste, not only because he sensed he was on the verge of a breakthrough with the Duke, but also because he was bored. He had never been one to sit around idle.

He stepped closer to the door and listened to the Duke and Landenberg arguing in raised voices. Or rather, listened to Leopold reprimanding Landenberg for botching a simple task.

A few minutes later, the door opened and Landenberg blustered out. He cast a contemptuous look in Gissler's direction.

"So, you are here. Leopold said to send you in, but I warn you. His mood is fouler than usual. Hold your tongue if you know what is good for you."

Gissler fought the urge to unleash his tongue on the

Vogt at this very moment, and managed restraint. He appeased himself by imagining how he would talk to the fat man if he were knighted, and settled for locking eyes with Landenberg as he pushed past the man into the hall.

Landenberg held his gaze, but stepped aside without a word.

Chapter 23

THE STARTLING BLUE eyes of Abbot Ludovicus went wide when Thomas took the quill from his hand, and instead of scratching an 'X', began writing his full name on the bill of sale.

Thomas took his time and formed the letters carefully. It had been some time since he had set ink to parchment, and if truth be told, had never achieved a high skill level in it. Reading and writing were as different as walking and riding to him. But the mere act of writing his own name was something even most bluebloods were incapable of performing.

Thomas set the quill down. Pleased with himself, he stepped back to appraise his work. He turned, and when he saw Anid, his good mood fled. He stepped in and let the horse nuzzle the left side of his neck; for some reason he always favored the side of Thomas's scar.

"Easy boy. The monks will treat you well. You will have all the mares you could ever wish for and food aplenty."

Thomas ran a hand one last time over Anid's long, black head, to his velvety nostrils. He patted his neck and relinquished his grip on the bridle. Abbot Ludovicus took the reins and passed them off to another monk quickly, as though the worn leather were crawling with lice. The monk bowed his head to the Abbot and led Anid away.

Thomas watched until they disappeared through Einsiedeln's gates into the monastery courtyard. His throat tightened, but he reminded himself he had no need of a warhorse. It had been selfish to keep Anid for as long as he had. He was a ferryman now.

"He is a magnificent beast and will be in fine hands here, I promise you. Our farriers are the best in the Empire."

The Abbot of Einsiedeln was a round man with a fleshy neck and cold blue eyes that continuously wandered, as though he were impatient to be somewhere else.

"Remember, per our agreement, he is not to be sold," Thomas said. "I want him to finish his days here, on these green slopes. Stud him out all you like but Anid is not to leave these meadows. Understood?"

Ludovicus bowed his tonsured head. "As agreed. But we will of course have to rename him. We cannot allow a heathen name within our walls."

Thomas disliked the Abbot more with every passing second.

"He will not answer to another name," he said.

"How is it a good Christian like yourself came to possess a pure-blooded Arabian like him in the first place? I know horseflesh well enough to say that his kind can only be found in the stables of princes. *Infidel* princes."

Thomas looked into the Abbot's eyes and said, "A friend gave him to me. A heathen friend."

The Abbot's eyes flicked over Thomas, and his nose wrinkled. "Well, he is small for a destrier. But fast, and strong. Coupled with the right mare, he should produce excellent stock."

Thomas nodded. The man did know horses. In fact he reminded Thomas more of a horse trader than a monk. "When can I expect delivery of my lumber?"

"In five days time. Now if you will excuse me, I must make arrangements. Brother Titus will be along with your new mount shortly."

Ludovicus picked up the parchment from the low table and turned to leave, but Thomas interrupted him.

"It is a long way back to Brunnen. I had planned to partake of your hospitality this evening. Perhaps a hot meal, and a place to sleep would not be too much to ask?"

The Abbot turned and smiled, but his eyes were cold and unsympathetic.

"I regret that we are unable to accommodate you. Bandits recently ransacked our stores and we have little enough to see us through the winter. The brothers have taken up a vote and decided not to allow outsiders into the grounds for the time being."

Thomas bit his tongue and resisted the urge to lash out at the man. A traveler would never be denied refuge in a Hospice of the Knights of Saint John. In the fields behind the monastery he had counted over a hundred head of horses, most of them bred to be destriers, the ultimate weapons of any army, and each one worth more than a farmer in Schwyz could make in ten years.

Thomas looked at the high walls surrounding the monastery's keep. This was no true house of God; it was a house of war. He idly wondered what ruse Pirmin and Noll had used to get past the main gates and into the courtyard.

Thomas let out a breath to calm himself before he spoke. "The man who gave me Anid would see his own children go hungry before refusing a guest food and shelter."

The Abbot smiled and nodded sagely.

"Such is the way of the Infidel, I am told." He looked towards the gate and said, "Ah, here comes your mount."

Thomas turned to see a monk pulling a squat mule through the gate. The animal balked, reluctant to leave the courtyard and the comfort of the stables. Its long ears twitched and it let out an offensive snort, which sounded more like a donkey's bray than the proud whinny of a horse.

Thomas could not stop his hand from balling up into a fist. "Our deal was lumber and a *horse*," he said.

Ludovicus scrunched up his face. "Was it? Oh, well let me confirm. I would hate to be mistaken."

The Abbot held up the parchment and made a show of examining it carefully.

"No, I am afraid it simply says you will receive four wagons of lumber and one 'mount'. There is no mention of a horse." He held out the parchment to Thomas. "Written in Latin, the language of God, and witnessed here by your very hand."

Thomas glowered at the Abbot. He thought of the Schwyz harvest festival and suddenly wished he had had the foresight to stuff his belly with enough pork to feed ten men.

By the time Thomas coaxed the mule back to the remains of his lakeside cabin, the sun hovered behind the tallest surrounding peaks. In the twilight, he saw a shadowy figure move near the entrance to his tent.

He reined in the mule and his hand drifted to the knife at his belt. He scanned the area, while the mule plodded ahead, ignoring Thomas's leg commands. Smoke rose from a small cooking fire, and since Thomas doubted anyone wishing him harm would first prepare dinner, he allowed himself to relax.

As he approached his camp, Thomas recognized the figure as Seraina. His pulse quickened and he urged the mule ahead.

The beast increased his pace to a bouncing trot and Thomas found himself sliding around on the animal's back like it had been slathered in olive oil. He berated himself for not having the business sense to keep his saddle. Knowing how ridiculous he must look with his long legs wrapped around the underbelly of his long-eared mule, Thomas was surprised to not be greeted by a stream of laughter from Seraina.

She stood when she saw him approach and paced to and fro until he dismounted and stood before her. When she looked up he saw the trails of recent tears on her cheeks. She said not a word, but walked to Thomas and threw her arms around his neck, put her head on his chest, and let out a deep breath.

"Seraina, what is it? What has happened?" He tried to lean back and turn her head up but she only clung to him all the harder. Her slim frame shook with a few silent sobs and he surrendered, reaching his arms around to hold her close.

He realized he had yearned to be this close to her since that first day she had appeared on his ferry, but now, holding her tight, he experienced a paralyzing sense of dread. He squeezed her gently and was overcome with the scent of wildflowers and warm, dark earth. Finally, he moved his hands to her shoulders and eased her back.

Hesitantly, Seraina told him how Landenberg's men had beaten and raped Vreni and would have done much worse if Pirmin and Noll had not intervened. By the time she was finished, her voice had risen and a quiet anger flashed in her eyes.

"Why do men talk of honor and god yet feel they can take a woman anytime they wish? Is that something your god teaches?"

"What happened at Sutter's was the Devil's doing. Not God's."

"You are wrong, Thomas. It was men who raped Vreni. Men with power given to them by other men. Men from foreign lands who treat us like animals, because in their eyes, we are not true people."

"I do not condone their actions, but Sutter must have done something to incur Landenberg's wrath."

"What could he possibly have done to deserve such a punishment? What did Vreni do?"

"They harbored outlaws. Everyone knows Noll is close with Sutter."

Seraina took a step back. "Noll cannot be blamed for this. The Habsburgs are a festering wound on our people and Noll is but the dressing."

"I do not understand how you can have such confidence in a common thief."

Seraina's tone softened, but her eyes still burned with

conviction. "You underestimate him Thomas. I do not know when, or how, but Noll will make all the difference. Our people, your people, will remember his name for centuries."

Thomas shook his head. "History is the words of conquerors. That boy will conquer no one, but he will make the lives of many short and painful. Just ask Sutter and Vreni if you doubt—"

Seraina slapped him across the face. It was so fast and sudden Thomas doubted for a moment that it really happened. But then the residual heat of her hand registered on the left side of his face, and the skin burned everywhere, except of course, for the chord of scar tissue. It felt as cool as ever.

Seraina's eyes widened and she stared first at Thomas's face and then at her own hand. She shook her head and backed further away.

Thomas stepped towards her and reached out.

"Seraina, wait."

"No," she said, her voice breaking. "I was wrong to come here."

She opened her mouth to say more but it caught in her throat. Then she turned, and fled into the trees like a startled deer.

Thomas stood alone. His eyes scoured the dark woods for the slightest hint of someone's passing. But all he had for company was a stinging handprint on his cheek, and the soft scent of wildflowers dissipating into the cool night air.

And one long-eared mule.

Chapter 24

TO PUT SERAINA FROM his mind, Thomas threw himself into rebuilding his ferry. He had decided the ferry would take precedence over the cabin, for without the ferry he had no source of income. He would live in a tent all winter if need be.

Thomas was so focused on peeling the charred layer from a log with his double-handled drawknife that he did not hear a man and horse approach. When a voice called out, he jumped, gouging a long divot in the wood.

"You. Peasant. I am searching for a man feared in the lands of Islam. A leader of men and a keeper of the One True Word. Perhaps you know where I might find this man."

Thomas put the drawknife down and straightened up. He wiped his blackened hands on his breeches, squinted into the sun, and pointed southeast.

"You will find him a thousand miles from here. That way I believe."

Gissler leapt down from his horse laughing, and the

two men embraced. Thomas made a show of not touching Gissler's clothes with his charcoal-covered hands.

Gissler turned in a full circle and surveyed the burnt-out remains of what had once been Thomas's cabin and ferry.

"What in God's name are you playing at here?" Gissler said.

"Nothing that cannot be put off until we are sharing a meal and some drink. Let me wash up. Then, what do you say we ride to the local inn?"

"Only if we spend my coin, Thomas. I have been fortunate and come into a position."

"So it would seem," Thomas said, giving a nod to Gissler's outfit. He wore a thick, burgundy traveling cloak and a white, finely embroidered tunic, which almost completely covered his light chainmail vest. On his head was a sleek cap with a peacock feather stitched into the hatband. Thomas had seen similar caps on well-off merchants and nobles, but he thought it looked ridiculous on Gissler.

"You found your kin then? Well, I look forward to hearing it all."

Gissler's eyes blackened for the briefest moment. "Better than that. I am now a member of the Duke's household."

This news caught Thomas by surprise. He turned his back on Gissler and ladled water onto his hands from Anid's trough. Or what used to be his horse's trough. It now belonged to an ornery mule.

"And which Duke would that be?" he said, rubbing his hands together. Rivulets of water cut trails through the charcoal dust on his forearms and dripped off his

199

elbows in blackened streams.

"Which Duke?" Gissler said, incredulous. "Your Duke. The only Duke this land knows. Duke Leopold of Habsburg."

"Duke Leopold's man then? You have indeed done well for yourself, Gissler." Thomas ladled more water over his arms, scrubbed them once more, and gave them a vigorous shake. "So would you be here in an official capacity?"

Gissler laughed, and the sound set Thomas on edge. Gissler was never a man to be so receptive to humor.

"Yes, and no," Gissler said. "The Duke has been happy with my service, I suppose, and when I mentioned I knew of a Captain of the Order living in his lands, he suggested I seek out my friend and offer him a position. I thought that rather generous of our lord, would you not agree?"

"I am done with soldiering. I told you that before."

"I do not talk of guard duty for some noble's spoiled children. This is the Duke's household. And not just any Duke, mind you. Leopold is one of the most powerful princes of the entire German Empire."

He paused and put his hand on Thomas's shoulder. "He has the power to grant us knighthood, Thomas, and has promised as much."

"Knighthood? What use to me is a title? What I really need is some solid timber to rebuild my ferry."

Gissler's eyes clouded over and his top lip curled upwards into a snarl. In a way, this relieved Thomas, for it meant the Gissler he knew was once again standing before him.

"Ferry? Are you daft? I offer you a chance at a noble life, something all men dream of, and you would rather sit in the mud cutting wood?"

"You do not need to be a knight to live a noble life. We have both known enough knights to recognize the truth in that."

Gissler threw up his arms and began pacing. "If you wish to wallow in mud, I will not beg to change your mind."

Thomas eyed Gissler. "Is that truly the reason you came to Schwyz? To offer me a position with your Duke?"

Gissler stopped pacing. His lips stretched into a thin smile. "You have an uncanny ability to hear things people do not say. Very well. I also seek an outlaw. Arnold Melchthal. Do you know of him?"

"You are the Duke's manhunter then? Once a soldier of God, now you chase outlaws for rich men. Is that the glorious position you dangle before me?"

Gissler's face clouded over with the dark grey of a winter storm. "You dare to mock my path?" Gissler stepped back and held his arms out to the sides. His fine velvet cloak fanned out and floated in the breeze, and the sunlight glistened off his calfskin gloves.

"My lord keeps me in the finest livery and comfort I have ever known. I have my own quarters in the Habsburg castle itself. Servants cook my food and bring it to me whenever I desire. And meat, Thomas. I eat meat every day, on trenchers baked from flour whiter than snow."

Gissler's eyes were wild now. He had always been volatile and easy to anger, but Thomas saw something there that made a tremor run up his spine.

"And this is but the beginning. Look at the rags falling off you. What right do you have to say your life is so superior? The Hospitallers whispered half-truths and lies to us as children so they could use us. They lulled us into a dream. They twisted your mind and stole your life, Thomas. They did it to all of us, but I have woken up. And you had best do the same."

Thomas watched Gissler carefully. His agitation had grown as he spoke, and years of resentment for the Hospitallers, the Church, and perhaps Thomas as well, poured forth from the man like froth from the maw of a rabid wolf.

Thomas shook his head. "You scoff at the Divine Order. God made you a soldier, not one of the ruling class, and He has a reason for everything."

Gissler laughed, but it was built upon anger.

"I hear nothing but the voices of monks in your words. I should have known you were too far-gone to reason with. Well, I will not waste any more time, for I have a life to live."

He walked to his horse, a dun mare, grazing nearby. Gissler grabbed her reins and jerked her head up. She whinnied in alarm and danced a few steps as Gissler leapt into the saddle.

"When you change your mind, come to Altdorf and ask for me at the fortress. I will be staying there for a time."

Thomas looked up at Gissler. "Why is it that everyone always thinks I will change my mind? Am I so fickle in my ways?"

With one last stare at Thomas, Gissler whipped the ends of his reins on his horse's neck and jammed his heels into her sides. She took off, eager to be away from the source of her master's ire.

Chapter 25

*C*URSE THAT MAN'S *self-righteous hide.*

Gissler sat with Pirmin, sipping at his first flagon of mead, while the behemoth across from him was already half through his third. Only the lip of the tall, clay mug peeped out of Pirmin's heavily scarred hand.

Gissler tried to focus on all that spewed from Pirmin's mouth, but the memory of Thomas's disproving face kept stealing his thoughts. Thomas was trapped in the past. No longer a captain of the Order, he was nothing now. Worse than nothing—a ferryman! He had no right to press his will on a member of the Duke's household. All those years being captain of *The Wyvern* had swollen his self-worth far beyond his station. Gissler had every right to have him tied to a post and lashed.

"What brings such a smile to your lips?" Pirmin's words cut through his musings. "Have you got a woman to tell me about?"

Gissler looked up from Pirmin's scarred, misshapen hands to his grinning, chiseled face and twinkling eyes that only the strongest of women could hope to resist. It was a face that had been spared the ravages of war, but there are always roads leading back through a man's past, if one knows where to look.

It had been an easy matter to find Pirmin. So easy in fact he regretted ever going to Thomas first. He should have known Thomas's view of himself was too elevated to ever accept a master other than God.

Gissler had found Pirmin in the same worn out inn they had all said farewell in not so many months ago; the same one they sat in now. It was mid-afternoon and the two men were the only customers in the place. Gissler had no doubt that if he were to return in ten years, he would find Pirmin astride the very same bench. Such were the lives of men without ambition.

He had thought it better not to tell Pirmin about his employment in the Duke's service, opting instead to say he had been traveling throughout Austria and France competing in the tournaments. Pirmin had not doubted him for a moment. The best lies were always the ones harvested from a seed of truth.

"I may have met a woman worth remembering," Gissler said.

"Ah, well out with it then."

"It is true the tournaments have more prizes than shields and coin," Gissler said. "But you will not trap me into moaning over my conquests like some lovesick courtier."

"Conquests? More than one then, and sounds like a battle more than a tumble with a sweet maiden. Pray, tell the tale, Gissler!"

Gissler declined a few more times, and finally, Pirmin gave up, concluding it was going to take a great deal more drink to loosen the man's tongue.

"It looks as though the tourneys have indeed been good to you," Pirmin said, nodding to the velvet cloak draped over a nearby rack. "Would take me two years of cutting Sutter's wood to get one of those."

He quaffed the rest of his drink and wiped his mouth with the back of his hand.

"Maybe three," he added grinning. "If I keep drinking my wages away."

"Coin is easy to come by for men like us," Gissler said. "You could just as easily hire out your ax and make a fortune. But you do not, and I believe I know why."

Gissler emphasized his words with what he hoped was just the right mix of admiration and jealousy to pique Pirmin's interest. And it seemed to work, for the hulk's eyes brightened at Gissler's words. He leaned forward on his bench and it groaned under his weight.

"And why is that—oh wise man with the fancy cloak?"

"You have a good thing here Pirmin. You are fulfilled."

Gissler gestured around the room and nodded to the bar where Sutter was stacking wooden mugs and bowls onto a shelf. The door to the kitchen was open and someone was preparing a stew for the evening meal. Savory smoke trailed from the doorway as cubes of mutton sizzled and browned in a pot. The scene was tranquil, and the inn spotless. Amazing really, Gissler thought, considering the mess Landenberg and his men must have made mere days before. But then again, what choice did peasants such as these really have?

"You have built something here. These are good people. What more does a man need?"

"A fine cloak would be a start," Pirmin said leaning back against the wall. But his eyes had lost their smile. "You are right. A man could do much worse. But truth is I mean to leave Sutter's inn shortly, and most likely will not be coming back."

"And why in God's name would you do that? You just said how happy you were here."

"Had some trouble a few days back."

"Woman?"

Pirmin shook his head and looked to his hands. He stroked a crooked finger, which had been broken many times over. It was the thickness of a woman's wrist.

"Soldier trouble, if you catch my meaning. Staying here puts these people at risk."

"What have you got yourself mixed up in this time Pirmin?"

"Nothing I regret, that much I know." His tone was fierce.

Gissler let the silence build, before he broke it. "Well, I find myself with time and coin, both in abundance for now. If you want my help, you need but ask."

Pirmin looked up and stared at Gissler's face for a long moment, his eyes narrowing. Feigning interest in his drink, Gissler avoided the man's stare and let his ponderous mind reach its own conclusions. It was critical that Pirmin believe the next thought to be his own.

Finally, Pirmin spoke.

"I myself need nothing, you understand. But, there are those who need help, and we would welcome a man like you."

"What scheme do you have cooking Pirmin?" Gissler said.

"There is someone who can answer that better than

me, if he will agree to meet you. He is young, but I warn you, do not take him lightly. He is as sharp as a Spaniard's dagger."

"He would have to be to have you speak so highly of him. Who is this man?"

"His name is Noll Melchthal. Have you heard the name?"

Gissler pursed his lips and fixed Pirmin with a stony look.

"Never," he said.

Chapter 26

"THOMAS—WELCOME. We have missed your face around here for some time."

Sutter was caught off guard by Thomas's sudden appearance at the inn. "Little early for dinner, but I got some nice mutton stew Mera made yesterday."

"Thank you. That and some mead would make me a happy man," Thomas said.

He sat at a table in the corner and watched Sutter drift off to the kitchen. He was a man going through the motions; a gaunt shadow of his usual surly self, always full of energy and quick with his tongue.

He returned with the stew and a tall tankard of mead, and when Thomas held out a coin, Sutter shook his head. He looked at Thomas with the dark, red-rimmed eyes of a man barely holding on.

"Your coin is not welcome here. But you and your friends always will be," he said, glancing down and leaving words unspoken.

Thomas tried again to pay the man, but Sutter was

adamant in his refusal.

Thomas thanked him and after an awkward silence said, "I am sorry Sutter. How are Vreni and Mera?"

The innkeeper shrugged. "Well enough, I suppose. Lots of folk are worse off."

Thomas nodded, not knowing what to say. He offered up a silent prayer for Sutter and his family, and took a mouthful from the tankard. It tasted of happier times.

"I need to find Pirmin. Know where he might be?"

Sutter cocked his head. "Too bad," he said. "You just missed him and an old friend of both of yours, or so he said."

The spoon stopped halfway to Thomas's mouth. "Friend?"

Sutter nodded. "Man named Gessler, or Gissler, or something like that. Pirmin said you was all together over there in the Outremer. You know him?"

Thomas put the wooden spoon back in the bowl, and willed his heart to stop hammering in his head.

"Where are they now?" Thomas asked.

Sutter caught the flustered look on Thomas's face and sat down across from him.

"What is it? He not the friend he makes himself out to be?"

"Worse. Gissler is a manhunter working for Duke Leopold. He was sent here for Noll Melchthal."

Sutter leaned back in his chair and closed his eyes. He raised a shaking hand to his temple and let out an anguished breath.

"Well, he found him then. I set up the meeting myself." His eyes were haunted when he finally opened them and looked across the table at Thomas.

"Where? When?"

"This morning. But the location was Pirmin's picking. They could be anywhere."

"Sutter, listen to me. Gissler is an extremely dangerous man. Noll and Pirmin are both in more trouble than you can possibly imagine. If you know anything about where Noll might be, or the location of his camp, you have to tell me now."

"God preserve me, Thomas, I know nothing! I swear it. I arranged meetings at coded locations between Noll and his men. They move their camp all the time and I have never known where it was. I swear."

"Who would? You must know someone who does."

"I leave signals in secret places and then Noll or one of his men contact me. That is how it has always been done in the past."

Thomas stood from the table and Sutter jumped in his chair.

"Then get a message to them now. Tell them of Gissler."

"What will you do?"

"I have to find Pirmin. And since you do not know where he is, I must find someone who does."

By the Devil's black hand, how could I not have seen what Gissler was up to?

In his heart of hearts, Thomas knew the answer to that question, and it was a disturbing thought riddled in sin. Thomas wanted Noll out of the way, and that desire had blinded him. Noll Melchthal was a danger to those Thomas cared for most: Pirmin…and Seraina.

He pushed through the inn's doors and the afternoon light temporarily blackened his vision. When it cleared, he saw his long-eared mount leaning against the tether rail. The beast tried to stretch its neck down to some lush grass without giving up the comfortable support offered by the railing.

Thomas whirled around and his boots shook the floorboards as he stomped back inside. Sutter was still sitting at the table, his eyes focused on the uneaten bowl of stew. He looked up, puzzled at Thomas's reappearance.

"Sutter, I need a horse."

Chapter 27

PIRMIN WAITED AT THE TOP of a treeless slope for Gissler to catch up yet once again. Vex whimpered at his side, eager to be off. Pirmin crossed his arms and looked at the pup.

"Easy boy. He may be a terror in the tournaments, but Gissler is not used to running through these hills like us. Give him some time."

He watched Gissler scramble up the slope like a cat walking on ice; his feet slipping and sliding several times before finding firm purchase. Noll would not have approved, for he left the ground chewed up behind him. Pirmin knew the constant climbing and descending of the Alps' meandering trails was difficult for someone unaccustomed to them, but Gissler had always been light on his feet. Far lighter than Pirmin had ever been. But, perhaps following Noll these past few weeks, as he goated through the mountains, had strengthened Pirmin's own lungs and legs more than he realized.

They had set out an hour before dawn and three

hours later arrived at a meeting spot Pirmin and Noll often used. Pirmin turned his back on Gissler and looked down into a shallow bowl at the bottom of three hills. To the east was thick forest, and that was the direction from which Noll would approach.

Shifting his ax to his other shoulder, he made his way down the grassy slope with Vex bounding before him.

Once Gissler caught up to Pirmin and Vex, the two men eased themselves down onto flat boulders to rest. Pirmin broke a loaf of dark bread in two and produced a wedge of cheese from his pack.

"How long before your friend arrives?" Gissler asked.

Pirmin shrugged. "Never know for sure with him. Could be somewhere in the trees watching us right now for all I know."

Gissler glanced up at the hills they had just come over.

"Not that way," Pirmin said shaking his head. "He will come through the trees, yonder."

"Ah, yes of course," Gissler said quickly turning his head and looking where Pirmin indicated.

Pirmin sensed a change come over Gissler in the last hour of their journey. Whenever Pirmin looked at him through the corner of his eye, there seemed to be a tightness in his face twisting Gissler's dark features. It registered a memory somewhere deep in Pirmin's mind that he could not place.

Gissler stood and stretched his legs. He saw Pirmin's ax leaning against a rock beside him.

"The great ax," Gissler said. "It has been a long time since I have stood beside her in battle."

He leaned over and lifted the weapon from its resting place, grunting with the weight of it. Unlike most axes, the elongated handle of Pirmin's was made from a hollow tube of forged steel, all eight feet of it. The blade on top flared wide on one side and narrowed to a vicious pick-like point on the other.

"How well do you know this Arnold Melchthal? Is he a man to be trusted?" Gissler asked, resting one end of the heavy ax on the ground.

Pirmin looked at Gissler's face and realized what his subconscious mind had been trying to tell him. The change in Gissler, his dark expression; it was the same tight-lipped disdain that Pirmin had seen on the man's face a thousand times before. It was the mask that covered Gissler's face just before battle.

Gissler saw him staring.

"You called him Arnold," Pirmin said. "I have never called him that. He goes by Noll."

Vex began barking. Gissler smiled, but his eyes hardened.

"Perhaps Noll to his friends," he said.

"You were not lagging behind all morning. You were leaving sign." Pirmin stood and shaded his eyes. He scanned the hilltops.

"You mean to collect the price on Noll's head."

He could not stop his words. They flowed out of him, his voice deep and ragged. The signs had been there all along, but Pirmin had refused to see them. He had been a fool and allowed Gissler to use him. He had to warn Noll before it was too late.

Gissler's eye twitched and he took several steps back. He hefted Pirmin's ax with both hands and launched it as far away as he could manage.

Pirmin ignored him and instead jumped atop the closest rock. He turned towards the forest and held one closed fist high into the air. He heard Gissler make a shrill whistle sound behind him. Pirmin continued to hold his arm up until he heard steel clearing scabbard.

He turned to face Gissler, who held his sword in front of him. On the hill behind him he saw a solitary man, walking, crest the rise. He sauntered over the ridge and began winding his way down towards Pirmin and Gissler, like he had all the time in the world.

The tracker, Pirmin thought, flexing his fists.

And then the ground trembled. Fully armored soldiers on horseback began flowing over the hill, one after the other, like rapids over river boulders. One rider carried a standard with a flag bearing a red lion; Habsburg soldiers.

Pirmin glanced around and weighed his options. The forest edge was too far away. The riders would be on him in less than a minute.

"Too late Gissler. I have sent the signal. Noll and his men are long gone by now." In truth there was no such signal, but Gissler did not need to know that. Pirmin prayed Noll had the sense to stay clear.

"Not all his men," Gissler said, leveling his blade at Pirmin.

Animals, especially dogs, sometimes display senses only their masters understand. Vex must have received at least a small portion of the hate and betrayal Pirmin was feeling towards Gissler, because before either man could speak again, the young pup growled and launched himself at Gissler.

He snapped at Gissler's thigh, and although his jaw muscles had not yet fully developed, his teeth were sharp. Gissler cursed and knocked Vex away with the pommel of his sword, but not before the dog had torn a hole in his breeches and drawn blood.

Pirmin shouted at Vex and ran at Gissler.

Gissler's eyes went wide as he saw the enraged giant charging at him. Even though he was unarmed, he knew what Pirmin was capable of. Ignoring the dog, he stepped to the side and almost eluded danger, but Pirmin reached out one tree-sized arm and snagged Gissler. The two men crashed to the ground, and Gissler lost his sword. Pirmin grabbed the small man and flipped him onto his back like he was nothing more than flatbread on a grill.

Gissler reached for the knife at his belt. The two combatants did not speak, or curse, or utter idle threats. That was the way of farmers in a fistfight after a night of drinking. For Pirmin and Gissler, each man knew he was in a fight for his life. Vex ran circles around them, barking and whining in distress.

Gissler freed his knife but Pirmin grabbed his wrist and head butted him flat on his nose. Blood splattered each man equally, like a giant mosquito had been crushed between them. Pirmin pushed against Gissler's broken nose with his forearm to create space, and moved into a sitting position on Gissler's chest. He began raining blows down on Gissler's head.

A noose slipped around Pirmin's wrist, and another around his neck. He had run out of time.

He screamed in outrage as men on horseback with pole nooses lifted him off the bloodied Gissler. Grabbing the end of the staff holding the noose around his neck, he twisted and yanked the man on the other end off his horse. Pirmin ripped the man's helmet off with a flick of his hand and then crushed his head with a knee drop.

Gissler pushed himself up from the ground and

staggered to his sword. He stepped in and thrust it through Pirmin's shoulder. Pirmin grimaced and turned on Gissler. He tried to reach him but Gissler jumped back and the void was filled with more riders with heavy staves and nooses. They beat Pirmin's arms and legs into positions so their ropes could be slipped on his feet, his wrists, or over his neck. Like hunters trapping a dangerous animal, they immobilized Pirmin's limbs one by one.

The blonde giant twisted and fought, and although several unmanned staff nooses dangled off his neck and limbs, eventually a fresh soldier would gain control of it once again. Pirmin was forced to the ground, where they stretched him out and beat him mercilessly with their staves.

Eventually, bloodied and battered, he was splayed wide on the ground with his face turned to heaven. He fought back no more.

"Enough!" Gissler had to yell to be heard above the grunts and cursing of the soldiers, but the effort caused a painful vibration in his smashed nose. He held a cloth to his face to stem the flow of blood and walked over to where Pirmin was held down by a dozen men, every one of them sweating and breathing hard.

Pirmin turned a hideously swollen face to Gissler. He had to spit blood from his mouth before he could speak.

"You worthless bastard, I piss on you," he said.

Gissler pulled back his leg and kicked Pirmin in the face.

Vex appeared out of nowhere and latched onto the hem of Gissler's cloak. He shouted and spun around while Vex growled and clamped on tighter, but Gissler found his range and kicked the dog hard in the ribs. Vex seemed to fold in two and yelped from a type of pain he had not felt in his short life. He stumbled back out of harm's reach and bared his teeth.

Gissler looked down at a tattered hole in his cloak. He drew his blade and walked towards the dog.

"Vex get out of here! Go home!" Pirmin shouted and thrashed against his bonds.

Vex's ears perked up at his master's voice and he looked at Pirmin with hope in his eyes. Then he wined in confusion at Pirmin's tone.

"Vex, go home!"

The dog bared his teeth once more at Gissler and then loped a few steps away. He turned back and did not move further until Pirmin yelled at him again.

"Come here, boy!" One of the soldiers called out. Several of the men laughed and started calling the dog. A thickset, older man came forward with a loaded crossbow and lifted it to his shoulder.

"Leave him be," Pirmin said. His voice sounded strange to his ears, as he forced the words from his swollen mouth. "I have coin in my pack."

The man with the crossbow sighted down the length of his weapon. "Is that so? Good. I will get that as soon as I shoot your dog."

He pulled the release. More men laughed and Pirmin closed his eyes.

"Give me another bolt," the man said.

"You better take a few," someone else said and laughed.

Pirmin opened his eyes and saw Vex standing further away. He paced back and forth at the forest's edge.

"Take three men and search those woods for any sign of Melchthal," Gissler said.

"Waste of time," Pirmin said, his voice barely a whisper.

"And kill that damned dog."

The four men mounted up, grinning at each other like boys about to get into mischief. They took off after Vex like nobles on a foxhunt. When the dog bolted into the woods, the soldiers dismounted and followed on foot.

***

"Here, boy. Got a nice biscuit for you." The grey-haired soldier held out his hand and Vex raised his head, catching the scent of the biscuit.

"That is the way boy, come on out from behind that tree."

He tossed the biscuit to the ground half way between himself and the large tree sheltering the dog. He heard his men move into place behind him, making far too much noise. He waved them back with one hand behind his back, and then raised his crossbow to his shoulder. He was determined to be the one to put a bolt between the mutt's ribs.

A youth stepped out from behind the same tree, but on the opposite side of the dog.

"Hello," he said raising a hand in greeting.

The soldier hollered in surprise, re-aimed his crossbow, and pulled the tickler. But the boy had already ducked back behind the tree and the quarrel tore off a heavy piece of bark as it glanced off the trunk.

"Shoot! The outlaws are—"

"Right behind you," Noll said, finishing the soldier's sentence.

The man-at-arms whirled at the sound of the voice and saw Noll standing with his sword drawn. It was red with blood and there was no sign of the other three soldiers. He threw the crossbow to the ground and reached for his sword, but Noll was faster. He stepped in and held the man's wrist, preventing him from drawing the blade. Then, taking his time, he thrust his own sword into his throat.

The last sound the soldier heard was the bark of a dog.

Chapter 28

"**W**OULD YOU SAY he was one of the more virtuous brethren in the Order?" Leopold asked.

"Pirmin? Virtuous?" Gissler could not help himself. His half smile turned into a chuckle before he could gain some measure of control.

"What I mean to say, my lord, is Pirmin was never one for following rules. Whether they be those of his superiors or God."

"Ah, that is unfortunate," Leopold said.

He turned to Bernard, his scribe standing behind him. "Be sure to make a note of that before we begin tonight."

The scribe bowed his head and did not look up until Leopold addressed Gissler again. "But he was initiated into the Brotherhood of Saint John. There is no doubt in that, correct?"

Gissler grew tired of all this talk of Pirmin. Forced to breathe through his mouth because Pirmin had broken his nose, Gissler wanted to forget about the man. He had arrested him, his task was complete. Why did the Duke insist on pestering him with all these questions?

"Yes, he was ordained as a brother-sergeant. As were we all."

"How old were you at the time?"

The answer to this one did not come easily. It took Gissler a few moments to respond.

"Sixteen, my lord? I cannot say for sure but Pirmin and I both share an age, and I believe the ceremony was that year."

"So both of you served with the Black Knights for more than twenty years." It was not a question. "Excellent. You have done well, Gissler. I know it must have been difficult to bring a brother in arms to justice after serving together for so long. But he knew where the path would lead when he chose to follow Arnold Melchthal."

"What will happen to him my lord?"

Leopold shrugged. "He will be judged and punished according to his crimes. He is in God's hands now."

"As it should be," Gissler said and crossed himself.

Leopold held out his hand and the scribe placed a rolled up piece of parchment in his hand. Red wax held the roll in place.

"For your place in bringing a dangerous outlaw to justice, I have arranged to have twelve mares and a stallion transferred to your estate."

Leopold placed the scroll in Gissler's hand. His eyes grew as he accepted it and his fingers felt numb and awkward in handling such a light and brittle thing. The wax bore the mark of the Duke's own lion seal. He looked up at Leopold, who smiled and nodded.

Thirteen horses. It was a fortune in Gissler's eyes. He stood up straighter as the generosity of the payment overtook him. Then he remembered something.

"This is most Generous, my duke. But, I have no estate. No land to raise horses on."

"No, of course not. For I have not given you any, yet. But worry not Gissler. You will have ample opportunity to earn yourself that land. In the meantime, I have arranged for you to keep your horses in the stables at Habsburg. Of course, you will have to hire your own farrier to see to their care. And pay for their keep from your own purse."

"Of course, my lord," Gissler said. He could not believe what he was hearing. "Thank you."

Leopold pointed at him. "I told you before. Our futures are entwined Gissler. You serve the Habsburg line well, and we will raise you up from the crowd."

Thirteen horses! All manner of thoughts ran through Gissler's mind. He saw himself driving his herd onto his brother's filthy pig farm and introducing himself. Then he would take Hugo and his daughter Sara with him to his own estate, where he would give his brother a job. Together they would rebuild the Gissler name. But before that, Gissler would have to hire one of the best farriers he could afford. He knew a fair bit about handling horses but almost nothing when it came to breeding them. But with a good farrier to tend the herd, in time, Gissler was sure he would have the most respected horse farm in the Aargau.

Caught up in his own daydreaming, he realized the Duke had just asked him something.

"Gissler? Did you hear what I said?"

"I am sorry my lord. My head is still shaken up from

the fight this morning."

Leopold nodded. "Your face does tell a story. I wish I were there to see it. You said the four men you sent into the woods were all hanging from trees when you found them?"

Gissler nodded. "And their eyes were cut out."

Leopold sighed. "A nasty habit Melchthal picked up from Landenberg. I told the Vogt to be careful what he teaches these peasants."

"Judging from the tracks, I would wager it was six men that got them."

"And you followed them?"

"For a half hour, my lord. Then the tracks started crossing and doubling back on themselves. The men got spooked in the woods, and I did not want to walk into an ambush and lose any more, so I gave up the chase."

Leopold smiled. "And that is why I sent you this time instead of Landenberg. He would have chased Noll and his men over a cliff. The preservation of an army is often more important than victory. I appreciate your reasoning."

The praise was a little too sweet for Gissler's ears so he changed the topic. "What would you have me do now, my lord? Return to the Kussnacht?"

Leopold glanced at the scroll clutched in Gissler's hand. "In a hurry to inspect some horse flesh are you? I am afraid you will have to wait another day or two. I have some business to finish here, but then you will accompany me back to Habsburg. In the meantime, stay near. I may need you."

Gissler bowed, "As you wish."

Leopold dismissed Gissler and after the newly mounted twelve-foot doors closed behind him, he turned to his scribe.

"Get the manuscript and meet me at the dungeons in one hour. Bring a priest and one of *my* judges. Be sure Judge Furst knows nothing of tonight's proceedings."

Bernard bent his grey head and scurried from the room, looking like a nursemaid who had left her child unattended for too long.

Chapter 29

THE YOUNG BOY had pressed himself up so tightly against the wall in the far corner of the cell that Pirmin, half blinded by his swollen eyes, thought he was a stone at first.

"No need to fear me boy. It is your jailers who wish you ill. Not I."

His throat, dry as rock dust, made Pirmin's voice come out as little more than a rasp and did little to reassure the boy.

Pirmin tried his best to look as harmless as a seven-foot giant covered in blood chained hand and foot to a wall could. When that did not work, he shook his shackled arms to demonstrate he was going nowhere. This seemed to relax the boy a little, and he lowered himself into a squat but kept a watchful eye on Pirmin.

Pirmin's chains had enough play that he could stand or sit, but neither comfortably. The beating he had suffered at the hands of Gissler and his soldiers had left him bloodied and sore, but he had known worse. His main concern was the sword wound to his shoulder. Although the bleeding had stopped, there was no way for him to clean the wound. Being an ex-Hospitaller, that thought disturbed him as he glanced around the filthy cage he and the boy shared.

"What would be your name lad?"

The boy eased himself down onto a pile of blackened straw.

"You can talk to me, or just listen to me. Either way suits me fine," Pirmin said. "I suppose the bastards already got your tongue then, eh?"

"My name is Matthias," the boy finally said.

"Is it now? Well, a good name that one. Right from the Holy Book itself."

"You talk funny," Matthias said.

Pirmin started. He turned his better eye toward the boy and looked closely. He wondered if the boy was a trick of the mind, like when men saw an oasis in the desert. Perhaps he was hurt worse than he thought. Maybe even dead.

"What did you say?"

"Your words, you say them strange."

Thomas had told him the very same thing when they had first met. The memories of the long march came to Pirmin and he smiled, grateful to have them. For a moment they took him away from his dank cell and the pain wracking his body.

"A good friend said those same words to me when I was about your age."

"What happened to him?"

"What do you mean?"

"Is he dead?"

"No. Why would you say that?"

227

The boy shrugged. Pirmin grunted and changed the topic. "Tell me what you did to land in here Mathias."

"Why should I?" The boy looked at Pirmin and stuck out his jaw. Pirmin noticed the beginning of a black eye and the remains of a handprint on the side of his face.

"Because you and me are going to be friends. Whether you like it or not."

Mathias squinted at the big man across the dark cell. "I stole three bottles of wine," he said.

"Wine?" Pirmin started laughing, but forced himself to stop because his ribs hurt something fierce. "Thought you were going to say bread, or a chicken, or something sensible. But wine? A lad like you is too young for wine. Who was it for?"

"I am plenty old enough. I was nine at winter's end. And I drank a whole half before the Duke's men found me." He puffed out his skinny chest and sneered at Pirmin.

Pirmin laughed, and this time he welcomed the pain.

Chapter 30

THOMAS RODE west from the village of Schwyz until he hit the road leading south from Brunnen. A wave of anger passed through him as he thought of how much time he could save if only his ferry were operational. A half day at least. For now he would need to turn south at Brunnen and follow the road all the way to the end of the lake. From there he would curve around its lower arm until the road turned north once again towards Seelisberg.

It was well after dark by the time he came to the overgrown path branching off the main road that led into the grove where Seraina had her cabin. Thomas never would have found it if Sutter had not given him detailed directions.

The path itself was virtually invisible, but it was marked with a menhir, a man-sized, cylindrical rock moved to this location centuries ago by people long since forgotten. Some said the menhir were markers that warned of places best avoided, others said they were waystones that helped the dead pass from this world into the next.

Thomas dismounted and set flint and steel to the wick of his lantern. Pushing aside some low-hanging branches, and holding the lantern aloft before him, he led Sutter's sturdy mountain pony into the bushes. Even though Thomas believed the stories surrounding menhir were nothing more than ridiculous Pagan beliefs belonging to another time, he found some measure of comfort in how his horse plunged onto the dark path without hesitation.

Fifteen minutes later the path branched off in three directions, forcing Thomas to choose one. Minutes later it branched again, and the trails seemed narrower. Another thirty minutes and Thomas was forced to admit he was lost.

At some point he had become turned around, and was no longer sure in which direction the road lay. Without the sun as a reference point he had no way of knowing. He slapped his open palm against the rough bark of a tree, one of many that crowded his path, and cursed himself for being so careless.

Thomas realized he had no hope now of stumbling upon Seraina's cabin in the darkness, so he hung his lantern on a high branch and began scrounging for firewood. He would have to wait until morning.

Some time later, with his horse unsaddled and hobbled nearby, he huddled in front of his campfire. He rubbed his hands together and when he looked up a figure stood before him on the other side of the flames.

Startled, Thomas jumped to his feet, drew his knife and took a step back from the fire. Unfortunately, a low line of saplings tripped him up. With a yelp he crashed over backwards and landed in the undergrowth.

Lying on his back, with plants crisscrossing all around him like a spider's web, he heard a woman's surprised laugh.

"Seraina?"

He was answered by more laughter and finally, when she had herself under control, Seraina said, "Oh, Thomas. I am sorry, but the look on your face was wonderful. Something I shall never forget."

Thomas sat up from his mattress of ferns and Seraina, after stifling another giggle, held out an arm and helped him to his feet. In her other arm she held a wool blanket.

"I thought you might need this tonight," she said. "And when you failed to turn up at my door, for some reason or another, I decided to come to you." Her eyes glistened in the dark with playful mischief, and Thomas was reminded of tales of men being seduced by beautiful creatures of the Fey.

He took the blanket, mumbling his gratitude, and for the first time in many hours felt himself relax. He had found Seraina, or rather, she had found him, and looking at her reflected in the flickering light of the fire, he felt a great weight lift. Then he remembered why he had come.

"Seraina, I need to find Noll. He and Pirmin are in trouble."

The playfulness in her eyes faded, and as sorry as Thomas was to see it go, the concern for his friend took precedence.

"Well look no further ferryman," a voice called out from the darkness, and this time Seraina jumped as high as Thomas. Her hand latched onto his forearm and stayed there.

Noll slipped out of the woods and walked towards them. "Noll, if I did not know better, I would say you were spying on us," Seraina said.

"I wish I had time for that," Noll said, stopping in front of them. He dropped his pack near the fire and leaned some sticks against it to shield the light. "Your fire is inviting every wanderer on the road for miles around."

He avoided looking at Thomas. There was more movement behind Noll, and Vex wandered out of the woods. He made a circle around the campsite, hot on the trail of some forest creature, and then came to sit at Noll's feet. Seraina's nails bit into Thomas's forearm.

Thomas looked down and something different about the dog caught his eye. The fur around his mouth seemed much darker than he remembered. He glanced at the dark woods, expecting Pirmin to come bursting through at any moment.

"He is not coming, ferryman," Noll said, shaking his head.

Thomas looked back at Vex's mouth, and in the flaring firelight realized it was lined in dried blood. A lot of blood.

If Seraina did not still have her hand on his arm, he would have killed Noll where he stood.

"*Where* is Pirmin?"

Chapter 31

THE JAILER, a compact, stoop-shouldered man with a tired face came for Pirmin and the boy that evening. Six Habsburg men-at-arms accompanied him; stern, disciplined soldiers who methodically locked Pirmin in a set of walking irons and then unchained him from the wall. As they hammered the bolts into place on his ankle cuffs, Pirmin eyed the jailer. He squinted and tried to bring his puffed up eyes into focus. He knew the man from somewhere.

"Heller. That your name? We met at Sutter's in the Spring."

The jailer raised his head and straightened up slowly, like a man with a secret who had just been found out.

"Was hoping you forgot," he said.

"I never forget someone I drink with," Pirmin said. "Unless he joins in late and I am so far into my cups there is no climbing out."

Heller started to say something but was interrupted by the shrill hammering of a soldier driving a pin into place on one of Pirmin's cuffs. When the hammering died off, Pirmin said, "I recall now, you said you were from Altdorf."

Heller nodded. "Wish I could say I was glad to see you here Pirmin."

Pirmin held out his manacled wrists. "So unfetter these and we will both feel much better."

One of the men-at-arms stepped in and backhanded Pirmin across the face. "Enough talk, outlaw." The blow dislodged a tooth loosened during his capture and opened up a cut on one of his gums. Blood trickled out of the corner of his mouth and then slowed to a standstill, like a hillside stream in the dead of winter.

The man who hit him wore a patch over one eye and he was bigger than any man in the room save Pirmin. His eye took on a mad glow when he saw Pirmin bleed and spit out his tooth. He laughed and Pirmin, smelling decaying meat on his breath, turned his head away.

He saw Mathias still standing against the far wall, shivering; his thin arms wrapped around himself and his eyes wide in fear.

"Hey, Mathias. Did you just run over here and slap me?"

The boy almost grinned, but the soldier's face twisted and the glow in his one good eye turned to fire. He punched Pirmin in his wounded shoulder. Lightning coursed through Pirmin's blood, sending a shockwave of pain throughout his entire body, and he doubled over, grimacing.

"That better big man? That feel like a boy's fist to you?" The soldier grabbed the mallet from the soldier putting on the shackles and raised it over Pirmin's uninjured shoulder. "Maybe we should even out the pain a bit so you can stand upright."

"Put that down or the Duke will hear how you crippled his prisoner," Heller said.

He strode between the men-at-arms and snatched the mallet from the one-eyed soldier, though he needed to raise himself on his toes to do so. The soldier glared down at Heller, but the threat seemed to register with him, and after a series of chest-heaving breaths he calmed himself. Turning back to Pirmin he grabbed a handful of his hair and yanked him upright. He leaned in close.

"Hear that, big man? The Duke wants to see you." He pushed Pirmin towards the door, but with his ankles hobbled by the short length of chain between them, Pirmin stumbled and fell. He reached out with his hands to break his fall, but his shoulder caused him to scream out in pain. His arms folded and he collapsed onto the flagstone floor amidst a pile of filthy straw.

He closed his eyes and clenched his teeth, pretending he had a strap of leather between them. He would not give these bastards the satisfaction of hearing him scream again.

The pain lasted an eternity. When it finally subsided, he did not have the strength to get to his knees, so he remained with his cheek pressed against the damp floor and breathed through his mouth to minimize the stench of human waste.

"Come on Pirmin. Let us get you up," Heller said softly. He placed his hands on Pirmin's uninjured arm and tried to lift him. "You," he said, nodding at one of the men-at-arms. "Give me a hand here. The Duke awaits."

It took three of them to finally get Pirmin to his feet.

The one-eyed soldier put a rope around Mathias's neck and they marched the two prisoners out of the dark cell.

They went down a long corridor lit by flickering torches in metal sconces on the wall. Cells branched off on every side and faces peered out between iron slats. A few voices called out, but most knew better, and remained silent.

"Where are you taking us, Heller?"

"To the Duke. That's all I know."

Pirmin worked his tongue over his split lip and around the inside of his mouth. He looked at the shadows of men moving in the crowded cells.

"More men in here than a slave galley. What are you doing here, Heller?"

"They have all been sentenced to labor on the fortress. Work day is over and they are back for the night now."

"No, I mean you. Why are you here?"

Heller shrugged, and kept his eyes fixed straight ahead down the long corridor. "I follow my lord's orders. Is that not what we all should do?"

The hallway ended in a high wooden door, reinforced with strips of iron riveted in place. Heller fumbled with a ring full of long iron keys and unlocked it. The door swung inward on protesting hinges and light spilled into the corridor. The air pouring out of the room was thick and damp, and as Pirmin felt the moist heat on his face, a shiver ran through him.

The men-at-arms herded Pirmin and the young boy through the doorway. Torches lined the walls and a single cell occupied the center of the large room. A table with leather restraints took up one corner, a weapons rack filled with flails, hammers, and pointed poles of differing lengths took up another. But what held Pirmin's attention, as he shambled into the room, was a large iron cauldron suspended above the ground on four sturdy iron legs. Flames from a healthy fire licked at the undersides of the metal pot. Steam rose above the cauldron and obscured the faces of four men standing on the other side.

Mathias looked at Pirmin, his face registering alarm. Pirmin did his best to calm the boy with a nonchalant nod, but he wondered what comfort he could really offer with his bloodied teeth and stringy hair. And added to that, was the fact that Pirmin was probably more terrified than Mathias, for he had a much better idea of what was to come.

The soldier leading the boy jerked on his rope and led them around the simmering cauldron to the four men. One was a cleric, who clutched a bible to his chest and chanted a constant stream of Latin. Pirmin tried to block him out.

Another man who could have been the priest's brother, stood at a podium with quill in hand. A thick leather-bound book lay open before him. The third man wore the black robe of a judge, and standing beside him, with his hands behind his back, was Duke Leopold. He ignored the boy but watched Pirmin closely with the inquisitive eyes of a hawk. The prisoners were forced to their knees in front of the Duke.

"Pirmin Schnidrig. I am told you hail from Wallis," Leopold said. "That is a long way from Altdorf, and beautiful I hear. I suspect you wish you where there now."

Pirmin looked straight ahead and tried to blank his mind, but it coursed off on its own. The snow-capped

Matterhorn flashed in his head, a small cloud skewered by its sharp peak, and then an image of him as a boy slitting the throat of a black-necked goat. He saw a field, and perhaps the face of his mother, but he could not be certain that it was she. Her features had faded over the years.

The priest's intonations and the sound of sap bubbling and spitting in burning logs drove away the few memories he had.

"You may yet return there if you answer my next question wisely," Leopold said.

Pirmin looked closely at the Duke for the first time and was shocked to see he was no older than Noll. But the similarities ended there. Noll was quick to anger, but he could be just as fast with a joke that would leave men laughing, or a smile that would have women swooning. Leopold, on the other hand, had the look of a man who had been angry his entire life. But he kept it deep, simmering, and let only bits and pieces of it out at a time. He had no light side.

Pirmin glanced at the cauldron and then met Leopold's gaze. "I expect this will be one hell of a question," he said.

"Where is Arnold Melchthal?" Leopold said.

"I will not fall in your hole," Pirmin said, nodding towards the boiling water. "You think I do not know the makings of *Lex Salica* when I see them?"

"Your Latin is good," Leopold said, and the way his face lit up made Pirmin cringe.

"As a lad, I learned enough to keep the monks and their sticks satisfied. Nothing more."

"You truly do not know where Melchthal is, do you?"

"Ah, now, you would like me to say that. But I will

not give you or your cursed priest any statement of mine to test."

Leopold shrugged and gestured to the table in the corner. "We could simply torture a confession from you if you prefer."

"Go foul yourself. I would rather die on that table with my guts spilling onto the floor than play your game."

"Very well," Leopold said, and turned to Mathias. "Boy. Did you steal from the food stores of the Holy Roman Empire?"

"Do not answer that!" Pirmin said. But it was too late. The boy's words came out in a torrent of fear.

"No my lord, I swear. Please! Do not cut off my hands. I need them to help me mam. Without them we will both starve before the first snows..."

Leopold nodded to the boy's handler, and the man jerked the rope and forced the boy towards the steaming cauldron.

"Bring a stool for the boy. And something to set the rock upon. The boy's arm is too short to reach the bottom," Leopold said to the jailer.

Heller's face lightened to a shade of grey, but he did as he was told. Moments later he lowered a metal stand into the bubbling cauldron and dropped a round stone the size of a man's fist into the boiling water, jumping back as he did so to avoid the splash. The rock landed on the stand, and rolled to a halt a foot below the water's surface.

"Come now! The boy cannot even lift a stone that size," Pirmin said. He made to stand up but three men forced him back down to his knees.

Mathias, bewildered, turned his dirty face from man

to man. "Please, lords. Do not cut off my hands," he said. "I took the wine, but I did not know it was the Empire's—I swear!"

Leopold leaned over the boy. "A moment ago you said you did not take the wine. How can I be sure you tell the truth?"

"I swear, I did not know it was my lord's. I would never take something belonging to m'lord. I swear it to God."

Leopold stood up straight and put his hands on his hips. "Well that is a comfort. For God is indeed the only one who can prove the truth of your words. Perhaps you can keep your hands, and we will send you home to your mother. Would you like that?"

Mathias nodded, but his eyes narrowed. "What must I do?"

"A simple test. If you pass, you go free." Leopold turned to the black-robed judge. "Explain the conditions."

The judge cleared his throat and, in an officious voice, recited from memory the rite of *Lex Salica*.

"You will be tried by the *Ordeal of Water*. You must reach your arm into boiling water up to your elbow, grasp the stone, remove it, and place it on the ground outside the cauldron. Twenty-four hours from the Ordeal, a priest and myself shall examine your limb. Some redness is to be expected, but if we perceive any blistering of the skin, or worse, we shall conclude you did not warrant God's protection, and shall deem you guilty in Our Lord's eyes, and therefore, guilty in this court. Do you understand the conditions of your trial?"

"Enough!" Pirmin shouted. All eyes turned to the man. Pirmin glared at Leopold.

"You are a snake, not a man." He turned his head and looked at every man in the room in turn.

"All of you. A nest of god damned vipers spitting and hissing, and weaving about the feet of a young lad for your own bloody entertainment." His eyes stopped on Heller, and the jailer quickly looked away.

Leopold's lips spread into a tight smile.

"Perhaps you would prefer to take his place? Surely a Hospitaller does not fear one of God's trials?"

Pirmin closed his eyes and nodded once. "I will submit to the Ordeal. But the boy goes free first and all charges against him are dropped. There. You have what you wanted."

"And why, pray tell, would I negotiate with a thieving outlaw?"

"Because you are a pox-carrying minion squeezed from the Devil's own arse. Now let us get down to it."

Leopold's eyebrows arched up at the insult but other than that he showed no emotion. The man had the features of a hawk, but the blood of a snake, Pirmin thought. Trusting someone like him would be a fast road to hell.

"Bernard, make a note that the Hospitaller offered to volunteer for *Lex Salica* to spare a young boy its discomfort," Leopold said to the scribe. He gestured to the soldier holding Mathias. "Take him outside the walls and release him."

"No. Heller takes him or our arrangement is off. I will not have your Cyclops giving the boy a farewell bugger at the walls."

The man holding the boy's rope, growled and stepped towards Pirmin with his arm raised, but Leopold cut him off and stared him down.

241

"Very well," Leopold said. "But remember, we can hunt him down easily enough if need be."

Pirmin nodded. His mouth was suddenly too dry for words.

Heller loosened the rope from around Mathias's neck, grabbed a handful of the boy's shirt, and guided him to a door opposite the one that led to the other cells. When he opened it fresh air blew into the room and Pirmin was sure he glimpsed a far off star.

Mathias spread his arms and legs in the doorway and cast a long backwards glance at Pirmin before Heller said something and propelled him through the opening into the cool night beyond. The door slammed shut and Pirmin was once again trapped in his inferno.

The guards put ropes around Pirmin's neck, tore the remains of his shirt off, and forced him to the cauldron's edge. Seeing that the cauldron's top stood at the same height as Pirmin's navel, the judge removed the unnecessary stool. When all were ready, they took off his hand chains. The soldiers spread out like the spokes of a wheel and kept firm grips on their ropes.

Finally, the judge took a long set of tongs off the wall and used them to retrieve the stand from inside the cauldron. The polished rock fell off and came to rest on the cauldron's iron bottom, four feet below the surface of the water.

Pirmin looked over the edge into the roiling water. Steam wafted up and flattened his wavy, blonde hair tight to his head. Through the steam and bubbles breaking the water's surface, he could see the distorted shape of the rock lying on the bottom. The thought of refusing to go through with The Ordeal flitted across his mind, but he knew that was just fear creeping into his soul. If he backed away now, they would simply find some other method of torture. And the Devil only knew what they would do to the boy.

He stared into the swirling waters, and for the first time in many a year, mumbled a heartfelt prayer. He took a deep breath.

Sometimes you just got to have at 'er until the job is done.

With a scream that vibrated the iron cauldron, Pirmin plunged his left arm into the boiling water.

***

Leopold watched Pirmin with rapt attention. He was an ordained member of the Hospitallers, a soldier of God, absolved of all sins in this life by the Pope himself. If anyone had a chance to survive the Ordeal of Water it was this man.

Morbid fascination gripped the room in silence as everyone watched the giant thrust his arm up to his armpit in the scalding liquid. He yelled bravely going in, but the pitch of his voice soon turned into a howling scream as he floundered along the bottom of the cauldron for the rock. Then he yanked his arm out so fast, the white-hot stone slipped out of his hand and flew straight at Leopold's head like it had been launched from a ballista.

The Duke managed to lean his head away in time to avoid the missile, but the man behind him was not so fortunate. The steaming rock caught him flush on the side of his face, sizzling as it made contact. He went down in a heap, cradled his head in his hands and began screaming from the pain of the burn.

Pirmin too was on the ground, moaning and

thrashing in agony, tossing the guards around on the ends of their ropes like kites in a windstorm. The room was in chaos for almost a minute until, finally, Pirmin passed out and the guard's own suffering reached its climax and his uncontrollable screams changed to muttered curses and groans.

Leopold leaned up against a wall and observed the room. He tapped his foot and waited for some semblance of order to return. Everyone breathed easier when the big man's thrashing eased and then stopped altogether.

The judge was the first to regain his composure. "Quickly now, gather straw to his arm and bind it to keep the heat in."

As the soldiers gathered dark handfuls of straw from the floor, Leopold walked cautiously over to Pirmin and inspected his arm. At first it appeared only ruddy, and he thought God had indeed intervened on the Hospitaller's behalf. But then the skin blackened before his eyes, and when the soldiers moved his arm to wrap it in straw, the whole outer layer of skin separated and the arm twisted inside it like a sword in a sheath that was too large.

Leopold backed away just as the first scent of burnt flesh watered his eyes. There would be no need to wait twenty-four hours. The Hospitaller had failed The Ordeal by Water. Disgusted, and more than a little disappointed, he turned and strode to the courtyard door. He threw it open and left the judge and soldiers to their pointless tasks.

Pirmin remained unconscious as the judge gave specific directions on how to pack straw around the arm and tie it in place. Once finished, they dragged Pirmin into the cell in the middle of the room. Before locking the door, the one-eyed soldier loosened his breeches and, to the snickers of his fellow men-at-arms, relieved himself on Pirmin's straw-covered limb.

Chapter 32

"WHERE ARE YOU GOING?" Seraina asked.

"To get Pirmin. Where would you have me go?" Thomas threw the under pad over Sutter's pony and then bent down and hefted the saddle. The horse regarded him with suspicious eyes. Being saddled after dark was not a normal occurrence for her.

"Did you not hear what I said ferryman? They have him in the fortress. You cannot simply march in and ask the fifty guards watching him if they will hand over their prisoner."

"What choice do I have?"

Seraina stepped in front of Thomas. "You mean what choice do we have. I am going with you. Noll would not get near the jails without someone recognizing him, but I can."

Thomas scowled at Seraina but she met his look with firm resolve. She would not be swayed and Thomas knew better than to attempt it. "Very well. I could use your help."

"Seraina is right when she says I cannot go with you, but that does not mean I cannot help. Pirmin is my friend too."

Thomas could take no more. He dropped the saddle and shoved Noll in the chest with both hands. Noll stumbled backwards, cursed, and had to leap over the fire to avoid falling into it.

"Thomas, please!" Seraina said, coming between them and putting her palms on Thomas's chest.

The heat of the moment passed, and when Thomas looked at Seraina his breathing slowed. "He is not welcome here. I want him gone."

"Or what ferryman?" Noll stood across the fire smiling, taunting. "What will you do? Sink down into the grass like a spotted fawn and pray danger passes you by? As you did when Landenberg torched your home?"

"We both know why he burnt my ferry," Thomas said.

"Just how much suffering do you need to experience before you see the truth? How many friends do you need to see hurt? Or raped?"

"Enough!" Seraina's voice boomed through the dark night like a thunderclap. Both men froze, then turned together and looked at her in surprise.

"You are both acting like children," she said, her voice once again her own. "And selfish children at that. Our friend is in trouble. We must do all we can to help him, and that means working together. Thomas, Noll has connections, and if he offers help, it would be wise to accept."

She kept speaking. Her words were soft, and much slower than Thomas remembered her ever speaking. Yet soothing, the way a warm bath is after a hard day's ride. His anger subsided, and Thomas once again felt in control. Seraina made perfect sense. He needed Noll. They would sort out their differences another time.

Thomas cast a doubtful glance at Noll across the fire. "Can you get us into the jails?"

"Perhaps. I will talk with Walter Furst. He may have an idea."

Thomas saw the beginnings of a plan coming together. Not a good one, but if he could get past the guardhouse and into the jails there was hope. He would have the long trip to Altdorf to worry about getting out.

"To the house of Furst then," Noll said. "If we leave now, we can be there by dawn."

Thomas glanced at Seraina and was surprised at the look of concern on her face. She turned quickly away when she caught him staring. No, not *concern*, he realized. For all her previous talk of selfish children, she had, for a moment, worn the expression of a child caught in a lie.

Chapter 33

"QUICKLY NOW. Get inside and bar the opposite door. It leads to the main cells and is where the guards will be patrolling. I have to get back to the gatehouse and make sure no one notices that key ring missing."

Walter Furst, dressed in his magistrate robe, ushered Thomas and Seraina through the heavy door and closed it behind them.

Seraina pushed back the hood of her cloak and allowed her eyes to adjust to the torch-lit room. The moment she stepped into the chamber her heartbeat quickened to a painful crescendo and the air stuck in her throat; every fiber of her being screamed at her to flee. The energy of the room was terrifying. She swayed on her feet and leaned against Thomas for a moment to catch her breath.

When she looked up into his face she saw him staring at a large cauldron on the far side of the room. It was blackened with soot. The remains of a burnt-out fire lay below it, now nothing more than a cold pile of ash. Before Seraina could speak, Thomas was moving. His long legs carried him across the room in a few quick strides. He stopped at a cell in the room's center and fumbled with the ring of keys Furst had given him. Seraina joined him and peered into the blackness of the cage. Someone was chained to the floor.

Someone huge.

She ran to the nearest wall and pulled a lit torch from its sconce. By the time she returned, Thomas had the door open and was crouched in the darkness at Pirmin's side.

Seraina's torch bathed the two men in light and what she saw made her gasp.

Pirmin, his ankles chained to an iron hoop embedded into the stone floor, lay on his back unmoving, his arms splayed out from his sides like a giant bird fallen from the heavens. One was wrapped in a thick layer of straw held in place by twine cinched tight in several places. His once handsome face was beaten and swollen beyond recognition, and his blond hair was caked and matted in blood and dirt.

"Oh God, what have you done?" There was panic in Thomas's voice, and although it frightened Seraina, it also shocked her into action. She jammed the torch into a holder inside the cell and dropped to her knees beside Pirmin.

"Pirmin! Can you hear me?" Thomas said. He pulled his knife and began cutting the twine encircling Pirmin's left arm. His hands shook.

Seraina put one hand to Pirmin's forehead and the other to his heart. He stirred under her touch and moaned. He whispered something that sounded like a name. *Mathias? Who was Mathias?*

Although Pirmin lived, he was burning with fever. His right shoulder had a wound that had soured. Even in the low light, she could see his upper arm beginning to darken. Soon the poison would drain into his torso and then it would be too late. She dug into her pouch and removed a small knife and several vials. They did not have much time.

Distracted by the task at hand, she was unaware that Thomas had unwrapped Pirmin's other arm, until a rotten stench assaulted her nostrils, forcing the contents of her stomach into the back of her throat.

She turned to see Thomas sitting with his head in his hands, his knife on the ground beside him. He looked at her with vacant eyes.

"Oh God. Seraina…"

She looked down at the source of the odor, already fearing the worst. A blackened log of flesh, bloated to three times its normal thickness, had replaced Pirmin's left arm. Scattered over his arm, a demonic harvest of straw poked up from the congealed mass. Seraina realized that what she had thought before was dirt and filth on the left side of Pirmin's chest, was actually rivers of decay flowing through his blood.

Thomas stared at her. His dark eyes big and round, begging her to do something for his friend. She put her hand once again to Pirmin's heart, though she did not know why.

"I am sorry, Thomas," she said, shaking her head.

He closed his eyes, and after a moment, nodded.

Pirmin moaned again and his leg spasmed.

"Can you do something for the pain?" Thomas asked.

But Seraina was already reaching into her pouch. She popped a handful of ditch nettle leaves into her mouth and chewed them quickly, taking care not to swallow. Once moistened, she spit the leaves into her hand and formed them into a ball.

"Help me open his mouth," she said. Together they tipped Pirmin's head back and Seraina wiped his gums and the insides of his cheeks with the leaves.

Pirmin coughed once and his eyes fluttered. "Mathias?" he said.

Seraina held the big man's head in her lap and Thomas scrambled around to his side.

"Pirmin. It is me, Thomas."

He grunted and his eyes opened halfway. "No need to yell at me," he said.

His voice was thin, not much more than a whisper. He closed his eyes and opened them again.

"Thomi? Ah, Thomi. I was wondering when you would appear."

"Save your strength, Pirmin. I am here. So is Seraina."

"Stay still," Seraina said, using the power of her voice to bring him some small amount of comfort.

"They put me to the Ordeal," Pirmin said and tried to move his left arm, which only caused him to grimace in pain.

"I know," Thomas said.

"It did not go so well."

Thomas's mouth stretched into a smile. "You did well enough."

"Had to use my sinister arm. Right was hurt too bad."

"That explains it then," Thomas said.

He closed his eyes for a few heartbeats, and when he opened them they appeared clearer. Seraina could see the ditch nettle was in his system now.

"They got Vex."

Seraina placed her hand on Pirmin's forehead and said, "No, Vex is fine. Noll saved him. Do not worry yourself over him, Pirmin."

Relief washed over his agonized face. Whether it was because his dog was safe or the herb was dulling his pain, Seraina could not be sure.

"I wish to confess," Pirmin said.

"And I will hear it," Thomas said, his voice breaking around the edges. "Go ahead."

"I did some bad things. But I did a lot of good things too. I hope God will take that into account."

Thomas waited for Pirmin to continue. After a long pause Pirmin said, "Say your piece Thomi."

"That is your confession?"

"One other thing." He turned his head and looked at Thomas. "I lied to you, Thomi."

"That does not matter."

"I never intended to go to Wallis. I would have missed your miserable face too much. I think I made up most of those stories…"

Thomas nodded. His eyes glistened in the torchlight.

"The fighting cows?"

"Nay. That one is true," Pirmin said. He ground his teeth together against a fresh wave of pain. Thomas held Pirmin's right hand and the big man clenched with what little strength he had left. His face cleared after a moment, but was a shade whiter. Even though he took a deep breath, his next words shuddered forth like his lungs had all the air of a spent bellows.

"Do not mourn me, Thomi. I lived enough for ten men…just promise me you will live enough for one."

Pirmin's eyes slowly closed. His breathing became less labored, and the muscles in his face relaxed.

"I will," Thomas said under his breath.

Seraina felt tears building as she watched Thomas make the sign of the cross above Pirmin and then go on to absolve him of all the sins he had committed in this life. It was a ritual she did not understand, but she appreciated seeing the comfort it brought to Thomas.

Pirmin never opened his eyes again. When he died a few moments later, Seraina felt a great saddening within the Weave; a collective tremor that only occurred with the loss of one who had touched a great many. The world would be a poorer place without Pirmin Schnidrig, until the Weave could usher in the likes of him once again. It may take years, but it would happen.

They sat with him for a few minutes more and then Seraina convinced Thomas they had to leave. Judge Furst would see that Pirmin was removed from the cell and buried properly, not simply thrown on the garbage heap outside the walls. She promised.

Seraina led Thomas out of the cell and back to the door that opened into a corner of the fortress's courtyard. She threw open the door and pulled Thomas behind her into the bright mid-day sun.

Into the midst of a dozen armed soldiers with crossbows and bristling spear points leveled their way.

"Welcome to the light," Duke Leopold said.

Chapter 34

"THAT IS NOT Melchthal," Landenberg said, his words heavy with disappointment. He rammed his sword back into its sheath.

"Bring them before me," Leopold said. A page stood behind him holding two saddled mounts, one for him and the other for Gissler. Leopold was to return to Habsburg this day, but when he got news that Walter Furst had been caught stealing keys to the jails, he decided to postpone his journey for a short while.

"Wait!" Gissler stepped forward and shouted at the soldiers surrounding Thomas and Seraina. "No one take another step. Remove your belt knife, Thomas."

"You know this man?" Leopold took a closer look at the man and woman who had emerged from the prisons. He had seen the girl before, but could not place where. The man however, he was sure he did not know. His scarred face would not have been easy to forget.

Gissler nodded, but did not look at the Duke. His eyes were fixed on the man he called Thomas.

"Aye, my lord. And he is not a man you want within arm's reach of a dagger."

At first Leopold thought the man might be simple, the way his head was bowed, and his movements unsteady. But when he turned his face up and met Gissler's eyes with a cold glare, Leopold immediately recognized him as a soldier.

"Yet another Hospitaller? It is no wonder the Holy wars go badly—you are all here."

"Pirmin is dead," Thomas said. The words, quiet and menacing, were directed at Gissler.

Leopold was not surprised by this news. He had seen the man's wounds, but Gissler flinched, and did not immediately respond.

"He chose his path," Gissler finally said. "Do not make his mistakes your own. Resist and it will not go well for you," he nodded in the girl's direction, "or your pretty friend."

Thomas assessed the situation with fresh eyes, seeing the spear points within thrusting distance of himself and his companion. Leopold had no doubt that if Thomas were alone, his actions would have been quite different. As it was, however, he edged his hand away from his knife handle and undid the clasp on his belt. He held it out and a soldier hooked it with the point of his sword and backed away. The soldiers pushed them toward the center of the courtyard, where Leopold, Gissler, and Landenberg stood.

"On your knees. You are in the presence of your rulers," Landenberg said, he sidled closer to Leopold, giving the girl a lascivious stare. She held her head up high and refused to meet the eyes of either man. Leopold smiled. Landenberg would have his hands full indeed if he tried to take this one.

"Bend your knee," Landenberg repeated. When neither the man nor the woman moved to do so, a soldier forced them down by rapping each one in turn between their shoulder blades with the butt end of his spear.

A crowd was beginning to gather. Work on the walls had come to a standstill since Landenberg had pulled some of the guards away to ambush who he had assumed was Arnold Melchthal, come to rescue his outlaw lieutenant. It was a motley group: condemned men and women, paid laborers, master masons, and even the parish priest of Altdorf milled about curious to see what the commotion was about. It was also market day in Altdorf, so the town was busier than normal. Since the fortress was situated just outside of town, vendors had been coming and going from the fortress with their wares since early morning.

"They caught the witch!" a woman said. "As I thought, she is in league with the ferryman."

Leopold turned to see an old woman pointing at the auburn-haired girl on her knees. "I knew God was listening," the woman continued. She ran forward and spit at the side of the girl's head. She flinched and regarded her assailant with a hurt look in her striking green eyes. People began murmuring, and the word 'witch' traveled through the mob like wildfire.

Interesting development, Leopold thought. He turned to Gissler.

"Return to the stable master and procure a cage wagon, with two guards provisioned for the road. And find Bernard. Tell him to pack my manuscript in the wagon and follow us as soon as he is able."

The soldiers opened their circle and Gissler pushed away into the crowd.

"She-Devil!"

The old woman took another run at the girl, but Landenberg intervened and pushed her away.

"Get the Menznau woman away from here," he said to a soldier. The man turned his spear sideways and was about to push the woman away when Leopold spoke up.

"Hold on. Mother, are you accusing this girl of witchcraft?"

The old woman fell to her knees and clasped her hands before her chest. "I do my lord. She said she would help my son, instead she fed his soul to the Devil!"

Gasps could be heard from the onlookers.

The girl shook her head, her eyes wide. "No, it is not so. I never even saw—" Landenberg cut the girl off with a hard slap, and her hand went to her mouth. His breathing quickened at the sight of a thin line of blood from her lip and the remains of his handprint on her skin. The man, Thomas, reached out to her, and simultaneously narrowed his dark eyes at Landenberg.

"Do not speak in front of your betters, girl." Turning to Leopold he said, "Perhaps we should search her for the Devil's mark, my lord."

"Seraina is no witch!" Thomas said.

Landenberg raised his arm and stepped forward.

"Stay your hand, Vogt," Leopold said. "The man is a Hospitaller. He has earned the right to speak."

Landenberg grunted and stepped back.

"So tell us. Why do you defend this woman when she has so many accusers? A man of God should know better." Leopold said.

"She has done nothing. I demand you set her free."

Landenberg laughed. "Not bloody likely. Better chance of pissing uphill in a föhn."

Thomas slowly eased himself off the ground to his feet and locked eyes with Leopold. The soldier next to Leopold followed Thomas's every move with his crossbow.

"I am Thomas Schwyzer, a Captain of the Knights of Saint John of Jerusalem, subject only to the commands of His Eminence, the Pope. In His name and that of our Lord Jesus Christ, I demand you set this woman free and trouble her no more."

The crowd was silent. More than a few crossed themselves. Leopold was impressed with the faith and conviction he heard in Thomas's words, but he also sensed something else. *Desperation perhaps?*

"Well, Thomas…*Schwyzer* was it? Hardly a blue-blooded name. I would think someone of your exalted rank could do better. But putting that aside for the moment, I certainly do not wish to upset the Pope, in the off chance you do indeed have His ear."

He raised his voice and addressed the crowd. "So I offer you a chance to prove yourself. Here, in front of these good people of Altdorf and in the presence of God."

The crowd erupted into a chorus of shouts and cheers.

Now, where was that damned Bernard?

Chapter 35

SERAINA'S KNEES ACHED and although her lip had ceased bleeding, her face still throbbed from Landenberg's blow. She heard someone curse her name, and the word 'witch' rang out all around her. The energy of the crowd was dizzying and she felt herself panic. She closed her eyes, but found no peace in the darkness, for the image of the villagers of Tellikon feeding a crippled newborn into flames only became so much more vivid.

She thought of running. If she could make it to the trees she would have a chance, for they would conceal her. But her heart fell when she craned her neck and saw nothing but broken walls and open land in all directions. *Killing fields*, the engineers called them. It had been a moment of fantasy, for she knew she could not leave Thomas.

"Do you know the story of Palnatoki?" Leopold asked Thomas, but he spoke in a voice that carried throughout the crowd. A soldier at each of his arms held crossbows loaded and aimed at Thomas's head. Others formed a circle to keep the crowd of people in order.

"It was a favorite of mine as a child, told to me by my father's greatest military advisor. His storytelling abilities, I must say, rivaled his military genius."

Thomas glanced at Seraina. His hard expression melted for the briefest of moments.

"I think I like this one," Landenberg said. "Palnatoki was a warrior in Dane's Land, am I right?"

Leopold blinked, obviously surprised.

"Right you are. But he was much more than a simple warrior. He was the bravest, fiercest, most skilled soldier in the land. So skilled, that his own king became jealous of his exploits and plotted against him."

As he spoke Leopold began walking. The guards opened up the circle for him.

"One day, when Palnatoki was drunk, the king overheard him boasting about his archery abilities. He claimed he could shoot an apple off the end of a stick at a hundred paces. The king called him on his claim, saying he would not have liars in his personal guard."

Leopold stopped beside one of the saddled horses his page still held, and rooted through its saddlebags.

"The king arranged a test." Leopold pulled out a red apple and held it up for all to see, and then pushed his soldier's spears aside and re-entered the circle. He stopped in front of Seraina. He reached down and put his fingers under her chin like he was caressing a lover. Seraina twisted her head away and averted her eyes. She heard Landenberg's deep-throated laugh.

"Stand her up," Leopold said. A large, one-eyed soldier grabbed her left arm and a smaller man her right, and they jerked her to her feet. Her legs ached as the blood returned to them and she stumbled. The soldier

261

with the patch put his arms around her from behind and chuckled as he ground himself against her. Seraina broke free of his grip and pushed him back. He winked at her and grinned with a mouth full of broken yellow teeth.

Landenberg had watched her brief struggle with interest.

"Think your legs are weak now, girl? Wait till you spend the night in my jails." He laughed at his own joke until he caught Leopold staring at him.

"I will continue my story," Leopold said, "if your courtship is over."

Chastised, Landenberg nodded and stared at the ground.

"The king called in Palnatoki's young son and placed the apple on his head. He then told Palnatoki he had one shot to prove himself. The archer removed three arrows from his quiver, and on his first try, split the apple in two. The king then asked him why he took three arrows when he was allowed only one."

Leopold tossed the apple up once and caught it. He turned to Thomas. "And do you know what he said?"

"To avenge myself on thee, in the event that I caused harm to my boy," Thomas said, as though reading the words. "It is a common enough tale."

"It is good you are familiar with it," Leopold said. "As you may already suspect, we shall use it as the basis for my test."

Seraina could see Thomas's jaw muscles twitch, but he said nothing.

"You and I together shall play the part of Palnatoki. There will be no evil king in our story." He smiled and held up the apple. "Only two heroes."

"This is how it shall work. We place the apple on the

witch's head and take turns shooting until one of us hits it. The apple, I mean."

"You are mad," Thomas said.

"God will protect the girl if she is truly innocent. If, however, she is a witch, well…we will just have to see. Now, since you are in my future home, I give you the choice. Would you prefer to shoot first or second?"

"I refuse," Thomas said. "This is utter madness. The girl is innocent."

"Fine. I will shoot first." Leopold grabbed a loaded crossbow from the nearest guard and as he did so his hand brushed the tickler and the bow went off. Everyone within earshot of the loud twang ducked or flinched not sure where the bolt was going. But Leopold had had it pointed at the ground and the heavy shaft thudded harmlessly into the hard earth.

Leopold smiled at Thomas. "I suppose it has been some years since I last shot one of these. But I expect it will come back quickly enough. Someone load me another quarrel."

Seraina knew what Leopold was doing, as, she suspected, did everyone else watching the young Duke.

"Thomas," she said.

His face turned and their eyes met. The weight bearing down on each of them lifted for the briefest of moments. She stepped away from her captors and walked to stand in front of Leopold. Ever so slowly she reached out her hand and plucked the apple from Leopold's grasp. His lips spread into a thin line and he mocked her with a bow.

"Seraina, no…" Thomas began, but she leaned in and put her finger to his lips.

"Do not let him choose my fate," she said. "I would

leave that to the Weave. And you, Thomas."

She backed away a few steps and then the guards were on her arms once again. They led her in the direction of the main keep and left her standing in an open work site with shattered rocks and dusty ground chewed up by the hooves of oxen.

The only flower she could see was a half-trampled autumn crocus. A *naked lady*, bent and withered.

***

Leopold handed Thomas a drawn crossbow with no bolt and showed him where to stand. Anticipation was growing in the crowd, and Leopold could feel the people's excitement building and mixing with his own. Gissler had returned with the cage wagon, and he now stood holding the horses, a scowl on his face. He was not a man who appreciated theatrics, Leopold decided.

He set a spearman on Thomas's left and a crossbow wielding guard on his right, with his weapon trained on Thomas's head just a few feet away.

"Precautions you understand. I hope they do not interfere with your concentration," he said to Thomas.

"Give him a bolt. *One* bolt," Leopold said and someone snickered.

All conversation died down as a soldier stepped in and held out a black, leather-fletched quarrel, to Thomas. He took the bolt in his hand by the iron tip and let out a deep breath. In his other hand he held the crossbow down at his side. Still holding it by the point, he raised the bolt to eye level and sighted down it, checking for defects. Satisfied he turned towards Seraina.

As he turned towards the crossbowman at his side,

Thomas reached out with the leather vane end of his arrow and flicked it against the tickler on the underside of the man's bow. There was an audible click and the crossbow jumped in the man's hands as it ejected its missile.

Thomas leaned his head an inch to the side and the bolt whirred by his ear, taking the spearman on his left high in the chest. Thomas stepped inside the dying soldier's spear and drew his belt knife before he slumped to the ground. A spin and a step later, the crossbowman's throat was cut, but with a crazed look on his face, he continued squeezing the trigger on his spent weapon until he finally collapsed.

Leopold did not recognize what was happening until both men were dead on the ground and Thomas was moving unerringly towards him, his black eyes focused on Leopold's throat.

Fortunately for Leopold, a young soldier, with reflexes better than his lord, jumped in front of him with his sword drawn. His death gave Leopold enough time to back out of immediate danger. Other soldiers rushed in.

Thomas sliced a man's leg in three places and sent him screaming to the ground. One soldier shot at Thomas but his bolt missed and hit one of his comrades in the shoulder.

"Hold your fire!" It was Gissler, sitting atop his horse with his sword drawn. "Give him room. Back up, but close the circle."

Thomas stood in a half crouch, one hand stretched out before him and the other one clutching the knife close to his body. Leopold was shocked at how calm he appeared. He had just killed at least three men, but he wore the unconcerned expression of a man sampling cheeses in the marketplace.

"Give up the weapon, Thomas," Gissler said.

Thomas heard nothing, for his eyes were fixed on the same thing most everyone else was watching.

Seraina had suddenly appeared outside the circle of spears and crossbows. She reached out one slender hand and lifted the point of a spear enough to allow her entry. She stepped over a wounded man as easily as a breeze blowing through deadfalls and walked slowly up to Thomas. She raised a hand to his face and held out the other. He looked into her eyes, closed his own, and with only another moment's hesitation, he set the knife in her palm. She let the blade fall to the earth and then pulled Thomas's head to her breast.

The soldiers were on them a second after Thomas's knife hit the ground. They pulled the couple from each other's arms and began beating Thomas with fists, hobnailed boots, and spear shafts. The girl screamed as leering soldiers manhandled her into the cage wagon and padlocked the door.

Gissler rode his horse into the midst of the soldiers beating on Thomas and drove them back.

"The next man to put a boot to him will find himself quivering on the end of my blade," he said. He gestured with his sword to emphasize his words. The soldiers grudgingly backed away from the prone figure in the dirt.

And while all this was happening, Leopold sensed a shift in the crowd about him. One that he did not care for.

"The ferryman is right. Seraina is no witch. She is a gifted healer. Nothing more," Leopold heard a voice saying.

He would have paid it no heed, except it was the

parish priest of Altdorf doing the talking. Others nodded their heads and murmured curses at the soldiers under their breaths.

Leopold beckoned Landenberg over from the cage wagon.

"Send the Hospitaller to Habsburg by boat. Then disperse this crowd. I do not like the looks of it. Gissler and I will take the wagon and the witch to Habsburg now."

Landenberg's face fell like that of an unwanted child.

Leopold rolled his eyes. "Very well. Follow us tomorrow. We will wait for you before we proceed with the girl's trial."

Leopold was well aware that sometimes you had to let your dogs run wild.

Chapter 36

GISSLER'S MEN MARCHED Thomas down the steep slope to the edge of the lake where their boat was tied to the dock. It was a sleek craft designed for speed and to carry no more than seven people, one steersman at the rear and the other six crowded onto three bench seats spaced out equally down the length of the boat. It had one large triangular sail, lateen-rigged to a twenty foot mast and the bottom to a ten foot boom that swung from side to side depending on the wind, and which caused the passengers to sit slightly hunched over to keep from banging their heads on the heavy wooden beam.

It was a new boat; its overlapping plank hull not yet darkened with age. Even though Thomas's head throbbed and his wrists burned where the ropes were cutting into the flesh, he still found a moment to pause and appreciate her fine workmanship—until 'One-eye' jabbed him in the center of his back and sent him stumbling. Thomas caught himself with his tied hands on the side of the boat, but a shooting pain burst through his shoulder to match the one in his back.

"Something wrong? Afraid of the water? Get moving Schwyzer scum."

Since there were already seven soldiers, One-eye pushed Thomas down to the floor of the boat at the helmsman's feet, on top of several spare coiled up lines, and sat backwards on the first bench to watch him. The rest of the men clambered into the packed boat. It had one set of oars in the middle and with a man on each side heaving to, they pulled away from the dock.

They soon stowed the oars and the helmsman shouted curses at a soldier in the middle as he fumbled with the sail. Obviously not a sailor, he finally succeeded in trimming the sail properly and the boat shuddered to life. It creaked for a moment, until the sail filled completely, and then the boat sprang forward and picked up speed. The helmsman skillfully pointed the bow as close to the oncoming wind as the boat could manage while still making good forward speed.

Thomas kept his eyes on the floor of the boat as he flexed his fingers trying to work some circulation into his wrists. The rope binding his hands was slick with blood. He could feel One-eye staring at him, looking for any excuse to hit him again. He wracked his mind to come up with a plan to escape, but could not focus. He was too worried about Seraina. She had been accused of witchcraft, and as sure as there was a god in heaven, she was headed for a painful, horrible death. And Gissler knew that all too well. He had betrayed them all. Thomas, the entire crew of *The Wyvern*, and of course Pirmin....

Thomas cringed and felt grief and rage course

through his blood in equal measures, paralyzing his mind. He tried to blank them out and concentrate.

Think, man. Think!

He squeezed his eyes shut and took a deep breath. For a moment he was on his own ship, with the smell of saltwater and the heat of the Palestine sun on his face. He saw Pirmin's laughing face, and heard the cry of a sea gull, and when he opened his eyes he heard it again.

But this was no local sea gull—it was the shrill cry of a black-crested gull.

Ever so slowly he raised his head to look over the side of the boat. *Either there was one very lost bird out there or....*

One-eye cuffed Thomas across the face.

"Stay down there. I do not want any good folk to see me traveling with a dog like you." The helmsman laughed at this, and Thomas grunted and eased himself up to his knees to face the man.

The helmsman was the only true sailor on the boat.

Thomas raised his hands up over his head and groaned as though injured, then, lowering them until they were level with the helmsman's face, he traced a slow cross in the air.

One-eye laughed and said, "Looks like you just got blessed by a witch lover. Or maybe he cursed you."

The man shook his head and swatted Thomas's hands away.

"Save your prayers for—"

His words were cut short by a hiss, followed by a wet plop, like the sound a smooth, round rock makes when thrown into a pond. A high-powered crossbow bolt had entered one side of his neck and exited the other, leaving no trace of its existence save for a plume of blood spurting from the exit wound.

The helmsman's eyes rolled up inside his head and he pitched forward. As he fell away from the steerboard, the boat began a lazy arc off course. One-eye stared dumbfounded at the helmsman until another crossbow bolt whistled through the air over his head. He threw himself backward to the floor of the boat and yelled, "Ambush!"

Thomas leaned over the helmsman's body and fumbled with his bound hands to draw his belt knife. He could hear One-eye shouting at his men as they scrambled over one another in confusion. Two more bolts pounded into the side of the boat near the front. He tried to focus on cutting his ropes with the knife, but the going was awkward with his hands tied. He glanced up to see One-eye glaring at him and drawing his sword. The heavyset man crouched and stepped over the seat separating them. He tried to cut his bonds again but the knife slipped out of his hands and clattered to the bottom of the boat. Thomas realized he was out of time.

He grabbed the dead man's body and pulled it between himself and One-eye. The soldier hacked at it once with his sword and screamed obscenities at Thomas.

"A corpse will not protect you for long, Schwyzer!"

As he attempted to clamber over the body in the narrow confines of the boat, Thomas grabbed the steerboard handle and pushed hard, keeping his eye on how the sail fluttered and died as the boat came around. He felt the wind move to the other side of his face and he ducked. With a groan of protest the heavy wooden boom holding the bottom of the sail swung from one side of the boat to the other, catching One-eye square in the chest and launching him and one other man out of the boat. Dressed in full chainmail, they screamed and hit the water hard, surfaced once, thrashed silently for a moment, and then disappeared below the surface, their heavy armor dragging them down.

The four men in the front of the boat managed to avoid the boom. One pointed at Thomas and shouted something to the other two. They all drew swords and began moving towards Thomas in a crouch. Thomas looked to the shore and estimated they were over three hundred yards away; far out of crossbow range.

They had been moving steadily towards deeper waters since the helmsman had been killed, and that was why there had been no bolts hitting the side of the boat for some time. There was only one man in a thousand that could have made the shot that took out the helmsman, but Thomas could expect no further assistance from his benefactor on land.

Thomas glanced briefly at the dead helmsman's sword, still in its scabbard, and then dismissed the idea just as quickly. Four armored men against one in the cramped space of a rocking boat would be a glorious but stupid death. He gritted his teeth and felt the scar on the side of his face tighten.

If he knew Seraina was already dead he would not have hesitated. But so long as there was a chance she yet lived, he would do everything in his power to survive. Yes, he could jump off the boat and swim for the shore. He might survive the cold water, and looking at the awkward swaying of the four soldiers he doubted they had the skill to turn the boat quickly enough and catch him, but he could not take the chance. Besides, Thomas had to get to Seraina quickly.

And for that, he had need of a fast boat.

Thomas stood in the back of the boat, his hands still bound in front, and watched the four armed soldiers close the distance. They would be on him in seconds. The time for planning was over.

He took a deep breath and reached his tied hands down to snatch up the helmsman's knife resting on the coils of rope at his feet, then raising his arms up high, he drove the blade deep into the helmsman's wooden seat. He rubbed his bonds up and down once against the sharp blade and his hands snapped apart.

He was free.

He picked up one of the coiled lines, put it over his head and shoulder, and then pulled the steerboard hard to one side, wedging it in place with the helmsman's body.

The boat began turning across the wind again and the boom began moving across. The soldiers were past the midpoint of the boat now, and when they saw the boom swinging around they ducked beneath it, well aware of how it had knocked their comrades over the side of the boat. Grim-faced, they continued their approach. A few more steps and they would be in sword range.

But Thomas had no intention of waiting. As the boom reached the end of its arc and slammed into place, the boat leaned dangerously. With the rudder locked in place and the sail filling with wind, all she needed was the slightest encouragement and she would go over. Thomas hopped up onto the side of the boat, took a couple of quick, agile steps and jumped out just past the mast as high in the air as he could. As he hurtled by the mast he reached out with one arm to snag the tall pole, letting his body weight tip the boat even further into the direction it was already leaning.

"You fool! You will capsize us," the nearest soldier shouted. There was a moment when the boat resisted, but the combination of Thomas's weight and the wind blowing into the sail, proved too much. It swayed, faltered, and then fell over sideways, slowly at first, but soon picked up speed, until the mast and sail slapped the water throwing up a wall of spray and tossing everyone into the cold alpine lake.

The cold water shocked the breath out of Thomas. This was no Mid-Earth sea, and he knew water this temperature could sap the strength out of a man in minutes. He needed to work fast, but at least he was not in as much peril as the armored men around him splashing, fighting for their lives to keep their heads above water. Swimming with thirty pounds of steel and leather dragging one beneath the waves was no easy feat. It was for this very reason that the crew of *The Wyvern* had adopted the use of the Saracen's lightweight Damascan mail shirts for their own armor.

As the soldiers thrashed and kicked, struggling to remove their heavy armor or swim to the side of the tipped over boat, Thomas fastened one end of his line around the narrow top of the mast. He swam back to the boat and clambered up onto the side sticking high out of the water, and then took up the line's slack. Gradually, like a man climbing a rock wall, he leaned back and heaved on the rope. With his body parallel to the water, the mast began lifting out of the water, encouraging him to ignore the pain in his shoulder and pull harder. The line dug into his hands, bloodying them, and every muscle in his body felt like it was going to snap off his skeleton, but still the boat would not turn over that last bit to right herself.

"Come on girl," Thomas said, his voice a hoarse whisper. "Do not let us down now." He could feel himself weakening. He leaned back further, his hair brushing the water, and pulled for all he was worth. The boat shuddered, but refused to flip upright. He did not have the strength, or the weight.

A strong hand grabbed his hair, twisting his neck painfully and dunking his head under the water. He lashed out blindly with one hand and felt it connect with a fleshy nose. The hand released him and as he pulled his head up he caught sight of One-eye reaching an arm out to grab him again.

Somehow, the veteran soldier had managed to remove his chainmail hauberk and boots, and with the frenzied strength of a drowning man, was now clawing his way through the water towards Thomas. Thomas knew he did not have the time, or the will, to fight off the crazed man. But perhaps he could enlist his aid.

Still holding the taut mast rope wrapped around one arm, he leaned back and extended his other arm. One-eye latched on and began dragging himself up Thomas's limb. Thomas screamed and with all the strength he had left, pulled One-eye as far out of the water as he could while simultaneously heaving on the mast line.

The extra weight lifted the entire length of the mast out of the water. The sail followed, shedding water as it rose, and then the boat popped upright like it was the most natural thing in the world.

Thomas half-rolled, half-collapsed into the boat as she righted herself, but One-eye remained hanging over the side still clutching Thomas's arm. The boat creaked and rocked from side to side, showering them with lakewater that hid in the folds of its canvas sail. Both men remained motionless breathing hard through their mouths, exhausted.

Finally, Thomas forced himself to his knees and leaned over the edge of the boat. One-eye had both his arms wrapped around Thomas's arm. His skin was ashen and his lips thick and bluing around the edges.

Thomas hit him hard in the face once, twice, and finally, after a third time, the one-eyed soldier slid off his arm like an over-ripe carcass from a meat hook. He sunk below the water without a sound, his eyes wide in terror.

Thomas collapsed backward into the boat and wrapped his arms around himself. He groaned and tried to rub some feeling back into them. He felt like he had been pulled apart by horses.

Finally, once his chest stopped heaving, and he could feel the blood moving again in his limbs, he poked his head up and surveyed the situation.

He immediately picked out a bearded figure waving on the shore. One Habsburg soldier still clung to the side of the boat. There was no sign of any others.

"Please…help me up," he said. "I was only following orders. Please…"

Thomas leaned over and undid the chinstrap on the man's helmet.

"I got nothin' against you Schwyzers." The man spoke faster when Thomas did not answer. "Nothin' against you, or the girl. It was just orders."

Thomas removed the man's helmet and threw it into the boat. There was a lot of water in the boat and he would need something to bail with. Then he retrieved one of the two stowed oars.

He stood up and stared down at the man. He clung

to the side of the boat with only the tenuous grip of his fingertips.

"No please! I got a family. Like I said, it was just orders." He was so cold he no longer shivered, but his words flowed slowly, like winter cream.

Thomas shook his head. "Orders you *chose* to follow. You have taken sides, and I can respect that." Thomas hefted the heavy oar in his hands. "But forgiveness is another matter."

"God, please…" Thomas cut off the man's words by bringing the oar down hard on his head.

***

It took only a few moments to set the sail and get the boat moving towards the figure standing on the edge of the lake. Thomas worked the steerboard with one hand and used the soldier's helmet to bail water from the bottom of the boat. Soon he was tossing the bowline to Ruedi, who deftly secured it around the exposed roots of a crooked pine tree growing too close to the water's edge.

"This was not exactly what I had in mind when I suggested we go hunting, you and I Cap'n. But I must say, you do flush out interesting game."

Thomas stepped ashore onto a large flat rock and the two men embraced, and then Thomas wasted no time in quizzing Ruedi on what he knew of Seraina's whereabouts.

"You saw what happened in Altdorf?"

"Saw enough. I came very close to shooting Gissler through that mutinous heart of his."

Thomas shook his head. "If you had I would still be

in chains on this boat, and you beside me. Did you see where they took her?"

"Aye Cap'n. Gissler threw her into a cage wagon then him and the Duke took the north road out of Altdorf. They will be taking her to Habsburg I imagine."

Thomas nodded. With the fortress in Altdorf still under construction, the Habsburg castle was the safest place for a member of the royal family. If they reached the castle with Seraina, Thomas knew he would never see her alive again. Leopold and his clerics would try her as a witch and torture a confession from her. And if she survived the tortures, she would be burnt at the stake. He had to get to her before they reached Habsburg.

As though reading his mind, Ruedi said, "We had best be off then. She looks to be a fast boat. If we leave now we may be able to cut them off at the Kussnacht. Be just like old times, eh Cap'n?"

Thomas placed a restraining hand on Ruedi's shoulder to stop him from climbing into the boat.

"I would like nothing more old friend. But I need this boat as light as possible. She will not make the speed with two of us."

Ruedi looked at the boat and then back at Thomas with a hurt look in his eyes. But he knew Thomas was right. Gissler and Leopold had too much of a head start. He removed his belt, with its dangling hook on the front for working a crossbow string, and gave it to Thomas. Then held out his crossbow and two bolts.

"These are all I got left. Gissler and Leopold were riding, and there were two soldiers driving the wagon."

"Thanks, friend. You have come through for me more times than I can count."

Ruedi's lower lip trembled just enough to be visible

beneath his red moustache and beard.

"Now you listen to me Cap'n. This is the best crossbow I have ever owned. Made by a Genoese master, and I will be expecting it back, so you heed what I tell you. You shoot Gissler with your first bolt. You shoot from behind cover and without him ever seeing you. If you miss your first shot you take him out with the second. Pay no mind to the other three until Gissler is down. You hear me Cap'n?"

Thomas looked into Ruedi's pleading grey eyes and was overwhelmed with the impression his friend was saying goodbye.

Chapter 37

SERAINA SAT HUNCHED in the low wagon, her eyes fixed on the narrow, hard-packed road through the carriage's barred rear door. Occasionally she heard voices above her but could never make out the words as the iron-rimmed wheels rattled and ground out the miles, snaking a ponderous route along the heavily treed coastline of the Great Lake.

She closed her eyes, ignoring the pain of her cracked lip, and focused on the trees. It took a great deal of time to still her mind and tuck away the emotions clawing to the surface, demanding to be acknowledged. Mile upon mile passed, and she knew with every passing moment she was careening closer to Habsburg Castle. Further from Schwyz, her people, and from Thomas, if he yet lived.

She clenched her teeth and bit down on her split lip, letting the pain clear her mind and refocus her energies. He was alive. She was sure of it, but she needed all her strength if she were to ever see him again.

She focused on her breathing and allowed her body's rhythms to merge with the swaying movement of the wagon. Then, when she was ready, Seraina closed her eyes and reached out to the trees.

She pushed her essence beyond the rolling cage that would keep her imprisoned, and found herself hovering outside the wagon; free, but unable to move, as though still tethered to her physical self. Her spirit kicked and screamed, grasping at every branch and leaf whipping past in a desperate attempt to disengage her spirit form from her body. She grew weak, and felt the cold iron bars press up against her back, threatening to pull her back within her prison of flesh and bone once again.

Then wind caressed her cheek. It danced through her hair, and brushed away her tears, and without warning, snatched her away, sweeping her straight up the side of a tall pine. Breathless, she floated high above the world on clouds of green.

The strength of the natural world replenished her spirit. Invigorated, she leapt and pirouetted from one lush dome to another, rejoicing in her freedom. On some distant plane she was aware of her physical body collapsing onto its side, and the scent of moldy straw and human excrement invaded her senses for a moment. But then she turned her face to the sun and leapt to hover above the leaves of a giant cherry tree. She laughed and gazed over the canopy of the forest. The tops of the trees undulated far into the distance like gentle hills, but then they began to move and reform. The treetops took on the shapes of heads, in a crowd of giants, gathered to admire the azure waters of the Great Lake shimmering below. And off to the right, rising higher than them all, were the ancient Mythen Mountains, majestic mates of stone and earth.

Seraina felt herself whisked forward along the green-topped crowd until she hovered a thousand feet above the shore, the edge of the forest rustling at her feet. Movement caught her eye. Farther away than any human eye should be able to see, a speck marred the perfect blue-green waters. Tiny, inconsequential, yet Seraina could not pull her eyes away. She tried to avert her gaze, but there was something about that speck she knew she should remember.

Thomas.

She fell to her knees. The stink of the prison wagon filled her nostrils once again and the bruises and cuts on her body sapped her strength and called out, begging her spirit to return. She clasped her hands together at her chest, and not knowing what else to do, called upon the Mythen.

***

The wind was not with him. Thomas angled the bow of the boat as close to the wind as she could manage and sat high on the edge to keep it flat on the water as he pulled the sail in tight. After a few minutes of making decent headway across the water, he pushed the steerboard away from him and ducked under the boom to sit on the other side of the boat. The boat shuddered as the heavy boom swung across the boat and snapped into place with the sail once again filling with wind.

He continued tacking back and forth across the point of the wind, his eyes fixed on a stand of trees on the shoreline far ahead in the distance, at a spot where he knew the road ran close to the water's edge. If he had any chance at all of catching up to Gissler, it would be there.

At that point the road narrowed before branching into two, with one route continuing along the shore of the lake and the other pushing east, leading away from the water and further into the Kussnacht, and eventually, to Habsburg Castle. If Gissler made it past that fork, Seraina would be lost to Thomas forever.

He focused on making the tightest turns possible, making the most of the feeble wind. Only the faintest tendrils of white floated across the blue sky and the slight breeze rippled the top of the water without breaking it. The horizon was not coming fast enough. In his heart he knew he would not make it. The boat was fast and well built, but he was running out of time.

Still, he would not give up. His mind raced with calculations and angles, trying to come up with alternate scenarios that would get him across the lake faster.

At the front of the boat, tucked into the bow was a cache of supplies stored under an oiled leather tarp. Most probably water and foodstuffs, perhaps a few tools for making emergency repairs. Whatever the items were, they were heavy and keeping the bow of the boat low in the water. They had to go, but he could not let go of the rudder without losing speed. Sailing into the wind required constant minute adjustments on the steerboard to keep the speed up, or worse, to prevent the boat from capsizing. What he really needed was a steerboard extension.

After tacking yet again, he wrapped the sail line around a cleat on the side of the boat to hold it in place. He picked up one of the oars and lashed it onto the steerboard, effectively extending it by the entire length of the oar. He tested it by moving a few feet away and steered the boat to see how she responded. Satisfied, he freed up the sail, tacked once more, and cleated the sail into place once again.

Moving quickly, he picked up his sword and scrambled to the front of the boat. He cut the restraints on the tarp and threw everything overboard he could with one hand, while he held the steerboard steady with the other hand. It was awkward and a balancing act, but it worked well enough. The items turned out to not be foodstuffs after all, but were sets of mason and carpenter tools: mallets, chisels, drawknives, and such. Thomas threw out half the items before deciding he needed to go back to the rear of the boat and tack again in order to stay on course.

The bow rode higher now that it was lighter, and after one more trip up it would ride higher still. Thomas tacked and was scrambling under the sail to the leeward side when the boat leaned heavily and almost capsized as a sudden gust of wind caught the sail. He eased off on the steerboard and scrambled to the high side to bring her back into contact with the water. The boat settled down and flattened out with the redistribution of his weight.

Thomas allowed himself a breath. It took a moment for his heart to stop hammering. If he capsized the boat now, there would be absolutely no way to make up the time.

He had almost lost her.

Looking around him, he noticed the ripples in the water had grown into small whitecaps. Preoccupied as he was, he had failed to recognize the change in weather. Turning his face to the sky he was shocked to see a bank of clouds rolling in fast. There had been no sign of them earlier.

Within minutes the entire sky was smothered in billowing grey clouds with dark, swollen underbellies. This was like no storm he had ever seen. It had to be a föhn, one of the unnatural warm winds that blew over the Alps. The locals had warned him to never be caught out on the lake when a föhn appeared.

Well, it was too late to heed that advice.

He felt the first drop of rain and tightened his grip on the sail line. The whitecaps grew and the water bubbled like some great titan stirred it from below.

I have my wind now, Thomas thought, his face grim. He looked out over the churning water and swallowed.

The gale blew so fierce it drove the rain hard against his skin, leaving painful welts like one of the sandstorms of the Levant. He had seen all manner of weather in twenty years on the sea, but never the likes of this. One moment the sky had been clear as far as the eye could see, and the next the storm waged around him, the unnatural wind changing direction and swirling without notice.

Thomas was convinced God had set his wrath against him. Was it because he fought to save Seraina? Was she truly Lucifer's servant as Leopold had called her? Thomas threw back his head and shook the water from his eyes. He shouted into the gale in defiance, his voice registering in his ears as a whisper.

Thomas made his way to the center of the boat, using the long oar extension to steer. Then he jumped up onto the side of the boat, balancing there for a moment to get a feel for the wind. He took up the slack in the sail line and looped it under the backs of his legs in a makeshift harness. When he was ready, he trimmed the sail and adjusted the steerboard until the boat lurched ahead and its one side lifted out of the water. With his feet perched only on the four-inch wide side of the boat, Thomas leaned flat out above the water in his harness. He tweaked the steerboard in small increments, and the boat leveled out and shot across the waves.

Thomas yelled in terror and exhilaration.

If this was God's attempt at sending him to Hell, He was about to be disappointed.

A wave caressed the back of Thomas's hair, as though reaching for him, but he raced by far too fast. With the dark waters heaving and jumping around him, a terrible laugh escaped from his lips.

He screamed at the elements and at God, both in equal measure, like a man possessed by some malevolent spirit.

Chapter 38

"SHE IS A QUIET ONE. Hardly made a sound since we took her," Gissler said to Leopold.

The two men rode side by side in front of the wagon. The Duke had kept to himself since Altdorf, and Gissler had hoped the long ride to Habsburg castle would have afforded him the opportunity to broach the subject of when he could expect to see his new horses. His first task would be to hire a farrier, as Leopold had mentioned before. He needed someone dependable, who knew about breeding, but would not drain his purse too quickly. He would have to ask around, for he knew very little about what constituted a good farrier.

"What did you say Gissler?"

"The woman. She's been quiet, my lord. Perhaps we should check on her condition?"

Leopold grunted. "No need. She lives, for her kind do not leave this world so easily."

The forest road was narrow, more a path really, that

had been carved into the sloped land by centuries of use. As the driver slowed the wagon to navigate a switchback, a crossbow bolt caught him high in the chest, lifting him off the bench seat and depositing him deep into the foliage where he disappeared from view.

When Gissler heard the distinctive twang of a crossbow tickler being released, his instincts forced him low over his mount's neck at the same instant the guard took the quarrel in the chest. Ignoring the panicked shouts of the other soldier in the wagon, he scanned the woods and whispered to his horse to keep her calm. Thirty yards to his left he saw a man bent over. He stood up stiffly, using his body to pull a heavy crossbow string back with a hook on his belt. The man straightened and Gissler found himself locking eyes with Thomas.

Impossible.

Leopold was shouting something but he did not comprehend the words. *How could Thomas be here?*

Thomas slotted a bolt into the crossbow and raised the heavy weapon to his shoulder. He pulled the trigger. The second man on the wagon screamed as the quarrel tore into his abdomen, slamming him back into the seat and careening off the side to land on the hard road. Thomas threw his crossbow into the woods and picked up a sword at his feet.

After a quick glance around, Gissler relaxed slightly and sat up in his saddle. Thomas was alone. Leopold pulled alongside Gissler and grabbed his arm. The Duke's eyes were wide and wild.

"That man is all that stands between you and a life of nobility. Finish this, here and now and I swear you will be ordained a Knight of Austria on this very day."

Gissler looked into Leopold's face, searching for

deceit, but saw none. The young Duke gave him a knowing nod and gestured at the wreck of a man running to the back of the prison wagon. He cleaved the lock off the door with a single swing of his blade.

Gissler stared at the man who stood between him and his future. He looked like a survivor of a hellhound savaging. Water and sweat ran off him in torrents. His tunic was in tatters and did little to cover the bruises and cuts on his arms and upper back that he had suffered at the hands of his captors. His left eye was hideously swollen, and a crusted-over cut above it threatened to reopen at any moment. Added to this was the ever-present scar marking the entire side of his face. He appeared more apparition than man.

The soldier with the bolt in his belly lay on his side and groaned. His hands pressed over the entrance hole of the shaft, while the bulk of the wooden missile extruded from his back with only the leather vanes still lodged somewhere within his torso. Every few moments he would let out a gurgling scream of pain.

The noise was beginning to irritate Gissler.

Thomas kept his eyes focused on Gissler and Leopold while he walked over to the pain-ridden soldier. He placed the tip of his sword in the hollow between the moaning man's collarbone and the left side of his neck. He leaned on the blade, and the woods became silent.

The girl stumbled from the wagon like she was drugged and Thomas went to her. He caught her as she collapsed, and eased her to the ground. He gave the two mounted men a dark stare and took a few steps toward them, moving remarkably well, considering his appearance. Ten paces away he set the point of his sword into the hard-packed earth of the road and rested his hands on the pommel. Leopold's horse whinnied, and danced to the side a couple steps until the Duke reined her in.

Gissler dismounted and drew his blade.

"What happened to you Thomas? Since when did you become protector to the Devil's spawn?"

"Say what you will, Gissler. But we both know why you are doing this. And it has nothing to do with the Devil."

"Spare me your lectures, *Captain*. Is it so wrong to want a better life for yourself? I have served God as well as any man and I will not be judged by the likes of you."

"You have traded your allegiance to God for that of a man."

Gissler laughed. "And you think serving the Hospitallers was so much more? We fought and died for French nobles, not God. The knights were all blue-bloods who saw us as little more than dogs."

"So, you would raise arms against a brother just to be welcomed amongst the ranks of those you despise?"

Gissler raised his sword to a low guard and said, "You consort with witches. And you are not my brother."

Gissler struck first: a straight thrust followed by attacks to either side of Thomas's head. Thomas knocked Gissler's blade aside easily, with quick, deft blocks. Gissler danced back and smiled.

It had been an exploratory attack to get a feel for how comfortable Thomas was with his weapon. To any normal observers Thomas would seem highly skilled, and they would not be wrong. However, in Gissler's mind, Thomas had taken the second slash too near the tip of his blade, where it had no stopping power.

Thomas had always preferred fighting with mace and dagger, much shorter weapons. He was nowhere near Gissler's equal when it came to the long blade, and Gissler saw that very thought mirrored in Thomas's eyes. The man was smart enough to know when he was outclassed.

"I will say this only once. Drop your blade and submit or I *will* kill you. But I believe you know that," Gissler said.

In response, Thomas yelled and charged at Gissler, swinging left and right with powerful overhand attacks. Gissler backpedaled and brought his sword up in a series of awkward blocks until he managed to sidestep the frontal assault and regain his balance. The quick attack had caught him off guard and he cursed himself for being so lax. Thomas was no ordinary opponent. He would not underestimate him again.

Gissler attacked. Two straight thrusts at Thomas's abdomen followed by a reverse cut to his head. Thomas parried them, but then Gissler swept his blade down and drew a line of blood across Thomas's thigh. Thomas grunted and stepped back. He dropped his sword to a low guard and met Gissler's next attack with a parry and two counter strikes of his own.

Gissler blocked the attack with ease and stepped around the left side of Thomas. His blade flicked out and he sliced Thomas across the ribs. Thomas leapt back lessening the depth of the cut, but not the pain. He grimaced and backtracked further to gain some room. Thomas was breathing heavily now, and looking into his eyes, Gissler knew the man was finished. But to Thomas's credit, he did not give in. He launched a flurry of strikes, but Gissler was ready.

He moved in circles and casually met his blade with crisp blocks at the end of each swing's powerful arc, and when Thomas stepped in too close, Gissler raised his elbow and smashed it across his mouth. Then he stepped away to create distance and slashed Thomas across his sword arm's shoulder. Thomas screamed and his blade flew through the air, landing on the ground near one of the dead wagon guards.

Breathing heavily, Thomas limped after his weapon, one hand pressed against his shoulder to stem the flow of blood. Gissler watched the pathetic man with a detached calm. So this is how Thomas Schwyzer, Captain of *The Wyvern*, the finest fighting ship in the Levant, was to meet his end. What would Grandmaster de Villaret say now of his favored son?

Gissler allowed him to pick up the sword with his left hand before attacking again. Thomas was on the defensive immediately but he was far too slow and clumsy with his off hand. Gissler slashed his chest and then rode the length of Thomas's blade with his own all the way to the handle's crosspiece. With a flick of his wrist he snagged Thomas's sword and sent it spinning from his grip. He placed the point of his blade against the front of Thomas's throat and forced him to his knees.

Thomas gulped in air through his bloody open mouth. His dirty tunic was now soaked in red and he had the forlorn eyes of a man who had lost everything. To Gissler, Thomas had already been dead a long time. His life had been spent in blind servitude. He could not bring himself to feel sorry for his old captain because Thomas had accepted his fate with open arms. Never had he fought to better his position or change his lot. He was little more than a slave to be used by those God truly favored. Those who struggled to further their station in life.

Thomas looked up at him and pulled the neck of his tunic to one side exposing the hollow between his collarbone and carotid artery.

"Make it fast," he said, his stare defiant to the end.

Gissler nodded. "You deserve that much."

He lowered the point of his sword from the front of Thomas's neck and stepped to the side to deliver the killing thrust. But his sword would not move.

Thomas had thrown his arm over Gissler's blade and held it pinned under his armpit against his side, while his hand Gripped Gissler's wrist. His other hand snaked towards the body of the caravan guard next to him and yanked on the crossbow bolt protruding from the dead man's back. It came free with a wet pop and before Gissler had time to react, Thomas leaned back reaching far behind his head with his right arm holding the crossbow bolt, its iron point and shaft slick with dark blood.

With a loud cry, Thomas drove the hardened iron point into the base of Gissler's throat, just above the spot at which his chainmail vest ended. The wind blew out of his lungs and Gissler stumbled back, dropping his sword while his hands wrapped around the base of the thick bolt protruding from his upper chest.

Gissler stared at the shaft with wide eyes and his head shook back and forth in disbelief. Blood poured from the wound and seeped under his chainmail, only to emerge at his waist to turn his white under-tunic a vivid red. He stumbled to his knees and his eyes lost all focus before he fell onto his back. He looked up at nothing, still clutching the crossbow bolt.

**

Gissler's lips moved, and with his ruined lung, he had hardly any wind left to make words, but Thomas heard them all the same. Though, like most men's last words, they made little sense.

"No… I must… hire a farrier…" Gissler gave a last shudder and his hand fell away from the crossbow bolt's shaft.

Thomas pushed himself to his feet and looked down at his boyhood friend. They had traveled to the end of the world together, faced the mightiest Saracen warriors ever assembled, and survived when so many others, most in fact, did not. Only to come back here, where it all began, and kill one another.

Where was God's Will in all of this?

A horse whinny caught his attention and he looked up. Leopold stared at him, disbelief blanketing his face. Thomas raised a blood-soaked arm and pointed.

"You," Thomas said. His voice rasped in his throat. "You… are *poison*."

Leopold looked once again at the fallen bodies on the road, then back to the specter walking towards him. He reined his horse in a tight circle away and kicked his heels into her side.

Long before the sound of galloping hooves had disappeared into the distance, Thomas collapsed face-first onto the hard road, amidst an ever-growing circle of crimson.

Chapter 39

THE MOONLESS NIGHT allowed the twenty figures to crawl over the barren landscape of the fortress's killing fields like darkness overtaking a desert. They flowed through gaps in the half-built walls, shrinking well back of the torchlight from the main gates, and continued inexorably forwards, until they came before the walls of the prison. There, they merged with the night, and waited.

A door opened, and Heller, the jailer stepped out. He glanced about, craning his neck to take in all corners of the courtyard, and then beckoned to the shadows. Noll and his handpicked group of men and women passed by him wordlessly and poured into the depths of the large stone prison. It took only seconds to overcome the three sentries in the guardroom, but a full half hour to unlock the countless cell doors and manacles of the hundred condemned wide-eyed inhabitants.

They armed themselves with chains, flails, torches, pointed staves, forceps, sharp cones of iron, and other tools readily available in a house of torture. When the distant sounds of fighting could be heard at the main gates of the fortress, Noll and Heller opened the doors of the prison and set their army free.

There were less than forty Habsburg soldiers at the fortress that night. Eleven survived to be thrown into the very cells they used to guard. Vogt Berenger von Landenberg was amongst their number. He had been found in his room in the keep, hiding in a wardrobe.

Noll had him dragged into the courtyard, and at first the man cursed and screamed, demanding to be set free or he would bring the wrath of the Holy Roman Empire down upon them all. But he sang a different tune when Noll held a hot iron up to his face.

Noll wanted nothing more than to take the Vogt's eyes, as he had taken those of Noll's father. But Landenberg was the only true bargaining piece he held. He needed him to trade for Seraina, and perhaps the ferryman, if he yet lived. And a fat Vogt with no eyes would make a poor offer, indeed.

Impromptu fires had sprung up all over the courtyard. His army had found the keep's stores and people all around Noll were singing and feasting. Children and wives had raced up from the town to welcome their previously imprisoned loved ones back into the world.

Yes, Noll was now in control of the Altdorf fortress, something far more valuable to the Duke than Landenberg. And if Noll knew relinquishing it to the Austrians would ensure Seraina's release, he would have given it up in a heartbeat. But it was not Noll's to trade. It belonged to the people.

In the end, he threw the poker aside and settled for

whipping Landenberg's back until it frothed with blood, and the man's screams faded into unconsciousness.

The mess on his back was nothing a good tunic would not cover.

Chapter 40

AFTER RIDING ALL NIGHT, a road-weary soldier from Altdorf limped into the Habsburg throne room early the next morning. A purple-haired Fool trailed along behind him, mimicking his inebriated-like gait, with an added flourish or two.

The bells on the Fool's shoes seemed especially loud to Leopold on this day.

The Duke, with the hulking and grizzled form of his man Klaus standing once again at his side, listened to the soldier's report. Leopold sank further into his chair with the telling of every detail. The Fool pulled up a chair beside the Duke and began copying Leopold's posture.

The soldier was in the midst of describing how Vogt Landenberg had been captured by the villagers, and was perhaps even dead, when Leopold sprang from his chair and wrapped his hands around the Fool's throat. They fell to the floor kicking and thrashing, and by the time Klaus managed to break his lord's grip on the jester, the little man was blue in the face and a crowd of servants had gathered at the door.

The soldier stood straight, his wide eyes fixated on the coughing Fool still lying on the floor. Leopold straightened his clothes and ran his hands through his hair once before turning to Klaus. He looked refreshed, like he had just stepped out of a bath.

"Make arrangements to leave at once," he said.

"To what destination, my lord?"

"Salzburg. And send runners before us. I want an entire War Council convened before we arrive."

Klaus bowed and turned on his heel. He waved his arms at the gawking servants and they fled before him as he left the room.

The Fool jumped up from the floor and began to follow them.

"And where do you think you are going?" Leopold said.

The painted man turned and faced Leopold with one hand on his hip. "Why to pack of course, my lord. For what War Council would be complete without a fool?"

He flashed Leopold his best entertainer's smile and scurried from the room. The bells on his shoes made not a sound.

Chapter 41

*T*HE SUN WAS OUT, BUT *it did little to cut through the searing cold frosting the beard and mustache of the old trapper as he made his way towards the one-room cabin in the distance. His rhythmic breathing drowned out his muffled footsteps as his snowshoes floated in and out of the fresh powder. As he came down out of the trees and started across a hillside clearing that would be a field in the spring, the trapper paused and leaned on his walking stick.*

A thunderous crack boomed through the woods behind him and echoed throughout the forest. The sap in a tree had frozen, and expanded freeze after freeze, until finally, the trunk gave in and exploded.

Without looking back in the direction of the sound, the old man pushed off on his walking stick and headed to the cabin.

The door was stuck, frozen in place. He chipped away at it with his walking stick until it yielded to his shoulder. Air considerably warmer than the outside temperature rushed past him, carrying with it a stagnant odor. Against the far wall, a spruce-bough bed held two still forms, covered up to their necks with a single threadbare blanket. A man and a woman; her head on his chest and him on his back with his white, beardless face turned toward the rafters.

The trapper crossed himself and then covered his nose with the same hand. Idly, he wondered why it was so much warmer in the room than it should be, until a flicker of light caught his eye. On the small table in the center of the hut, burned a single tallow candle. And just past the candle, peering out over the rough table, a pair of dark eyes stared back at him.

A boy, who looked to be around four, stood at the edge of the table and did not move. The pupils of his already dark eyes were dilated so wide they appeared midnight-black.

The trapper attempted to speak, but his voice came out in a croak. He had not used it for speech since the summer. And then only once, while he traded for supplies. He cleared his throat and tried again.

"Nothing to fear, boy. Tell me your name."

The dark eyes narrowed and bored into the trapper's own for so long the trapper thought the boy could not understand him. He was about to try again, but in French this time, when the boy's chest heaved and he finally spoke in a voice as dry as the trapper's own.

"Thomas."

"How long you been here like this?"

The boy turned to look at the figures on the bed. He pointed at them.

"They look cold so I covered them. Might be they are still sick."

The trapper's eyes followed the frail little arm to look at the gaunt figures embracing on the handcrafted bed. The fever got them long before the cold ever did.

The old man crossed himself again and averted his gaze. "The cold cannot reach them anymore, Thomas."

Thomas came awake with a jerk that sent a spasm of pain racing down the length of his arm and under his ribs. The old trapper's face hovering above him faded and was replaced with Seraina's. Her auburn hair fell across one of her green eyes and he could make out the light freckles on her sun-browned skin.

She smiled and held a cool hand to his forehead. She smelled of violets and spoke words he did not understand, but were comforting. His body became heavy, and staring up at her, he fought hard to keep his eyes open, wanting nothing more than to remain lucid in the moment. But within seconds, her skin and hair blurred together and those brilliant eyes faded like stars on a cloudy night.

The scent of violets, however, remained with him long after the darkness returned.

###

The story continues in "MORGARTEN"

Available now!

www.jkswift.com

***

...a message from the author:

Thank you very much for reading my work. Reviews and personal recommendations from readers like you are the most important way for an author to attract more readers, so I truly am grateful to anyone who takes the time to rate my work. If you could take a moment to rate my story and/or leave a review where you purchased it, I would greatly appreciate it. It doesn't need to be long—a sentence or two about why you liked it or disliked it would be great. Feel free to contact me through my website and sign up for my **New Releases Mailing List**. Thanks very much!

Contact info for J. K. Swift: www.jkswift.com

If you enjoyed this story, you may also like:

HEALER: Keepers of Kwellevonne Vol. 1

(a short story series)

Why would anyone try to kill a healer?

Deenah's quiet life as an apprentice healer in the remote village of Brae's Creek is shattered when a stranger gravely wounds her master and flees into the wild. For all her skills, Deenah is unable to identify the strange forces at work on the injury. To save her master's life, Deenah must join the young Warder Kaern, and an aging veteran tracker, as they set out on a manhunt into hostile lands.

A 7000-word (28 pages) short story

Historical Notes

The William Tell story that most of us are familiar with, has William Tell being forced to shoot an apple off his son's head by an oppressive Austrian Governor named Hermann Gessler. We have the playwright Friedrich Schiller to thank for this. He wrote his hugely successful play *William Tell* in the early 1800's. In 1829 Rossini premiered his opera of the same name. The opening piece was the *William Tell Overture*, portions of which would be brought into popular culture by its adoption for use in *The Lone Ranger* radio and television shows.

Most historians doubt William Tell ever existed. He does not show up in any historical documents until one hundred and fifty years after the time he was supposed to have shot the apple (around 1307), and there is absolutely no mention anywhere of a Governor named Gessler. This is very unusual, as written records did exist at the time detailing the names and positions of even minor officials. The apple scenario itself is most definitely an embellishment, for strikingly similar tales of a tyrant forcing a hero to shoot objects off the head of a loved one appear much earlier than the 1300's, in several different cultures, from Denmark to India.

The only thing we know for sure, is that the regions of Schwyz, Uri, and Unterwalden rose up against their Austrian overlords in a rebellion that culminated in the Battle of Morgarten in 1315. My own feeling on the matter is that the legend of William Tell arose based on the exploits of more than one man or woman. William Tell was invented to personify the bravery and perseverance of a small group of people who, even when faced with overwhelming odds, still chose to make a stand for what they believed.

And those men and women, did exist.

***

The Malleus Maleficarum

There is, in fact, a treatise on witchcraft known as the *Malleus Maleficarum*. However, it was published well after Leopold of Habsburg's time by Dominicans named Heinrich Kramer and Jakob Sprenger in Germany in 1487. It was a collection of witch lore from several different sources, and became a bestseller of its time.

The reason I exercised my right as a fiction writer to so blatantly pluck it from its time period and thrust it into the hands of Leopold of Habsburg, is because I discovered it actually had a story in it about a witch-archer being forced to shoot a penny off his son's cap by a despicable Prince.

With this tenuous connection to the William Tell legend, I couldn't resist using it. I hope the true historians out there can forgive me.

About the author

J. K. Swift lives in a log house well off the beaten path in central B.C., Canada. He has worked as a school teacher, jailhouse guard, Japanese translator, log peeler, accountant, martial arts instructor, massage therapist, technical editor, and has called a few Bingo games. He gets his story ideas while traveling in Europe, feeding his chickens, and cutting wood.

J. K. Swift's website and blog: www.jkswift.com

The Forest Knights website: www.theforestknights.com

Made in the USA
Columbia, SC
27 October 2020